"*Drowning* tells a compelling and al. ....-.. ....
suburban domestic violence. Maloney gives a hauntingly realistic
look into the struggles of too many victims and their perpetrators
who are living a life of lies presented in pretty pictures and a
scrapbook that tells only half the story. It is my hope that this
novel will invite readers to see the issue of domestic violence in a
new light; with compassion not disdain for its many victims." Alli
O'Malley, Domestic Violence Survivor and Executive Director,
RESOLVE of Greater Rochester

"Katelin Maloney keeps you in suspense until the last page
wondering if Rebecca will take her friend's advice and leave her
abusive husband or will she stay with him and continue to be
emotionally and physically abused? Ms. Maloney does a marvelous
job of portraying the inner thought life of an abuse victim, whose
life gets smaller and smaller as she hopes against hope her
husband will miraculously change." Caroline Abbott author of A
Journey Through Emotional Abuse: from Bondage to Freedom
and A Journey to Healing After Emotional Abuse.

"*Drowning* is an avid page turner. Katelin Maloney's writing is
beautiful. Her story is deep; and its message is poignant. Readers
will not want to put it aside until they reach the last page." Lauren
Makarov, Author of Reflecting on Domestic Violence:
Understanding the Emotional Aftermath

Drowning

Katelin Maloney

COPYRIGHT © 2015 by Purple Ribbon Publishing

EDITOR: PT Editing

COVER DESIGN: Sprinkles on Top Studios

ISBN: 978-0-9963307-0-1

This book is dedicated to all of our sisters

Chapter 1

Rebecca checked the digital clock. 7:05 pm. Three hours until Mitch returned from his shift at the hospital. Plenty of time. She rummaged through the dresser drawer, her pulse racing, and from beneath a pale pink cashmere sweater, pulled out the course catalog.

Taped to the booklet was a note. *Don't even think about it.* Mitch's precise handwriting. The catalog fell from her fingers onto the beige carpet. She spun around, sure to find Mitch watching. No one was there. She was alone.

Bare feet poking from pajama bottoms carried her into Mitch's office and to his computer. It was risky, but she couldn't stop herself. If Mitch truly discovered her signing up for the online college course … she could almost feel the punch of his fist on her cheek.

The online class wasn't ideal, but with Mitch's bouts of jealousy and her need for anonymity, being on campus was out of the question. The accounting course flashed on the screen. Rebecca hit the registration button. Scout, their calico cat, jumped onto her lap and purred. When the spring semester confirmation popped up, she clapped her hands, then quickly cleared the cache and logged off, making sure Mitch's pen and glasses were exactly in their place. After nuzzling with Scout, she coaxed her down. She turned off the light and closed the door, leaving the room just as she had found it.

Time to return to the day's tasks. There was a lot to complete before Mitch came home. She grabbed the heaping laundry basket from the floor of the master bedroom and hugged it against her hip, navigating toward the basement stairs, feet patting on the hardwood. The wedding picture on the wall in the hallway caught her eye.

They were married on a chilly October Saturday five years ago, surrounded by their family and closest friends. Candles illuminated the small church as they spoke their vows from memory. Perfection. Rebecca remembered the way Mitch had beamed at her. That was then. Things were different now. Very different. She now yearned for his appreciation.

When she touched the frame, *The Way You Look Tonight* by Frank Sinatra played in her mind. Their wedding song. It had been the first time they'd danced as a married couple. It had also been the last.

The face of a woman smiled from the picture. Confident and strong, so unlike today. A stranger. Although Rebecca still wore her light-brown hair long as per Mitch's request, the blond highlights had faded and her pale-blue eyes no longer sparkled. Circles under her eyes made her look older than her twenty-eight years.

Her index finger outlined Mitch's face. Handsome, neatly cropped black hair, he looked distinguished. She had given him her heart. Hadn't he given her his? Why couldn't she stop making him angry?

Dust gathered on her finger. Another job to do before Mitch noticed. A strange noise came from the basement. Down the stairs with the basket, her feet touched the wet rug, and a sensation of worry as cold and mushy as the rug hit her.

What had happened? Rebecca shoved the basket onto a metal chair, but it tipped sending the clothes spilling onto the wet floor. She rolled up the hem of her pajama bottoms, and hurried to the far corner where water from the hot water heater flowed from the tank.

Mitch's baseball cards! No, they were safe in waterproof totes.

The fluorescent light flickered, taunting her with further problems. She rescued the clothes from the floor, ran back up the stairs and grabbed her cell phone. Mitch didn't like interruptions while at work. He was a doctor, an important person. She chewed at her fingernails, her teeth piercing the skin and drawing blood.

Her husband answered his cell on the fourth ring. Muffled voices in the background made it difficult to hear him. "Go ahead." His brisk tone sent chills through her.

"The water heater's broken, and water is flowing out. What do I do?"

"Dammit, Rebecca. Turn off the main water valve."

Her stomach knotted. "I'm sorry, Mitch. Where is it?"

"In the far corner of the storage area, by the metal shelves. You should know that."

She paced back and forth. "There's water everywhere. At least an inch covering the basement floor."

"Don't touch anything after you turn off the valve. I'll be home in fifteen minutes." He hung up.

The drive from Rochester General Hospital should take half an hour. Rebecca found the valve and turned it off. The flow slowed to a drip and water swirled into the drain, leaving large puddles and a soggy carpet.

Back upstairs, she hid the wet clothes in the guest bathroom tub. They would have to wait until tomorrow. Rebecca quickly scrubbed the kitchen tiles, removing marks left by the sodden basket.

She peered out the side window and down the snow-covered street. No cars coming yet, but Mitch would be home soon. She needed to stop screwing up. She needed to change.

Chapter 2

Rebecca tightened the white belt, pulling the gi closer around her waist. Spectators watched as the instructor and student sparred on the blue mat.

She rubbed her arms and said to the teenage boy next to her, "This is intimidating. I don't know if I can do this."

His big, brown eyes looked into hers. "The sensei knows you're new. He'll just walk you through the movements."

"Still, I'm worried." She couldn't shake the uneasy feeling.

"Next!" The sensei called.

Rebecca moved to the edge of the mat and bowed to her instructor. It was a mechanical movement. Their eyes met. Don't look intimidated, she thought. He's only going to show me some karate movements. Her feet plodded onto the spongy training area. His expression was evil.

Fighting the urge to flee, she took her position, waiting for instructions. They didn't come. His leg slammed into hers causing her body to crumble onto the floor. She grabbed her thigh screaming in pain. Her eyes shot to his just as he connected again.

She scrambled away, but he was right there, ready to strike. He pulled her pony tail, dragging her toward him. She clawed at his hands, nails ripping into his flesh. He jerked his hands away and she rolled over, thrusting her legs in front of her to block another strike.

Her belt came loose. It was no longer white. It was pink cashmere and ripped like paper.

He moved toward her with more vengeance than before. She kicked her legs at him, trying to connect. He pushed them out of his way as if they were air and yanked her wrist, pulling her hard toward his face.

"Don't ever call me at work again."

*****

"What happened to you?" demanded Anna, late the next morning.

Rebecca motioned her into the dining room and walked into the kitchen.

"Want some coffee?" Without waiting for a reply, she poured hazelnut coffee into Anna's favorite mug, the Mickey Mouse one. Anna had worn a Mickey Mouse sweatshirt the first time they'd met, three years ago. Anna loved coffee, and Rebecca presented the extra-large mug as a gift. She placed it in front of Anna, then poured herself one.

"What's going on, Bec? Tell me." Anna's spoon clicked against the mug as she impatiently mixed creamer and coffee together.

Rebecca turned from her friend's stare, and played with a wooden baby lamb figurine Mitch had carved after the fight last night.

"Bec?" Anna's soft voice coaxed as if Rebecca were a wounded animal. "Talk to me. I'm worried about you."

Rebecca looked out the window at the swirling snowflakes, fearing the upcoming conversation. They'd talked about it too many times. Anna would take action on her own soon. Part of Rebecca wanted to give her all of the details. Another part, the part that wished the abuse had just been one of her many nightmares, wanted to keep quiet.

Anna reached across the table and touched Rebecca's hand. "I can see the bruises on your wrist, you know? I saw you walking with a limp. I know Mitch hurt you. Again."

Rebecca jerked her hand away and rubbed her neck, hair falling across her eyes. "I shouldn't have interrupted him at work. He's a busy man."

Anna tapped her foot on the floor. "What happened?"

She uttered a quick laugh. "The stupid water heater burst. Water leaked all over the basement."

"And?"

"I called Mitch." Rebecca's stomach churned at the memory. "I should have called a plumber."

Anna massaged her temple. "Your basement flooded. Of course you'd call your husband. That's the normal thing to do."

"I have to be strong and handle problems on my own. I shouldn't bother him while he's busy." Rebecca couldn't look at her friend. She studied the *Water Lilies* print behind Anna. They had seen the painting at the Museum of Modern Art during a trip to New York City to celebrate their engagement. Mitch bought her the framed print as a wedding present. They also visited Chinatown. He'd fed her Lo Mein using chopsticks and insisted she try to use them, too. He made fun of her lack of success. Her fortune cookie read, 'Fear not waves that crash on you. You will rise above them.' They had laughed and Mitch warned her to stay away from the ocean.

"It's no excuse." Anna's protest interrupted Rebecca's thoughts. "You've been married for five years, and he's been pushing you around for how many? It's getting worse." Anna pointed to Rebecca's bruised arm. "When was the last time? Never mind, I know the answer."

"Please, don't make me relive bad memories. I should have realized my phone call would set him off. Mitch just has a few … quirks."

"Quirks?" Gesturing toward Rebecca's arm again, Anna said, "Nothing you do gives Mitch the right to treat you like this."

Rebecca wiped at the tears she didn't give permission to fall. "Don't get upset with me."

"I'm not upset with you. I'm worried about you and this existence you're claiming as your life. This is no way to live."

Rebecca tucked a loose strand of hair around her ear. "I'm trying to figure out the best way to deal with him. I have to learn not to upset him."

"And in the meantime?" Anna tapped her fingernails on the table.

The noise echoed in Rebecca's head. "In the meantime, I'm going to be stronger and more careful about what I do. I always manage to screw things up."

"Rebecca, this isn't your fault. It never is."

Heat rose to her face. "I love him. I love how he used to be. In the beginning, he was so kind and thoughtful. We bonded and shared stories of our upbringing. He opened up to me about his alcoholic mother and his sister Maddie's cancer. Oh, how he loved her. I still see glimpses of that good man in him, but then the violent side appears." She continued, although not liking the words tumbling from her mouth. "I have to take better care of Mitch, be a good wife and not add to his stress."

"It's not you. He's solely to blame. You have to talk to someone. Please."

She gripped her hands around her coffee cup ignoring the intense heat, and forced a smile. "It's complicated."

"You know I'm here for you whenever you need me." Anna hesitated, and then added, "But you've got to get away from him."

Rebecca grimaced. "If I could change—"

"You aren't the one who has to change."

"I've got to be at the bank by noon."

"You're in danger, Bec. Don't you understand?"

Anna was quiet for a moment, but Rebecca could feel her stare.

"I have good news. I signed up for an online class at the community college."

Anna gasped. "You did?"

"I did." Rebecca hugged herself. "Accounting. It's one of the requirements to finish my degree. I had earned fifteen credits before dropping out of Flagler College to take care of Nan. Now I can take classes at the local college here in Rochester."

"Wow, I'm impressed. Where did this burst of independence come from?"

"You." Rebecca smiled. "I've been thinking about how strong you are and I want to be more like you. I channeled my *inner Anna*."

Anna laughed. "I'm glad I was useful, but seriously, I'm proud of you. You need to do something for yourself like this. Just be careful and don't get caught."

Rebecca shivered.

"When does the class start?"

"End of January, right after Mitch and I return from vacation. I was secretly able to save just enough money to pay for the course. Joan has been talking about a new Personal Banker position opening up soon. She says if I can keep earning credits toward my degree, then maybe I can train to become a Personal Banker either at my current bank or another. It's a long shot, but if I move to another bank, I'd be away from Margo. Plus, my mom has really been struggling financially lately. I can support her."

"A win-win."

"Exactly."

"And you could leave Mitch."

"Anna, please. I still have to figure out how to tell him I might get a full-time job."

"What do you think he'll say? He wants you to be pregnant and unemployed."

"I'm going to approach the subject while we're on vacation. He's so stressed right now studying for the exam. This isn't the right time. I'm hoping we can have a good conversation on vacation." She counted the weeks until his Board Certified Medical Exam. Five more weeks. Then vacation.

"Nothing will change because it isn't your fault. When will you see that?"

Rebecca ignored the statement. The grandfather clock chimed. "I've got to get ready for work."

After Anna left, Rebecca took the wooden figurine to the living room and opened her hope chest. It was a gift from her father. He made it for her sixteenth birthday. She felt closer to her dad when she touched the carvings on the chest. Her mother had filled it with antique linens, silverware, a charm bracelet, her baby booties and baby blanket. She hid the lamb with the other figurines, under the linens and blanket, not wanting it to touch her precious heirlooms.

She hobbled down the stairs and carried up the laundry in her arms, breathing in the fresh scent of clean clothes. Because the plumber had fixed the water heater earlier that morning, she was able to get the clothes washed and dried. She needed to fold and put them away before she left for work.

When she tossed them on one of the twin, white leather sofas, Scout was frightened from her resting place and followed Rebecca into the bedroom, the cat's bell jingling as she trotted behind. She resisted the urge to climb into bed, pull the pale-blue comforter over her head, and cuddle with her cat. She wanted to stay home and work on her mother's Christmas present. The quilt was being modeled after her antique quilt.

She pulled the long, brown skirt up her legs, then struggled with her tan sweater, trying to maneuver it over her arms without further hurting her wrist. A roll of bandages, the sleeves of her sweater and her thick gold and silver bracelets did a good job concealing the bruises. Before leaving, she took two ibuprofen.

On Rebecca's drive to work she remembered the laundry. It would be the first thing she did when she returned home.

She parked. When stepping out of the car, she slipped on the icy pavement, but caught herself. Her warm, wool coat provided protection from the bitter cold temperature. As she walked through the parking lot, she took in the exterior of the building, marveling at the intricate architecture. She never tired of absorbing its beauty. Western New York had some striking structures, but this was the finest.

Taking a deep breath, she walked in. Tile murals depicting the early settlers covered the high ceilings. She touched a cool marble pillar and stopped to straighten the customers' deposit slips on the giant, cherry tables.

Spotting her co-worker, she said, "Hi, Kelly. How's work?" Rebecca admired her soft, black A-line dress. Kelly's short, auburn hair and high-heeled shoes completed the stylish look. Mitch wouldn't approve. The dress was above the knees.

"Busy today." Kelly counted money, writing down figures as she worked. "How have you been?" She looked up.

"Fine," she lied. "How are classes?"

Kelly set down the pile of cash. "It's almost time for finals. I'm a little overwhelmed with projects and papers, so I'm taking next week off. I can't believe today is only Tuesday, though. I've got the rest of the week to go."

Single and in college. Not married to an abusive man.

Forcing Mitch from her mind, Rebecca said, "The week will go fast and I'm sure you'll do great."

"Thanks. I appreciate it. Hey, want to go to dinner Monday? I only get a chance to talk to you when we switch shifts. We can catch up." Kelly's eyes surveyed the room. She added in a whisper, "And talk about Margo."

Rebecca smiled.

"I'll call you Sunday and we can discuss the details." Kelly grabbed her purse and heavy winter coat. "I'm excited."

"Rebecca, do you have a moment?" Joan played with a button on her navy suit jacket.

She followed Joan into her office, admiring her dark-brown, bob hair style.

"When are you coming back from vacation?" Joan asked.

"The end of January."

She scribbled on a notepad.

"There is a training program that starts around that time. If I pull some strings, I might be able to get you in. You might be able to get the promotion we were discussing last week."

"Thank you so much for pursuing this, Joan. I really appreciate it."

"I know you do. You're an outstanding teller with so much potential."

If she could get into the training program, she'd be on her way to fulfilling her dreams. Her goal of being a career woman had been derailed when Nan became too ill to care for herself. Unfortunately taking care of Nan also meant she didn't finish her college degree which meant not helping support her mother as she would have liked. Her father's death was her fault—no matter what other people said—and she wanted to make up for it in a small way. But what to do about Mitch?

Joan led her out of the office.

Rebecca strolled behind, the vanilla scent of Joan's perfume lingering. Rebecca breathed it in, remembering when she baked sugar cookies with Nan in the house Rebecca now called her own.

Margo interrupted her thoughts. "Rebecca, are you with us? That program you installed for the tellers, it has a glitch."

The program Rebecca devised had been a success. Margo simply didn't know how to work it properly.

"Do you want me to fix it now or wait on customers?"

"The line is growing. You'll need to wait on customers. They come first. When they're gone, come to the back office and fix it." Her eyes narrowed into slits and her lips pursed. Margo's high-heeled shoes clicked on the floor as she stormed away.

Rebecca approached her line with a frown until she saw David Morris. David dusted snow from his bulky tan jacket and waited for her to help the customer in front of him.

David was a close friend of the family. Rebecca's grandparents had taken him in when he was a problem child and raised him in his teenage years. Her father had grown up with David and referred to him as his brother.

Rebecca considered David her uncle. He was the father figure she'd longed for since her dad's death ten years ago. David had walked her down the aisle and had given her away.

She knew he would do anything for her family. Retired for fifteen years, he served twenty-five years with the police force. He was a well-groomed man, handsome in a rugged way.

"How are you?" He handed her his deposit slip. Ocean-blue eyes, so like her father's. Her father's Irish eyes had sparkled whenever he smiled. He had smiled often. She missed his calm demeanor and laid back attitude.

"I'm good. When are you leaving to visit Vicki and your grandkids?" Rebecca took his checks, entered the information into the computer, and waited for the receipt to print.

Snow fell from his gray hair as he leaned in. "Next Friday. I have to rest so I can keep up with the kids."

"How long will you be visiting?"

He blew warm air into his meaty hands. "Until the second. The kids go back to school then."

"My mother is coming here on the twenty-third. I can't wait to see her." Rebecca worried about how Mitch would react to her mother's visit. During her last visit he was standoffish, and he made too many flippant excuses for his behavior.

"How's Evelyn doing?"

"Mom's okay. Working too many hours as usual. I wish she'd move either here or in with Michael and his family so we could ease some of her financial burden. There's no reason for her to live alone in Savannah."

"Well, she's like her mother-in-law was. Stubborn."

Rebecca thought about Nan. "I agree."

"Tell her I said hello and I hope we can get together next time she visits."

"I will."

"And how about us? We're going to resume our weekly meals when I get back, right?"

Nodding, she gave him his receipt, her hand brushing his. He looked down and furrowed his brow.

Her eyes traveled to where he focused. The bruised wrist peeked from under the bandage. Her mind flashed to Mitch's expression right before he wrenched her arm last night.

She had to be more diligent in the future.

A confrontation between David and Mitch would be disastrous.

Chapter 3

The gloomy sky matched Rebecca's mood as she drove home from work. She glanced at her bruised wrist and rubbed her forehead, the usual headache plaguing her. The constant pounding made concentrating more and more difficult.

As she switched on the headlights, the cell phone rang. It would be Mitch. She wasn't allowed to give her number out to others without his permission.

"Why aren't you home? I called the house and no one picked up." He used the same indignant tone as the night before.

"I'm a little behind schedule." Rebecca pictured Mitch shaking his head in his arrogant way. "I stopped to talk to Joan for a few minutes after we closed."

"About what?"

Her chest tightened. "Her mother is coming for an unexpected visit. I might pick up a few of her hours." Lying was both dangerous and necessary. "I'll be home soon."

"I'm leaving the hospital right now for a couple of hours and want to spend some time with my wife."

Dinner needed to be cooked. Clothes were left on the sofa. She accelerated. She had to beat Mitch home.

"When you get pregnant, you're going to stop working. I'll pick up all the bills. You'll have an allowance."

Would he take care of her, just as he had at the beginning of their marriage? Loving and attentive? She'd thought she found the perfect man. She still did. Things would get better. Of course they would.

But if Mitch controlled all the money, there'd be no way to continue with college courses. She wouldn't be able to move into a better position at the bank. Her mother's mortgage payments were behind. She had to get that job.

Pushing the thought away, she arrived home and quickly started making parmesan-crusted chicken. One of Mitch's favorites.

Ten minutes later, Mitch breezed through the door. Rebecca rushed to get the chicken breaded and into the oven. Mitch kicked a shoe out of his way and she cringed when it hit a wall. Had he noticed the laundry?

He walked into the kitchen, hummed a tune and picked up Scout who struggled to break free. His eyes settled on the tray in her hand. "Mmm, look's delicious." He kissed her on the cheek.

She slid the chicken into the oven. "It should be ready in about twenty-five minutes."

"Then there's plenty of time for my surprise before dinner." He grinned, gave Scout one last squeeze and placed her on the floor. Scout scampered away. He led Rebecca by the hand to the dining room table and pulled out a chair. "Please sit down. I want to talk to you."

Using the word *please* confused Rebecca more than him ignoring the laundry and cuddling with Scout.

"Don't you want me to finish preparing dinner?"

"It can wait. This is more important." He pulled a royal-blue box from his pocket. Sapphire Skies. Her favorite jewelry store.

"Mitch ..." Was this an apology gift? She never got those.

"Open it. I saw this when I was doing some early Christmas shopping and thought about how wonderful it would look on you."

On a small bed of satin lay a beautiful rose-gold necklace laced with sparkling amethysts. Her jaw dropped. Bewildered, she searched his face for meaning.

"It'll be stunning with the purple dress you're wearing to the party this weekend." He held her uninjured hand tight. Too tight, but she dared not pull away. "The amethysts are the same color as the sequins on your dress."

The amethysts were also the color of the bruises hidden by the bandage. "Thank you, Mitch. It's lovely."

"I can't wait to show you off at the party."

It wasn't an apology. It was insurance that she'd attend the party with him.

Mitch pulled her into his arms. "I love you. You know that, don't you?"

She leaned back and looked into his dark eyes before he squeezed her tight. He let go just as she sank into his chest.

After checking on the chicken, she glanced at Mitch, who'd pulled out a newspaper and sat at the dining room table. He hadn't apologized. He hadn't asked for forgiveness. She pressed her fist against her chest, trying to encourage the pain to abate. She needed things Mitch couldn't give her, things she wanted, things she craved. They'd come when she changed.

"It's getting rough dividing my time between work and studying. It'll be a relief to have this exam behind me. Vacation can't come soon enough."

"I agree. You need a break, and some peaceful time together will be wonderful." Rebecca brought the salad to the table.

"The party Saturday night should be nice. I'm excited to introduce you to my new boss Doctor Fields."

"Will Mrs. Fields be there? It'll be nice to talk with another doctor's wife."

"The party's at their home. They're expecting forty people, mostly doctors and interns and their spouses or dates. It's a thank you from the Chief of Staff to everyone for their hard work."

She brought out two glasses of wine, a loaf of bread and butter and the chicken. "I look forward to meeting everyone."

"I also want you to meet Derek Canton. He's become a close friend of the Fields since they've moved here." Mitch cut into his chicken and inspected the color of the flesh. The study took painful seconds. Rebecca was sure the meat was cooked through. She'd never make that mistake again. The consequences were agonizing.

"He's also a highly respected psychiatrist who came on staff about a year ago. He published an article in *Psychology Today* and has been asked to speak at the American Psychological Association annual conference in Houston in February. His specialty is borderline personality disorder." Mitch took a bite. It seemed it was to his liking. He broke off a piece of bread and reached for the butter. "We've become friends. He promised to take me golfing this spring at Windgate Manor. You know how I enjoy that country club."

*****

Rebecca walked into the guest bedroom with her phone and gently closed the door to make sure Mitch didn't hear. She sat in an antique rocking chair inherited from Nan. When she was alive, the chair sat in the living room near the fireplace. Nan embroidered there, while wrapped in a quilt. Rebecca remembered being rocked to sleep by Nan in the chair. As a teen, she'd pictured rocking her own children by the fire, but Mitch insisted it either be thrown out or moved from sight. It didn't fit in with the décor. She brushed off the thought.

"How are you, Mom?"

"Oh, Rebecca. I'm okay, I guess."

"What's going on? I can tell something is wrong." She picked up a doll saved from her childhood and caressed its hair. Betsy was her name. It held a special significance to Rebecca. David and Carolyn gave it to her on her tenth birthday, shortly before Carolyn passed. Nan had sewn clothes for Betsy. Rebecca had pretended she was the little sister she'd always wanted. Betsy always sat on the dresser, eyes focused on the bed.

"I don't want you to worry."

"Mom, please."

"I wake up in the middle of the night worrying and can't get back to sleep. I'm so tired."

Rebecca tossed the doll onto the bed, immediately feeling guilty. "What are you stressing about?"

"Bills. The mortgage. The usual. I'll be fine. You know how I am. I get anxious."

Rebecca rubbed her temple. "Why don't you think about moving in with Michael or me?"

"No, I won't be a burden to my children. Absolutely not. I wouldn't want to strap you and Mitch with my problems. You two have a perfect marriage and I'm not going to upend that."

"We don't." Rebecca stood. She walked to her sewing table and fingered the binding on the unfinished quilt.

"Rebecca, please. You do."

"I wish you would stop saying that." She plopped back in the chair.

"Just like your father and me."

Rebecca rocked a little harder in the chair.

Chapter 4

Darkness.

Water everywhere.

Surrounded.

Rebecca struggled in the body of water. Immersed, drawn under the surface. She gulped, choking as waves splashed around her head, pulling her down further. Strange noises, muted voices howled to her, but she couldn't understand the words, just the tone of caution. They beckoned, but she did not comprehend their intentions.

Surrounded.

Water everywhere.

Darkness.

*****

Holding a scarf to her face, Rebecca rushed into the clinic. She scanned the waiting room hoping not to discover familiar faces, someone who might report her presence there to Mitch. Quarterly visits were risky, but necessary.

She signed in, fingers trembling when she wrote her real name. The receptionist held out her hand. "Insurance and driver's license, please."

She thumbed through her wallet and pulled out her license. "I don't have insurance," she lied. "I'll be paying cash for the visit."

Rebecca eased into a chair and flipped through a brochure. Babies. Beautiful, precious pictures of babies stared out from the pages. She rubbed her eyes. Her fists just might push the threatening tears back in.

The bell on the front door jingled and the thump of heavy boots on the hardwood floor followed. Forceful boots, like Mitch's from the other night. She dared not look up. The man walked toward her and cleared his throat. Rebecca busied her fingers, opening and closing the zipper to her purse. The man sat down two seats away. A woman followed and sat next to him.

Not Mitch. Safe for now. How many more times could she go through this? But she needed that pill.

Mitch's desire to have a baby had turned into an obsession. He had already chosen a name. Madeline, his sister's name. They would be having a girl. He had decided. She would go to the best private school in Rochester, so she'd be surrounded by a higher class of people. Children of doctors, lawyers, executives. She'd have the best healthcare, toys, clothing.

What about love? Rebecca wondered.

Too many times during these visits, she considered leaving the clinic, but each time she drew strength from Anna's influence. Yes, she needed that pill. A baby had to wait. She felt penetrating eyes. A woman sitting across from her focused on the TV screen above Rebecca's head. Was someone else looking at her? She picked at her fingernails.

"Rebecca?"

After a weight check, the nurse led her to an examining room. The smell of disinfectant tickled her nostrils. Rebecca held out her good arm ready for the blood pressure machine. She was sure to hide her bruised wrist.

"Quite high." The nurse scanned her chart. "Last time it was much lower."

"Traffic was bad on the way here, and I'm running late."

"The doctor will probably want to see you back in one month and run blood work as well."

She averted her eyes and said, "Sure, no problem." Rebecca had no intention on following up with another visit so soon. High blood pressure was the least of her concerns, and she was sure it would drop as soon as she left the place.

"Put this gown on. The doctor will be in soon."

She changed. A baby cried down the hall. She touched a poster on the wall, outlining a pregnant mother's belly. Her finger swung easily, tenderly.

Shortly after they met, Anna convinced Rebecca to take birth control pills until Mitch became less volatile. Anna didn't think that time would come. Rebecca did. Rebecca yearned for a baby, but she couldn't bring one into her life, not just yet. Things had to change. She had hoped they would have changed by now. For almost three years, Rebecca had deceived Mitch. She hated doing so, but he'd left her no choice. The lie exhausted her.

Rebecca examined her bruised wrist, deciding she'd wait another five weeks until after Mitch's exam and their vacation.

She could talk to him then. See if he would accept her need to work full-time. She could then consider not taking the pill anymore.

Anna's voice played in her head. *Mitch is too unpredictable. You can't get pregnant right now.*

The doctor walked into the room and Rebecca climbed onto the examining table, moving her arm behind her.

"I see on your chart your blood pressure is elevated. How do you feel?" she asked.

"Fine. I'm just busy."

"Are you sure?" The doctor pulled her chair a little closer and wrote down notes. "Any dizziness or heart palpitations?"

"No, it's probably just work and it's been hectic with the holidays approaching."

She studied Rebecca for a long moment. "Sometimes it's good to talk about stress. You do know we have counseling services available here as well."

"I'm here for birth control pills, not psychological treatment." Rebecca heard the snap in her tone and immediately regretted the outburst.

"I didn't mean to upset you." The doctor rested her hand on Rebecca's. "I want you to be aware of the range of services we offer."

"I'm sorry. It's been a very demanding week." The base of her skull throbbed.

"I understand. Let me know if you need anything." She patted her knee. "We'll follow up in a month to check your blood pressure."

Rebecca tossed the appointment card in the trash can outside. She pulled the scarf over her face, kept her eyes down and rushed to the car.

Chapter 5

Rebecca picked up the newspaper, put the dishes in the cabinet, and swept the kitchen floor. The curling iron was heating. Everything had to be perfect if her night with Mitch was to be calm. She curled her hair per Mitch's request.

Mitch had surprised her earlier with a proposal to dine at a restaurant. A rare event. They celebrated their anniversary each year without fail, but beyond that annual affair, Mitch spent his nights at the hospital, balking at any social outing for just the two of them.

The garage door slammed. Rebecca dropped the curling iron. Scout ran into the bedroom and jumped onto the bed. Mitch moved through the house, calling to her.

"Ah, just who I wanted to see. I knew the sight of you would make me happy." He scooped Rebecca in his arms, his large frame embracing hers, spinning her around.

He was in a good mood. She breathed more easily. Mitch wore his form-fitting charcoal gray suit. Her favorite. They'd picked it out together on a shopping trip in New York City. His hair glistened and his eyes shone.

"I made reservations for six o'clock at Vincent's Restaurant. Will you have enough time to finish getting ready?"

Rebecca smiled. "We're going to Vincent's?" Mitch proposed at Vincent's over five years ago. She touched her one-carat, platinum engagement ring and brightened. "That's wonderful."

Memories swirled in her head. After they'd finished dinner, she had gone to the restroom. When she returned the plates had been cleared and a royal-blue box sat at her place. Mitch knelt on the floor. Rebecca's eyes watered.

He'd said, "Rebecca, I've found my soulmate in you. You're everything I've dreamed of in a companion. Kind, thoughtful, beautiful." He opened the box revealing a gorgeous diamond ring. "Rebecca, will you marry me?"

She nodded, and then said, "Yes!"

People nearby applauded and Mitch and Rebecca embraced. The server brought champagne and they toasted.

"I'm so happy," Rebecca said.

"To a perfect life. A perfect wife."

A carriage ride around the town completed the picture-perfect occasion.

Scout meowed, bringing Rebecca back to the moment. She looked around the room. Mitch had left.

She laid her black cocktail dress on the bed and slipped out of her work clothes, then rushed into the bathroom and applied her blush and eye shadow. She sprayed shimmering, rose-scented body mist on her skin.

Mitch poked his head in. "Almost ready?"

"Almost." She pulled on her pantyhose while Mitch combed his hair.

"It'll be nice to go back to Vincent's. We can celebrate."

"Celebrate what?"

"Our future together." Mitch put his arms around her. "Mmm," he said, as he breathed in her perfume.

"Did something happen today?" She slipped on the dress.

"Things are aligning perfectly in my life and I want to enjoy it. I have a wonderful wife who loves me, a promising career, and soon I'll have a family of my own."

"I'm sure it won't be long."

"I have no doubt. Any time now we'll have a little girl. That's why we're celebrating." He kissed her cheek and left the room.

She sat down on the bed. Scout nestled against her leg. Her fingers struggled with the straps, but she managed to pull on her black heels, and then she joined Mitch in the living room.

He smiled as he helped her slip on her long black coat. "Sometimes I just can't believe how beautiful you are. I could never lose you, Rebecca." He took her in his arms and whispered, "You'll never betray me like my father did."

Both were quiet on the way to the restaurant. As they approached the parking lot, Mitch put his hand on her knee and squeezed. Was he still thinking of his father? She hoped he could block out his past and enjoy an evening filled with romantic conversation. The mention of Mitch's father worried her. He was so bitter, and rightfully so. To be abandoned by him.

His parents had argued constantly after Maddie's death. Mitch would turn his music up to drown out the sounds. Had the fights been violent? Mitch never said. Would he have known? She thought of her own abuse. Yes, he would have. There'd be evidence. Had there been? If so, did Mitch think his father was justified?

Mitch had inherited his woodcraft skills from his father. They'd crafted furniture together when he was a boy. Maybe crafting was a way for Mitch to connect with his father on some level. Therapeutic.

She put her hand over his and caressed it, watching his chiseled expression soften.

The lights in the restaurant were dim. Red candles gave off a soft ambience at each table.

"Oh, Mitch, look at the garland and strands of little white lights hanging on the fireplace mantel. This place looks as beautiful as always." The restaurant hadn't changed its décor since the night Mitch proposed. Excitement bubbled inside.

She pointed and his hand pushed hers back down.

"Did I—"

"Don't point."

A decorated Christmas tree stood in the corner. The scent of pine permeated the air, reminding Rebecca of their first Christmas together. It had been just the two of them. After they'd eaten a large breakfast, Mitch started a fire. Rebecca snapped several pictures and had made a page in her scrapbook celebrating their first Christmas. Her favorite present from Mitch was a Bernina sewing machine. She'd squealed and explained the many functions it could perform. She could create beautiful quilts with the different tools. While the pot roast with potatoes and vegetables cooked, they'd cuddled on the sofa and watched movies. The evening was filled with love making.

"Good evening, sir and ma'am." A young server handed them their menus. "Today's specials are herb-crusted, prime rib with twice-baked potatoes and roasted asparagus, pan-roasted chicken with lemon-garlic green beans, and linguini with roasted red pepper sauce. Here is the wine and draft beer list." He held the wine menu out to Rebecca. Mitch took it before she had a chance to touch it.

His eyes shifted to Rebecca's. "Can I interest you in a glass of wine?"

Mitch shoved the wine menu at the server. "We'll take a bottle of the Vineyard Hill pinot noir to start."

The server took a small step back. "Yes, sir. Excellent choice. I'll bring that right out as well as two glasses of water." He gave a little bow and left.

"He was gawking at you. Practically drooling."

Rebecca tried not to react. Mitch grew jealous of any man. And with his jealousy came anger. But he surprised her, laughing.

"He's like twenty years old. You attract all ages, don't you?"

Rebecca placed her hand, bruises peeking out from the bracelets, on top of Mitch's. "And I'm here with you."

He pulled her hand to his lips, kissing gently, ignoring the purple and brown bruises.

Rebecca smiled, twirling her hair around a finger. "The decorations put me in the mood for Christmas. I can't wait to go to Pine Meadow Garden and cut down a tree."

"I'm looking forward to it, too. Hopefully the weather will cooperate. Last year's temperature was almost too cold to deal with."

"Fifteen-degree temperatures take the fun out of the hunt. Remember how white our lips were by the time we got back into the car?"

"I couldn't speak properly for half an hour."

The server returned with water and steaming rolls and butter. "Have you decided on your orders yet?"

"We will have the prime rib special, mine with mashed potatoes and hers with twice-baked potatoes."

"How would you like your steaks cooked?"

"Medium-rare for me and medium-well." He pointed to Rebecca.

"And the dressing for your salads?"

"Blue cheese." Mitch looked at Rebecca.

"Italian for me, thank you."

Rebecca nibbled on a roll as Mitch described the condition of a car accident victim brought in that morning. The man's car had veered off the road and hit a tree. A broken neck. Barely surviving.

She put the roll down. Her father died in a car accident. He hit a tree, too. But it had been instant death.

"He just turned sixty. Became a grandpa for the first time a few months ago."

Her father never saw his granddaughters.

"His wife is devastated, and rightfully so. He may never walk again. May not even survive."

Like her dad.

"The wife is worried about their home not being suitable for a wheelchair. I thought that was premature. Let's see how he progresses. Make sure he makes it through the night."

"Mitch, you didn't say that?"

"Of course not. I'm just thinking out loud. She shouldn't jump to conclusions. Prepare herself for the worst."

Rebecca's stomach turned, and she wished he would change the subject, though she wouldn't dare ask him to.

Mitch stopped talking when the server returned. After uncorking the bottle of pinot noir, he poured the wine. "Can I get you anything else?"

"Not for now," Mitch said, turning away from the server.

"I've downloaded a set of instructions for a cradle. I'll handpick the maple slabs."

Rebecca couldn't make eye contact. She nodded.

"I'll drive out to the lumber company in Bath to get the wood. It'll be an adventure. It's like going to the wilderness with no civilization, except a lumber yard." He sipped his wine. "You might like to come with me."

She picked at her fingers under the table.

"When I have time, I'll start to plane the wood, making it useable and smooth. It'll be a process."

"And you'll love every minute of it."

"Absolutely. I'll be using my new planer. Remember you bought me that for my birthday?"

"Yes, and I had no idea what it was for."

He smiled. "You can watch me use it. I've got lots of tools that I'll use. I can make some detailed carvings with them."

The hope chest. Her father's intricate carvings.

Rebecca's stomach sank. She drowned out his words, her mind drifting to her father. His passion. He had created amazing works of art. Chairs, end tables, a hutch, bedroom furniture, her mother's jewelry box, clocks, her hope chest. He had a workshop in the far corner of their garage where he built everything. It was common for saw dust to blanket their car.

Mitch was so like him.

But so unlike him.

"Rebecca?"

"Hmm?"

"Are you listening to me? I was asking you if you wanted the cradle painted or stained."

"Oh. I don't know. Can I think about it?"

"How long do you need to think about it?" Annoyance rang in his voice. It wasn't a question and he didn't expect an answer.

He continued to talk about each step in the process of building the cradle. None of it interested Rebecca. The cradle would gather dust for a while, just as her father's car gathered saw dust. Their meals arrived.

Mitch bit into a piece of his steak and nodded his approval. "This is delicious. So tender."

Rebecca agreed. "Mine, too. Cooked to perfection."

"The hospital is perfect for me. I have a good chance at earning the chief resident position. I know I can beat Ben out for the job."

Rebecca scooped up a forkful of her twice-baked potato. "You work so hard. You deserve the promotion." The potato was good.

"Doctor Fields congratulated me on my Munchhausen Syndrome diagnosis in the baby Shepherd case." He finished off his pinot noir. "He says I'm a great doctor and I make the hospital proud."

"Of course you do."

As Mitch talked about recent cases, Rebecca felt the prospects of her life improving. With every new case that came and went, so too did the time until their vacation. It would be a perfect occasion to talk about going back to college and a possible promotion. She didn't want to hide anything else from him. The birth control pills were enough.

"I have a sad case right now."

"What happened?" Rebecca actually thought all his cases were sad. Her husband dealt with pain and death and misery every day.

"This woman broke her hip and developed pneumonia while recovering. She's still in the hospital. I don't think she'll make it."

Nan. Did he remember that was how Nan passed? How could he not? Mitch was Nan's resident while she was in the hospital and Rebecca had leaned on him for support. He was much more than a resident doctor to the family. He'd bought them coffee from the cafeteria, given them magazines and books to read, and kept a constant vigil by Nan's side.

For Rebecca, he was a shoulder to cry on, especially in the end. He had pulled her away from the hospital whenever possible. She'd been so struck with grief, she didn't notice his growing interest in her until it was pointed out by her mother. He'd brought her small carvings he had crafted. Her favorite, a simple wooden heart painted red, rested in the hope chest. Mitch's hobby had attracted Rebecca. He was just like her father, or so she'd thought.

They'd gone on walks at Seneca Lake, discussing their dreams. Mitch's goal was to become chief resident in five years. Mitch had listened with interest when she told him her wish of returning to school.

The remnants of muddy snow crunched beneath their feet as they'd walked along the trails in the park. She'd enjoyed the serenity and solitude. Except for dog walkers, few people visited the lake during the cool spring. Purple and yellow crocuses peeked out from beneath the snow. The first sign of spring. They'd picnicked on their next visit. Tulips had taken the place of the crocuses. New life. Life ended for Nan, but had just begun for Rebecca.

Fate had brought Rebecca and Mitch together.

"Horrible," she said somberly.

"I shouldn't have brought it up. It's similar to your situation and she has family all around her just like Nan did before her death. One of the many things that attracted me to you is your supportive family. Among other things, of course." He smiled.

"I didn't know that."

"I'm thankful I was Nan's attending resident."

The server interrupted, clearing the plates. Mitch ordered them coffee and a slice of blueberry cheesecake to share.

"The pace in the emergency room has been hectic lately." He ran his fingers through his hair. "We're short staffed right now."

Rebecca sat back and listened. She knew he didn't want to hear about her job. He didn't even want her working. This was just another time for him to shine.

The dessert and coffees arrived, and they were silent for a few moments.

Mitch moved a piece of cheesecake around his plate. "I love your confidence in me. I need your support."

He positioned the remaining cheesecake on his fork and placed it in front of her lips. She opened her mouth and he slid his fork in.

Rebecca let the cheesecake melt in her mouth.

"I'm excited for you to meet Doctor Fields tomorrow. He'll adore you."

"Thank you."

When the server brought the check, Mitch handed over his credit card.

"I'd like to take you on a carriage ride around the village," Mitch said and took her hand.

Just like the night he'd proposed. She wove her fingers into his and they pressed their palms together. "I'd love to. That would be so romantic."

The server came back, handing Mitch the bill folder.

Mitch stared at the name on the credit card. "Daniel Stevens! What the hell?"

"What happened?" Rebecca asked.

"Nothing I can't address." Mitch's hand shot up in the air, motioning the server back to their table. When the server returned, Mitch stood, getting in his face.

The server took a step back. "Is there a problem, sir?"

"There certainly is. You can get my credit card back, and immediately. How could you make a mistake like this?" He shoved the bill folder into the server's chest. "I'm not Daniel Stevens!"

The server flushed. "Oh, I'm so sorry. I mixed yours up with another table."

"Obviously." Mitch's fists were clenched.

"I'll fix it right away, sir." He hurried away.

Mitch sat down and twisted in his seat. Rebecca put a shaky hand on his. "It's an honest mistake, Mitch. Don't let it ruin our evening."

"I'm going to talk to someone about this. It's ridiculous."

"Please, we had a wonderful dinner. It will all be sorted out."

"Someone needs to speak up." He pounded the table and the utensils clinked. "This is inexcusable." He stood.

"What are you doing?"

"Looking for someone in charge."

"It was an honest mistake."

"You're repeating yourself, Rebecca."

"Mitch, let's just get our credit card and head to the carriage ride. Please, let it go."

He glared at her. "You never stick up for anything. You have no backbone." He left, following the path of the server. Rebecca stayed at the table, biting the skin on her fingernails.

People stared in her direction.

Mitch came back. "Get up. We're leaving." He grabbed her wrist and dragged her away. She winced in pain.

"You won't believe it. They had to chase the other person down in the parking lot. He had no idea he had the wrong credit card."

"What did you do?"

"I gave the server a piece of my mind. He should be fired for that."

They retrieved their coats and headed out the door. Mitch stormed to the car, Rebecca barely able to keep up. She shivered in the cold. No carriage ride. It wasn't like the night he'd proposed.

Chapter 6

Falling. Rebecca opened her eyes, but there was nothing to see. A blank slate. When she lifted her hands to her face, she gasped. They'd disappeared.

As she fell, she became lighter and lighter, until she was like a piece of paper drifting in the breeze.

She drifted downward until she was gone.

*****

Rebecca rolled over in bed and caught Mitch staring her way.

"Is everything okay?"

"Yes, I'm just taking you in."

He wasn't thinking of the server from the night before. Relief. She stretched and a smile grew on her lips.

"I'm really glad ...." Mitch said. His forehead was creased and his eyes were intense.

"What is it?" She stroked his chest.

He pulled her close and gave her a deep, sensual kiss. He leaned back into the pillow, and said, "I really admire Doctor

Fields. I've gotten to know him a little since he joined the hospital last summer."

She snuggled closer. "It sounds like he likes you, too."

"He keeps telling me that I'm a great resident."

She moved her hand up to his face and gently poked his nose. "That's because you are, silly."

Mitch grabbed her finger and playfully bit down.

"Maybe you'll get to know him better at the party."

"Yeah, that's what I was thinking. I'd like to golf with him this spring. I know he played several times last fall with the review committee that hired him."

Mitch's interest was a curious thing. Rebecca wondered what the appeal of Dr. Fields was, besides being his boss. Mitch hadn't been interested in getting to know his previous boss.

"I wish life had worked out differently."

"How so?"

He stiffened and looked away. "I resent my father for leaving us. Getting a birthday card in the month of my birthday doesn't count as keeping in touch. No football games. No playing catch in the backyard. No movie nights. Nothing after I was twelve."

Rebecca caressed his cheek, turning his face slightly toward hers. "It must have been so hard on you, especially in your teen years."

His gaze met hers. "Yeah, I guess so. But, I don't need him now that I'm an adult."

Mitch was wrong. Rebecca knew he needed his father, just as she needed hers. Every child needed a good dad. Maybe that's why she was so sure the pill was the right thing. Mitch wasn't ready to be a good father. Rebecca still mourned her dad greatly. She'd never forgiven herself for his death, and carried the guilt daily. She blamed herself. It was pouring when her father drove to pick her up from the party. She shouldn't have been drinking.

The rain ... the cloudless day had transformed into a night sky blanketed by thick rain clouds. Why?

The day had been spent at the beach on Tybee Island. The group of eight friends climbed 178 steps to the top of Tybee Island Light Station as they'd done many times before. The friends filled the platform. Rebecca's bright yellow summer dress whipped in the breeze.

"One last time before we all separate." Josh had put his arms around Rebecca and her best friend Jen. "Let's not forget each other."

They were quiet as they looked out at the water. Rebecca's eyes teared. It was bittersweet. She'd miss her family and friends, but was excited to start a new life at Flagler College. She could visit on weekends. The drive was less than three hours.

Stephanie said, "We'll never forget each other. I think we should come back here at this time every June. A reunion."

And they did, until Rebecca married Mitch. It was then the visits stopped for her.

After they'd had pizza and beers back at Josh's home, they gathered around the fire pit, waiting for darkness to set in. Rebecca kept glancing up at the darkening sky, weary of the rain clouds moving in.

The temperature cooled and she retrieved her light sweater from her car.

"Hey, Bec, can you grab a case of beer from my car?" Josh asked.

"How many cases did you get? There are only eight of us." She struggled with the beer, but was able to bring it to the folding chairs sitting around the bonfire.

They had lit the fire at dusk. Rebecca was on her third beer. She leaned over to swat at a mosquito and wobbled in the chair.

"Bec!" Jen laughed. "You're getting drunk!"

Rebecca responded by taking another swig of beer.

The roaring bonfire couldn't shake the chills that kept haunting Rebecca. She pulled the sweater closer and scooted toward the fire.

After four beers, she'd had enough. Her stomach cramped and when she stood, she stumbled.

Jen was at her side. Raindrops started to hit their faces. Lightning filled the sky, followed by bellowing thunder. Rain came down in pellets and everyone rushed toward the house.

Drenched when she got inside, her dress and sweater clung to her and she shivered.

Josh handed out towels, but even as she dried, the shivering wouldn't stop.

"I need to call for a ride home," she said, her stomach cramping again.

She used Josh's phone. "Dad, I can't drive. I've been drinking. I'm so sorry, but could you pick me up at Josh's?"

She listened. "Be careful of the rain. It's pouring."

"Yes, Dad, I love you more than life, too." She hung up the phone and the shaking turned into trembles.

God, how she missed her father. She shuddered and Mitch tightened his hold on her.

Yes, Mitch was wrong. He needed … some sort of father. Maybe he saw Dr. Fields as filling that void.

"I could never lose you. I survived my father abandoning me, but not you."

She stroked his chest again.

"What are you thinking about? You seem a million miles away."

She closed her eyes and whispered, "My dad."

He pulled her so close she could hardly breathe. His heart beating in the same quick rhythm as hers. Did he feel her pain? Was he trying to relieve her heartbreak as he'd done years ago when they'd first met? She started to cry in harsh, broken sobs.

He wiped at her tears, kissed her wet cheeks with real tenderness. She felt he could take an ounce of pain away with each gentle kiss. She slipped her arms around his body, melting into him.

He rolled on top of her, his muscular arms surrounding her.

"I love you." They spoke the words in unison, the moment he entered her. Powerful words.

"I need you, Mitch. I need your comfort."

He grunted in her ear.

After they made love, Rebecca snuggled in his arms. "Mitch?"

"Hmm."

She hesitated, and then said, "Do you often think of Maddie?" She'd wanted to ask that question so often. Maddie, his little sister, had meant the world to him. He'd said she called him her protector. Rebecca knew it killed Mitch that he couldn't protect her from bone cancer.

"Sometimes, especially when I visit the children's wing."

"Oh, hon, why do you do that to yourself? It's torture." She outlined his lips with her pointer finger, then pulled her hand away. She found his hand beneath the sheets, and held it gently.

"I don't know. I guess I need to. Maybe I'm hoping to see her there. I know it sounds crazy."

"Nothing about how people react to tragedy is crazy. We all handle it in our own way. Grieving is such a personal process."

He looked at her with a pained expression. "True, I guess that's why I visit. I like to sit with the children and talk to them. I feel closer to her somehow. I don't go very often, just when I get in a mood, you know?"

"I wish you could talk to me when you get sad."

"I stop by the nursery and admire the newborns. Oh, Rebecca. I can't wait. I hope we have a little girl."

To replace Maddie? What if they had a boy?

He squeezed her hand.

She wanted to help him forget his painful memories. Her eyes watered and tears spilled onto Mitch's chest. She started to wipe them away, but Mitch stopped her.

"Let me feel your pain. I need to."

As she cried, she realized her tears were mixing with his.

He grabbed her hips and pulled her on top of him. They made love again, this time with even more passion. Afterward, he released her and she slid down next to him.

"I can hear the wind blowing. Another storm's brewing," Mitch said. "I hope we don't get bad weather for Christmas. I want Evelyn's trip to be safe."

"Does it bother you to have my mom around for Christmas?" The slamming doors, working in the garage the whole visit, picking up extra hours at the hospital, his cold tone.

"You mean because of my own dysfunctional mom?"

"Yes"

He kissed her cheek. "Your mother is nothing like mine. She drank her life away and could barely care for Maddie and me."

When did his mother start drinking? He'd always been brief when discussing her. She learned only snippets of that part of his past. When she had tried to probe in the beginning of their relationship, he'd shut down.

Once, he'd yelled at her when she asked him how old he was when his mother died. The outburst should have been a warning sign, an indication of future anger, but she'd dismissed it, only wanting to see the good in him.

She massaged his shoulder, trying to ease some tension. "I'm sorry. I know the holidays are hard for you."

"You make them better. And I'm fine with Evelyn being here. I'm looking forward to it."

He hadn't been looking forward to her visits before. Why the change?

"Soon we'll have little ones to care for as well," said Mitch.

Chapter 7

Rebecca's body tingled when she remembered how gentle Mitch had been while making love that morning. Opening up to each other made Rebecca feel more secure. He rarely discussed his family, especially since they'd married. She wished she could talk at a more intimate level with him more often, but his erratic ways caused her to hold her tongue.

She busied herself getting ready. Tonight was the party. After pulling on her dark-purple, sleeveless dress, she clasped the new amethyst necklace. She studied herself in the mirror. Would her appearance please Mitch? Being in a room full of doctors intimidated her. Would she forget people's names? Use the wrong spoon? Say something that sounded uneducated? And going to the Chief of Staff's home made her all the more nervous.

She finished her make-up and added touches of perfume to her neck. It was a floral scent. She unwound the bandage at her wrist. Faded bruises. She picked out bracelets to match her dress, and of a size to cover the marks. The bruises represented reality. Her outfit, her perfume, her make-up were true covers. That unwanted feeling of dread threatened to devour her. *Get a hold of yourself, Rebecca. Mitch is excited about tonight. All will be fine. Just check your behavior.* Yes, it should be a peaceful evening.

Ice clinked in the living room. Mitch sat on the sofa, holding a scotch in one hand while shooing Scout away with the other.

Mitch stood and touched her long hair. "You look amazing. The most beautiful woman will be by my side tonight." He pulled her close, kissed her cheek, and held her.

"I'm nervous about tonight. I hope to make you proud."

"Looking like that, I'm already proud." Mitch looked her straight in the eye. "I'm glad you're mine."

That last statement was spoken in a serious tone, one Rebecca was only too familiar with. That feeling of dread revisited her.

"Remember, the important people at the party are the Fields and Derek. You need to impress them. Everyone else is secondary."

"I understand. Who else will be there?"

"Some friends. Branden and his wife, Julie. And of course, Melissa."

Rebecca had heard all those names before, all except Melissa. Who was she? Was she someone else to be extra polite to, more attentive?

"Several other residents as well. You don't need to know their names."

"Okay, I'll do my best."

"Yes, you will."

They pulled up the long driveway, and the estate came into view.

"This is what I expected to see. I heard their house was stunning."

Evergreens adorned with festive Christmas lights lined the perimeter of the property. Sugar maples lined the enormous circular driveway. As they approached the house, Rebecca marveled at the cobblestone walkway peeking out from under the melting snow. A red light illuminated a giant wreath affixed to the front of the house. A candle glowed in every window.

"How beautiful. Look at how the snowflakes glisten on the evergreens." She moved to point to the scenery, then lowered her hand.

Mitch rubbed her leg. "The grounds are amazing, aren't they?"

"Oh, yes."

"Jonathon wanted something more personal than a restaurant."

"He got it. This place is incredible."

They drove to the center of the drive. A valet motioned them to the house.

"Valet parking? How many people are they expecting?"

"They're probably just giving the neighborhood college kids a job to do."

Lighted garlands decorated the doorway where another attendant escorted them into the entranceway, then took their coats. The chandelier highlighted the cherry walls. She ran her hand along the wainscoting, touching the ridges of the smooth wood.

She fidgeted with an amethyst on her necklace and stepped closer to Mitch. An elegant woman approached. She wore a long, flowing, emerald dress and a scarlet shawl held together with a large Christmas tree pin. Her black hair, streaked with gray, bounced around her shoulders.

"Mitch?" the woman asked.

"Hello, Mrs. Fields. It's nice to see you, again. This is my wife, Rebecca."

"Please, call me Barb. Welcome to our home." She took Rebecca's hand. The smell of lavender wafted. Rebecca loved that scent. It was soothing, and very much matched Barb's manner. "I met Mitch in August at the golf tournament fundraiser for the children's wing. I'm sorry you were visiting your parents at the time. It would have been nice if you could have joined us."

Visiting my parents? One is dead. Mitch cleared his throat. His arm on her back pressed more firmly than necessary. "Oh, yes, I wish I could have, too. Raising money for the children's wing is such a great cause."

"Rebecca is interested in getting involved with some of the volunteer organizations at the hospital," Mitch said.

I am? Why would he say that and put her on the spot? They'd never discussed her volunteering. What other falsehood was she going to be confronted with?

"That is, as long as she isn't too busy when she has our first child."

Mrs. Fields smiled, and her welcoming eyes shifted to Rebecca's belly. "Are you expecting, Rebecca?"

Mitch spoke before Rebecca could answer, "Not yet, but we're hoping she will be soon."

"That will be exciting. I have two grown daughters of my own."

"How nice," Rebecca said, delivering her own smile. Volunteering? Did he plan for her to work at the hospital? Or was it an addition to the conversation to simply impress? "Are you enjoying Rochester? You moved here from Cleveland, right?"

"Yes, similar weather. I enjoy all four seasons." Barb stepped forward. "I'm sure you want to mingle with the other guests. I'll show you into the living room. We can talk there."

It was an immense room. A tray ceiling outlined with crown molding. Walls were taupe in color. Family pictures covered a red-brick mantelpiece which housed a lit fireplace. A large flat-screen TV sat above. Floor-to-ceiling bookshelves stood to the sides of the fireplace, filled with leather-bound books, antiques and more framed pictures. A sitting area with two black leather couches facing each other was perpendicular to the fireplace.

A large table along the far wall held hors d'oeuvres, and several smaller tables with chairs were placed near the food arrangement. Rebecca eyed a huge Christmas tree. The tree was adorned with white candles and burgundy bows, with a nativity scene beneath.

"Your home is amazing. How large is that Christmas tree?"

"You like it, Rebecca? Twelve feet. I love to decorate for the holidays. It's a challenge finding enough ornaments to fill it."

Mitch touched Rebecca's elbow. A man dressed in a black sweater and khakis approached.

"Rebecca, this is my husband, Jonathon," Barb said.

"Call me Jon, please." Dr. Fields extended his hand.

"It's nice to meet you." Rebecca shook his hand. "You have a beautiful home. It's so generous of you to host this party."

"Barbara and I thought throwing a party would be a nice gesture to all the doctors who work so hard." He patted Mitch's shoulder. "Mitch is making us proud at the hospital."

"I'm trying."

"We'll have to golf this spring."

"I'd like that."

Jonathon laughed and pointed. "I see trouble coming. I'll let you guys catch up," he said and they walked away.

A stocky man several years older than Mitch, stumbled from the bar area. His tie was loose, too loose. He smiled broadly and extended his hand. He took another five steps before his hand reached Mitch's. They shook. Rebecca could smell the alcohol on his breath.

"Glad to see you," the gentleman said.

"Rebecca, I'd like you to meet Derek Canton, whom I mentioned to you."

Derek looked her up and down as if she were on display. "Rebecca, you're a vision. Do you have any sisters?"

"No. No I don't."

The two men laughed.

"You'd better keep her on a short leash. She looks quite the catch."

Mitch sent a confident smirk Rebecca's way. "She knows her place is with me."

Derek said, "Let's go get you two fixed with some drinks," and he led the way.

Rebecca chewed her nails. Mitch sent her a frown. She dropped her hand to her side.

The bartender wiped the counter. "What can I get for you, sir?"

"A double scotch for me and ice water for my wife." Mitch motioned to Derek's almost empty glass and added, "And I think he needs a refill."

"Thanks for noticing, bro."

They took their drinks from the bartender.

Derek patted Mitch's back. "See you in a few."

Derek rejoined a loud group, announcing his return.

Couples were seated on the black leather sofas talking.

"I would like to introduce my wife, Rebecca. I don't think she has met any of you. This is Lee. You're in your third year of residency, correct?"

"Yes." He stood and extended his hand to Rebecca.

"This is my wife, Michelle," Lee said.

Michelle smiled. "Hello, it's nice to meet you both."

Mitch gestured to the second couple. "Tim's in the same year as I am."

Something tugged at her and she rolled Tim's name over in her mind. During dinner about three years ago, Mitch had mentioned Tim Miller. The conversation came flooding back.

Mitch had said, "Tim is very talented in the ER, but ..."

"But what?"

He'd snickered. "He's choosing to become a general surgeon instead of working through to become a top notch surgeon like he could be."

"What's wrong with that?"

"Just general?"

"You're being silly, Mitch. That's a huge accomplishment."

"The point is, he's settling."

Rebecca had scoffed. "Settling? Please!"

She'd talked back. She could back then. Or so she had thought. It felt as if it was yesterday. Mitch had leaned across the dinner table and slapped Rebecca's face, warning her never to speak to him in that tone again. It was the first time Mitch hit Rebecca. He had continued eating as if nothing happened. Tim wasn't mentioned again in conversation.

Rebecca's hand touched her cheek. Yes, yesterday.

Mitch brought her back to the present. "You must be Emily. Tim talks about you all the time. What are you up to these days?"

"I'm staying home taking care of our two-year-old twins."

"Oh, how sweet. Do you have a picture?" Rebecca asked.

Tim laughed. "Picture? She could show you their pictures on her phone all night." He pulled Emily closer and kissed her. She seemed to melt into his arms.

Rebecca flipped through the photos. One in particular caught her eye. The little girls sat on a porch swing wearing matching, pink-fleece jackets and jeans. Their smiling faces tugged at Rebecca.

Michelle said, "We have a three-year-old boy named Noah. Would you like to see pictures of him, too?"

"Please," Rebecca said.

A photo of Michelle's son on a slide at the playground made Rebecca laugh. "How cute! His hair is sticking up from the static electricity on the slide." Moving to the next picture, she noticed it was of Michelle and Emily. They cuddled close to each other. Their intimacy showed.

She stopped at the last photo and stared. It was of Noah sitting on Lee's lap outside on the grass. Autumn leaves surrounded them. It was a stunning photo, shot from above, both engrossed with something in the distance. She saw love and contentment, and lots of it.

She returned Michelle's cell with a hollow feeling in her chest. "Your girls are adorable, and Noah, he is precious."

Mitch excused them both and they drifted toward the group Derek had joined. He squeezed Rebecca's arm. She winced.

"I thought you were going to look at those pictures all night."

Mitch introduced Rebecca to Melissa, another colleague. Her boyishly cut jet-black hair was a sharp contrast to Rebecca's long, lighter hair. Melissa didn't extend her hand.

"I'm Branden and this is Julie, my wife." He put his hand out for Rebecca to shake and Julie gave her a quick hug.

"When are we going out for drinks again?" Melissa asked the group.

Branden laughed. "Soon. Sunny's dartboard is waiting for us. Our game was interrupted the other night. Of course, I was winning."

Melissa nudged Mitch. "I want a rematch on our pool game, too. You're just too good."

Mitch didn't respond.

"If I wasn't so busy studying for finals at law school, I'd join you more often. You guys have so much fun," Julie said.

"Yeah usually at my expense." Branden faked a frown.

Everyone laughed.

"You're an easy target," said Melissa.

"Rebecca, you should join us sometime," Branden said.

Melissa turned quickly, but not before Rebecca caught a distasteful look.

Mitch didn't comment on the invitation. She didn't know Mitch went to Sunny's with them more than once every few months. She believed he was studying. Had he lied? He only discussed the stress and exhaustion of his job and his study. Nothing else.

Barb escorted a tall, strawberry-blond haired man to their group. Rebecca saw Mitch's lip twitch. Everyone shook his hand, except Mitch.

"Ben, this is my wife Rebecca." Mitch's tone was tight.

"I'm happy to meet you." Ben's voice was warm and his smile contagious.

Rebecca knew Mitch and Ben were in the same year of residency. Although they worked together for a long time, Mitch rarely spoke of Ben, and as far as she knew they never socialized outside the hospital. Ben asked if anyone needed refills.

"A glass of wine?" he asked Rebecca.

"She's the designated driver," Mitch answered.

"More water, then?" He spoke with a slight southern accent, and aimed the question at Mitch. There was an uncomfortable silence.

"Then I'll have to go to the bathroom." Neither man looked to her. "Well, I guess I'll take the risk."

Ben returned with the water. Rebecca put her hand out, bracelets clinking, and took the glass. Her eyes traveled to where he stared. The bruises, visible when the bracelets slid up her arm. Ben glared at her husband, but Mitch was oblivious to the heat. He was deep in discussions of a medical case. Rebecca moved the glass from her injured wrist to her free hand and the bracelets fell back into place.

"Thanks." She leaned into Mitch. He slipped his arm around her shoulder, still discussing the case.

At a break in the conversation, Mitch said to Rebecca, "Everyone I work with closely is here, except for the ones who have rounds. I think several younger residents haven't arrived yet. They'll probably be here any minute. Also, I just heard that Doctor Fields has invited some of the nurses who are off duty."

"I thought only residents and spouses were coming."

"As long as Doctor Fields is graciously hosting the party, he can do what he wants. Besides, there's plenty of room here for a few more people, and they're not going to run out of food or drink too soon."

New voices came from the hallway.

"Are they doctors?" Rebecca whispered.

"Yes and a couple of nurses."

One woman wore a skin-tight red dress that barely covered her large breasts. Lipstick matched the dress.

"Mitch, who's the woman?"

"Oh, that would be Amy. She's hard to miss. Stunning, but too showy for my taste."

"Is she a doctor, too?" She linked her arm in his.

"No, she's a nurse on the maternity ward. She had a personal invitation from Jon."

Jonathon moved toward Amy with a drink. She smiled at him seductively and brushed his hand. Jonathon didn't pull away. In fact, he then positioned his hand about two inches above Amy's rear.

Clapping hands grabbed everyone's attention.

Barb stood in the center of the room. "Can I have everyone's attention? Dinner will be served soon. Please stop at the bar on the way to your seats."

Six tables with six place cards at each. Golden fabric covered the chairs. Red bows were tied behind. Green linen tablecloths, red napkins, and green taper candles. Each place setting held a Christmas-themed cookie-cutter favor decorated with a festive bow.

Rebecca felt eyes aimed her way. Ben. His gaze moved from her eyes to her wrist. She fiddled with her necklace. He started to move toward Mitch.

She pulled her husband away from the discussion. "Let's go to the bar before it gets crowded."

When they found their table, Mitch said, "Let's see who we're sitting with. Oh, good, Derek, Branden and Julie."

"Seems I'm here, too," said Ben.

Mitch slammed his drink down, the scotch almost spilling over the side of his glass.

The silverware was sterling silver, similar to the set left to her by Nan. Rebecca never used the set, but Mitch made sure it was polished and in its place.

The servers were dressed in similar clothing to the servers at Vincent's. Sharp black tuxedo's and crisp, white collared shirts with a black bow-tie. They placed plates of filet mignon covered with mushroom sauce, baked potatoes and roasted mixed vegetables at each guest's place. Mikasa china. Rebecca thought it was almost too nice to use. She couldn't imagine the Fields owned forty place settings of the elegant dinnerware.

She looked up. A baroque crystal chandelier. Its lights sparkled. Maybe the Fields did have forty place settings. Maybe more. Mitch elbowed her. She looked at him and he motioned for her to pay attention to their conversation.

"I've been taking a cooking class in my spare time," Julie said, pouring herself some water.

Derek wiped his mouth with his napkin. "That must be a treat for Branden. I usually grab my meals at the hospital."

"I love going home and sampling Julie's *taste tests*. She's becoming a wonderful chef," Branden said, patting his stomach.

"Mitch, can't you brag about your beautiful wife's cooking?" Derek asked.

"Maybe Julie could give her the name of her instructor," Mitch said.

Rebecca's face burned.

"Well, that explains why I've never been invited over for dinner." Derek laughed.

"She's from the South. Georgia, specifically," Mitch explained. "They have many different tastes down there. Heavier meals. Lots of barbecue and greens."

Rebecca picked at her fingernails, until she felt Mitch's stare.

Ben interrupted, "Would anyone like another drink? I'm going to the bar. Mitch? Mitch?"

Mitch emptied his glass then moved it to the center of the table. "Double scotch."

Ben left with three empty glasses.

"Besides," Mitch continued, "I guess I didn't expect much from a southern belle. I thought it served me right."

Derek laughed.

Rebecca twisted her napkin. She looked at the women at the table. All eyes were down.

Ben returned with the drinks. "Are you okay, Rebecca?"

Mitch took the drink from Ben. "She's fine. She's just sensitive about southern jokes."

"Maybe because they aren't funny," Ben said.

Rebecca squirmed in her chair.

Mitch snickered. "Oh, that's right. You're from the south, too. Vanderbilt for med school?"

Surprised he knew, Ben said, "Yeah."

"You southerners like to stick together, don't you?" Mitch took a swig of his scotch.

"Mitch, please," Rebecca whispered.

"What's wrong, Rebecca? I'm just talking to Ben about southerners."

"Well, my ex-wife wasn't much of a cook either," said Derek.

"Which one?" Branden asked.

The group laughed.

Chapter 8

The main course finished. Mitch and Rebecca stood by the fireplace. *It's A Wonderful Life* was playing on the TV. Most of the nurses collected by the bar talking and laughing with some of the residents. Rebecca wrung her hands together.

"Mitch?"

No answer.

Julie, Michelle and Emily stood near a window whispering. When they caught Rebecca looking their way, they turned their backs. She didn't want to be there. Ben knew her predicament, she was sure of it, and he seemed unconcerned about showing his disgust. He could only make things worse.

Mitch pushed an empty glass toward her. "Get me another drink, would you?"

She did, and when she returned Mitch wore an indecipherable look. "Is everything okay? Did I take too long?"

"I was just watching you. I like to see what you're looking at."

"What I was looking at?"

He didn't respond.

Ben returned to their group and Branden asked, "Have you been skiing lately?"

"Whenever I can get away and the conditions are right."

"The slopes at Bristol Mountain have been nice lately, with all the fresh powder."

"I agree. With all this new snow, I'm in heaven," Ben drawled.

The southern accent drew a comfortable familiarity. A boyfriend left behind at Flagler College. His southern drawl had soothed Rebecca. He'd been gentle and kind. Laid back and calm. He was always happy to be with her. Would he still be or would she have messed up that relationship, too?

"Like I said, I like to see what intrigues you."

Mitch caught her. Caught her doing what. Daydreaming?

"I'm not sure what you're talking about, Mitch."

"Ben."

"Oh, really? It's just the accent. I was thinking of ... of Dad. Excuse me, please. I need the bathroom."

In the bathroom mirror, a pale face stared back. Tired eyes. A slender body way too thin. That wasn't the old Rebecca. *Her* skin was tanned from the southern sun. She'd worn bright pink lipstick and painted her perfect fingernails to match. She rinsed her face, applied fresh make-up and headed back out to the party.

Ben stood outside the bathroom door.

"Oh, you startled me. I didn't know anyone was waiting to get in."

His body blocked the entrance to the hallway. "I don't need the bathroom. I want to speak with you."

"Excuse me," she said, attempting to move around him.

"Rebecca."

"I can't."

"Why? Listen. I see things. Things you try to hide." His eyes dropped to her wrist.

"It's none of your business."

"Why? Do you believe you deserve this?"

"Please move."

"Where did those bruises come from?" Ben didn't wait for a reply. "At least let me give you a phone number to call. It's a support service. You don't have to go through this alone."

He held out a card. *Domestic Violence* blared from the print.

"I don't need—"

Derek's approaching snicker interrupted the exchange.

"You have someone to talk to if you need it." Ben walked off.

Derek grabbed her arm tightly as she tried to pass. "What are you up to?"

She tried to pull away. "What do you mean?"

"You and Ben were deep in conversation. What were you talking about?"

"Nothing. Let me go."

He released her with a jerk. She swayed, and caught herself.

"Were you two flirting? Was he giving you his phone number?"

"What? Of course not." She rushed away, hearing a drunk chuckle.

Mitch spotted her and shook his almost empty drink. She headed to the bar and returned with a fresh scotch.

"Well, we have to pay because some doctors screw up," Mitch said.

"Yeah, that's the way things work," said Branden.

Jonathon joined the conversation. "A few horrible mistakes and many doctors are made to pay higher premiums."

"At least premiums have fallen in the last couple of years," Melissa said.

Rebecca checked the clock on the mantel. It was 8:45. Trays of desserts were being placed on the tables. How much longer?

"Excuse me. I want to catch up with Derek," said Mitch.

"Mitch," said Rebecca, placing a hand on his arm. She didn't want Mitch to hear a word Derek had to say. That drunken man could blurt anything.

But Mrs. Fields interrupted. "Have you been enjoying your evening, Rebecca?"

She looked past Barb. Mitch and Derek headed past Jonathon and the nurses. "It's been wonderful. The food was delicious and your home is beautiful."

"I'm so glad you've enjoyed yourself." She pulled her shawl around her shoulders and her eyes followed Rebecca's.

"You've done a terrific job."

"I enjoy playing hostess."

Amy in the red dress slipped a finger around Jonathon's belt buckle.

Barb looked away from the spectacle. "You may have found that being married to a doctor has some disadvantages. It's very stressful, demanding work. Sometimes the hours can be ridiculously long. You probably wonder at times if you're still married. I find having my own hobbies and interests helps me get through the lonely and stressful times."

What was she trying to tell her? That a woman should understand her husband's affairs and flirtations? That a woman should expect and accept infidelities? "I have a part-time job for those reasons."

"The key is having your own identity separate from your husband. So many women make the choice to put their lives, their dreams on hold. Later they regret doing that."

"I'll think about what you said. Thank you."

She patted Rebecca's hand. "You're welcome. I hope you keep in touch after the party."

"I'd like that."

"I want to help other young women." She glanced in Jonathon's direction. "I just don't want you to be alone."

"Why would my wife be alone?" Mitch interrupted. His tone was steady, but his eyes penetrated Barb.

"Oh, Mitch. I referred to when you're working long hours at the hospital, that's all. It not only affects you, it affects those around you, especially your wife."

"Really?" Mitch asked.

"I was giving your wife a window into my past, so she could more easily get through the difficult times and the stresses associated with being the wife of a doctor. She can talk to me if she has trouble dealing with the pressures. Isn't that right, Rebecca?"

Mitch silently dared her to reply. How could Rebecca undo this? "If I ever feel lonely because Mitch is working and studying, I'll call you. He's a wonderful husband, and has made sacrifices to help others, and those sacrifices come at a price. It's kind of you to be so supportive of us. Isn't it, honey?" She took Mitch's hand. He squeezed it so hard she felt the bones roll.

"You've handled being alone since we've been married. Why is it a problem now?"

"Mitch—"

"Rebecca didn't say it was a problem. Actually, she didn't mention it at all. I'm just trying to help people in situations similar to mine. Is there a problem with that, Mitch?"

"Thank you for your concern, Barb." Mitch gave Rebecca's hand a tug. "Please excuse us."

Mitch grabbed her elbow and squeezed as they walked.

"Let me explain," Rebecca whispered.

"What in the hell were you thinking? She's my boss's wife. Everything you say goes directly to Jonathon's ears."

"I … I didn't say anything bad. Please, believe me."

"I could snap your neck in half right here."

She tried to wiggle free from his grasp.

"How dare you talk about me or our relationship to anyone?"

They stood waiting for their coats.

"I didn't. She started—"

"Do you think I'm a complete idiot? I heard the conversation." He backed her into an empty corner of the room, away from everyone's sight. "We'll go back to the party, say good night, and then leave. Can you do that without badmouthing me?"

Mitch located Jonathon and thanked him for his hospitality.

"Oh, you're leaving? You'll miss the dessert," Jonathon said.

"Thanks anyway. I have an early shift."

"I'm glad the two of you were able to make it this evening. Mitch, a fascinating case you had. We'll discuss it more some time."

"I'm looking forward to it."

"It was very nice meeting you, Rebecca. Mitch is a lucky man." Jonathon shook her hand.

Chapter 9

Rebecca could tell Mitch was a volcano about to erupt. The valet returned with his Lexus, leaving the driver's side door open. Mitch shoved cash in the valet's hand, threw the coats in the back seat, and climbed in.

Mitch had been drinking. Too much. He shouldn't be driving. They had planned for her to drive home. She couldn't say anything now, not in front of another person. She walked around to the passenger's side. Her heels clicked on the pavement as loud as her heart beat.

As soon as she shut the door, Mitch pushed his foot down on the gas.

Rebecca tightened her seatbelt. "Mitch, do you want me to drive?"

He scoffed. In the moonlight, Mitch's eyes looked like black glass marbles; cold and inhuman. He sped along the unfamiliar road.

Rebecca squeezed her hands together and prayed. *Please, God. Help me.* She knew what was to come. His anger meant serious injuries. He didn't blink and his face was twisted in a crazed expression. He misjudged a curve in the road. The car crossed the line and traveled into the other lane. A semi coming from the opposite direction blared its horn. Rebecca slapped a hand over her mouth. Tires screeched. Mitch yanked the wheel to the right, barely missing the truck's bumper. He over-corrected. The Lexus skidded across the road onto the snow-covered shoulder. Out of control, it spun into a one-eighty, snow flying everywhere.

When it slowed, Mitch somehow pulled it back onto the road.

"M-Mitch," Rebecca tugged at her seatbelt. "P-Please let me drive."

His white knuckles gripped the wheel.

"I really think—"

"Do you? Do you *really* think?"

A deserted parking lot was on the left and he swerved. She crashed into the door from the force of the turn, and grabbed at her elbow. He sped through the lot until he reached a corner, slamming his foot on the brake. The car came to a halt. Rebecca's head whipped forward and then back into the headrest. The regular headache returned.

"Do you really think, Rebecca?"

"I-I didn't drink any alcohol. Wouldn't it be better if I drove?"

"So, you know what's best now? What's best for our marriage and us, too, I suppose? You're an even bigger idiot than I thought." Mitch jammed the car into park.

Get out of the car and run, a familiar voice in her head yelled. *Anna?*

He'd catch her. Her dress. Her high heels. He'd catch her and beat her.

"I want you to know I didn't, nor would I ever say anything negative to Mrs. Fields about us. I understand and accept all aspects of your career."

"Really? Do you think I'm a fool?"

"No, I don't think that."

Get out of the car and run! Now!

"Out of all the people that you could bond with in this town, you choose my boss's wife? Are you trying to ruin my career?" Mitch banged the palm of his hand on the steering wheel. "A wife is supposed to be supportive, not look for allies that she can run to if I fail."

"I am supportive of you, Mitch. I do everything you want me to." Her fingers searched for the door lock.

"You betrayed me. How dare you confide in that woman about your loneliness?"

She put her hand to her heart. "She said those words. I'm not lonely, Mitch. I'm not. I'm happy. Really happy." Her voice faltered and she couldn't breathe.

"And Ben?"

"What about Ben? I hardly know him."

He grabbed her hand. She pulled it back as if it had been bitten.

"Don't give me that crap."

"Mitch, please. Can we just talk about this?" She worked harder to find the lock.

"Rebecca, you're the one who made me angry. You should have thought about that before you had private, intimate conversations with my colleagues. You did this to us, not me. Take some responsibility for a change."

Her voice quivered. "It was just small talk. Really. Barb won't think any more on it."

"But Ben. What was reported to me makes me believe that something is going on between the two of you."

She whispered, "Nothing happened. Nothing is happening."

"And I'm supposed to believe that?" Mitch shot back.

Tears rolled down her face. "Mitch, please."

He ignored her. His strength grew as hers declined.

"What do you have to say for yourself?"

Crying, Rebecca held onto the door with one hand.

"Answer me, you bitch!"

Run, the voice yelled again.

She unlocked the door and released the seatbelt. He lunged, grabbing for her, but missed. She ran through the dark parking lot, her heart racing. He was faster. She screamed when he grabbed her, but he put one hand over her mouth and his other arm around her waist and pulled her to the car, her shoes scuffing on the concrete. He backed up with her in his grip. The heel of her right shoe snapped off.

Fight! You can do it! Bite his hand!

She bit down on his finger with all of her strength.

He lost his grip. "You bitch! You'll pay."

She scrambled to get away.

He grabbed her hair, and yanked her back toward his body. He made his way to the car, pulling her with him. He pushed the seat back and threw her inside. Leaning in, he stood over her. She kicked her legs at him, but he shoved them aside. Yelling, his voice echoed so loudly she couldn't understand his words. She cried until she coughed. Mitch grabbed her throat and squeezed. She clawed at his arm. He didn't relent. She pulled, but nothing worked. Stars filled her eyes and she lost focus. Her lungs felt like they were about to explode.

"You are *my* wife, and don't you ever forget it."

Her limbs became heavy, the feeling spreading throughout her body. She felt as if she was drowning and couldn't get her head above the water, couldn't find the surface.

"'Keep fighting, keep fighting'," someone said.

Who was talking to her? She tried to fight, but couldn't. Her body gave out. Darkness took over.

The pressure on her neck eased. Mitch grabbed her shoulders and started shaking them. She heard Mitch shouting. He sounded far away. He shook her and started breathing air into her lungs. She was pulled from the darkness. She could feel life entering her body again and her muscles felt pinpricks.

"Rebecca!"

She unwillingly returned to consciousness. In the distance, she heard muffled voices. The sound grew louder and more distinct. Rebecca blinked. Mitch's face came into focus. Tears rolled down her cheeks. A deep awareness washed through her entire body and her skin tingled.

She gulped in air. "Mitch?" The word barely escaped her lips.

"Dammit, Rebecca," Mitch said, recovering his voice. "Why in the hell do you make me so angry? Honestly, it's as if you do it intentionally."

Her throat burned and her chest tingled. She wanted to sleep, return to that darkness and never wake. She wished the horrible experience was a bad dream. She turned in Mitch's direction. Gone were the piercing black eyes of an animal. What remained was tired and troubled. He looked older than his thirty years. He moved away from the car and yelled into the empty parking lot.

"Why? Why do you do these things, Rebecca?" He punched his fist in the air. Suddenly he walked back to her.

She hadn't done anything wrong.

It isn't my fault. Nothing has been my fault. It's all you, Mitch. It's all you.

He slammed her door, moved around the car, and got in the driver's seat.

It's all the stress you've been under. I just have to make it to his exam. Things will get better when the exam is done. It has to.

Once he pulled into the garage, he stormed out of the car, and disappeared into the house.

I am not to blame.

Chapter 10

"*I*t's beautiful out here," Rebecca said.

"Almost as beautiful as you." Mitch stood at the helm. Bandages were wrapped around the steering wheel. Bandages she'd worn. "But don't look behind you."

She turned, despite his warning. The sky darkened and lightning flashed in the distance.

"Are we safe?"

He laughed. "I am."

She walked to the stern. "Should I put the life-preserver on?"

"Don't bother."

Her arms prickled at the sight of his crooked smile. "Shouldn't we turn back?"

"But we're just getting started. Don't worry."

"The sky, Mitch. It's turning, and the clouds ..." She stood holding onto the railing. She looked up. Her college application was taped to the mast, sagging as it became wet.

Heavy rain started to pelt her skin and she rushed to pull on her raincoat.

Mitch laughed. "That's not going to do much in this weather. Trust me, you'll be soaked in a few minutes."

He took her in his arms. He kissed her. A long, deep kiss.

She closed her eyes, melting into the curves of his body, fear abating.

He whispered something in her ear, but she couldn't make out the words.

She felt pressure on her arms. Mitch squeezed and grabbed them tight. She opened her eyes and saw the face of a devil.

He pushed her backward, hard.

She started to fall, into the lonely ocean. Hands reaching out toward him, she screamed, "Why?"

"You know why."

*****

Rebecca stretched her sore body to make sure everything worked. Everything did, but the pain was excruciating. She wanted to block out last night, but everything kept needling, kept pushing to the forefront of her thoughts.

It wasn't her fault. Had it ever been?

A fight over a phone call. Slaps because of crumbs on the counter. A twist of her arm when his car wouldn't start. A beating in spite of a mistake. His parking ticket. A bad golf game. Burnt chicken. Wet laundry. No mayonnaise.

Before the beatings came constant yelling and putdowns. He threw an over-cooked meal into the kitchen wall. She couldn't do anything right, he'd said. She was a lousy cook, cleaner, wife, and lover.

He'd told her repeatedly his actions were caused by her wrongdoings. Why had she believed him? When had she lost her self-esteem?

Now, she'd have to spend an entire Sunday with Mitch at home. She sank deeper into the mattress in the guest room, and fear covered her like a blanket. Would she have to pretend last night didn't happen? Maybe he'd go to the hospital and study for a few hours. She could wait him out until he left.

Mitch knocked at the door and then entered. "Rebecca, the coffee is brewing. Why don't you come and get yourself a cup? It's getting late."

Late? Late for what? She obediently pulled herself out of bed and headed into the kitchen.

Mitch didn't make eye contact. "I'm running to the store to get *The New York Times*." Though his tone was less hostile than last night, his voice still had an edge.

He twisted the jacket he held as if he was wringing out a towel. Those were the hands and the actions she felt last night. Rebecca leaned on the counter.

"I'll be a few minutes. Save me some."

This was his Sunday ritual. Shower, make coffee, buy a paper as the coffee brewed, return and drink the coffee while reading the paper. No time wasted.

She watched the car disappear down the street. Could she make it through the day?

She sniffed the coffee as she wiped spilled grounds off the counter. The smell evoked memories. Making meals with Nan in this kitchen. Sipping coffee with David at Susie's Café talking about her father. The college cafeteria surrounded by close friends. How times had changed.

A wooden bunny sat on her placemat. When had he finished this one? Another reminder of the baby Mitch wanted so desperately, but wasn't going to get. She analyzed it, amazed at the talent Mitch had for his artwork. The hope chest would hold another heirloom. She placed it at the bottom of the chest with the others.

Rebecca went to the bathroom, sat on the toilet. Her period had come. *How ironic. I'm in control, if only over a small part of my body.* With everything that had happened recently, she hadn't paid attention to the number of pills left in the pack.

She pulled up her pajama bottoms and slid down the wall until she sat on the floor. Strangely, she giggled. And the giggles turned into laughter. She laughed so hard, she started to cry. She cranked the shower nozzle on to drown out the noise in case Mitch came home.

In her mind, she thanked Anna. Thanked her for her support, her advice, her friendship, her wise words.

After showering, she wiped steam off the mirror and examined her bruises closer. Deep purple fingerprints encircled her neck. When she touched the area, she winced. Aching consumed her and she rubbed her midsection. She dried her hair and ran her fingers through it. She grabbed her pink fleece bathrobe from the hook and pulled it on.

After breakfast, she sat at the dining room table, sipping coffee, with Scout at her feet. Her emotions alternated between fear and pain to strength and control, although terror remained at the forefront.

Mitch returned and slammed the garage door. Coffee sloshed out of the cup she clutched, burning her hand.

"Did you see the passenger side door, Re-bec-ca?"

She dabbed at her burnt hand with a napkin. "No."

He paced back and forth.

With a scratchy voice, she said, "What happened?"

He loomed over her. "I don't know, Re-bec-ca." He picked up her mug and threw it against the wall. It broke into large pieces, sending coffee spilling everywhere. Scout ran and hid.

She lifted her hands, covering her face, fearful of what was coming next.

"There's a dent in the side of the passenger door. It looks like someone opened their door into it."

She poured sincerity into her voice. "Do you have any idea when it happened?"

"It had to be last night. I got the car washed the other day and examined both the interior and exterior. The mark wasn't there."

"Maybe when the valet parked the car."

Mitch walked around the dining room table "I was thinking the same thing. Idiots!" He threw the newspaper down, poured himself a cup of coffee, then sat across from her.

"Maybe you should call Doctor Fields," Rebecca said. "Let him know what happened to the car."

"Oh, sure," he said. "It would be a great idea to let the chair of the department, the one who so generously opened his home to us, know that someone he hired for the evening damaged my car. Brilliant, just brilliant."

"I guess there's nothing we can do about it, unfortunately." She got up and pushed the pieces of the broken mug into a dustpan.

"I'll get it fixed myself, if I can. It'd be pretty tactless to dump it on Jon."

She bent down to look under the table for any missed pieces. Her body screamed in pain from the movement and she had to put her hand on the chair to pull herself up.

Mitch glanced to the floor, and said nothing.

She set to work on the day's chores. Clean clothes from the basement dryer. Folding. She heard 'Reba' spoken in the distance. It wasn't Mitch's voice. A fleeting memory of her father patting her head while her mother and she folded the laundry at the kitchen table drifted by. Her father would be horrified to see the life she'd made for herself. He'd intervene. He'd never let his Reba be treated poorly. Never. She quickly dismissed the thought and took some clothing to the bedroom for ironing.

Mitch liked all of his pants and shirts ironed with razor sharp creases. Ironing his clothes took at least an hour. It was one in a long list of chores that Mitch enforced, including polishing her silver and dusting the shelves that held his medical journals. Mitch stormed around the kitchen. He cursed and muttered, swearing about the valet. She didn't respond. She didn't dare.

She put the clothes away in the closet, ensuring everything was in perfect order. She made the bed and checked that the knick-knacks and trophies on his dresser were in their appropriate places. Mitch went to work at his computer.

"Come in here."

She rushed in.

Mitch was holding his cell. "Derek sent a text. He's coming over to watch the game this afternoon."

She didn't want to see him, of all people, especially today.

"We commented last night that we should get together more often. We're both big football fans."

"I have a lot of errands to run today, so I won't be around."

"Can't they wait? Derek would like to visit with you, too. He keeps asking if you have a sister."

"I have to finish our Christmas shopping and get groceries to make cookies. I need to get it done before my mom arrives on Friday."

Mitch's eyes narrowed. "Blow off our company to go to the mall. I'll explain to Derek that you prefer to shop rather than socialize with your husband and his friends."

"I didn't know you invited anyone over. Why do you need me?"

"I *need* you here because you are my *wife*. It's nice to show others that I'm able to spend time at home with you."

Arguing more would be dangerous. He would equate her leaving the house for any reason with her unwillingness to please him.

"I'll just go the grocery store. And when I get back, I'll make some appetizers for you both."

"You should wear a turtleneck. Your neck is red," he said, not even glancing in her direction.

She shuffled into the bedroom, her head hanging low. Tears welled in her eyes as she threw her robe in the corner, and she crumpled onto the bed wearing only underwear. She needed to explode. Rebecca squeezed a pillow, held it to her face and screamed. She held it close. Despair and grief fell into that pillow. It grew wet.

She had to stop. She had to stop before Mitch made her stop. She was trapped. A trapped animal. Tethered and kept on a taut leash. Unable to escape its keeper. She changed into a charcoal turtleneck and jeans, hung the robe in the bathroom, and called to Mitch. "I'm leaving for the store."

She stopped at an intersection and looked both ways. To the right was the store. To the left was the New York State Thruway. If she turned left, she'd be on the Thruway in moments. From there, she could go anywhere, be anywhere, anywhere without Mitch. No cars were coming in either direction. Her heart beat fast as she pictured life without Mitch. Promotion. No more abuse. No more fear. Freedom to choose what she ate. How she dressed. Whom she befriended. Complete freedom.

Rebecca turned right and drove to the store. Soon they'd be on vacation.

Chapter 11

Keep thinking about Anna. Anna's words. Anna is strong. Be Anna.

Thinking that way gave her the little bit of strength she needed. Rebecca pasted on a smile, grabbed two overstuffed bags of groceries, and headed into the lion's den.

She pushed her way through the door with bags in tow. "Hello! Hi, Derek." She gave him a quick smile. He was leaning back on the sofa. A pillow in his hands covered much of his Buffalo Bills shirt. He gave her too much attention in reply. Those eyes wandered north and south.

"I'll make a plate of munchies." She was more than happy to be away from that room, away from those ogling eyes, away from Mitch and his ... his outbursts.

Oven on. Fresh vegetables by the sink. Beer in the refrigerator. Chicken wings in the oven. She washed vegetables. She worked in slow motion.

"That wasn't a touchdown!"

"They'll bring it back after they view the replay," Mitch said.

Broccoli, celery, and red and green peppers cut. Rebecca placed everything on a festive Christmas tray, a plate that seemed abhorrent today. She added some ranch dressing, and a little extra. The dressing covered baby Jesus.

Rebecca put the veggie tray and two Corona's on the coffee table. Buffalo Bills were playing the Miami Dolphins. Rebecca didn't care for football. The screen told her Buffalo was up, ten to seven, and the second quarter had just started.

"Thanks, Rebecca," said Derek.

Her reply came with eyes set on the TV. "You're welcome." She left the men to their game.

The oven timer beeped. While the wings cooled, she cleaned the countertop and wiped the fingerprints off the stainless steel appliances, then took the wings into the living room. Buffalo was still up.

"Would you like to join us?" Derek asked.

"I'd like to finish a book."

"She doesn't like football," Mitch announced. "Damn! What sort of block was that?" he yelled to the TV.

"Let me know if I can get you anything else." She felt Derek's eyes leering again. Rebecca smoothed her jeans with her hands and headed for her room.

She plopped onto the bed and reached for her book. She was halfway through it. It was about a dysfunctional family who lived in the Civil War era. The year was 1864, the year before Lincoln was assassinated, and the main character, Susannah, was in love with one of her father's slaves. Reading was the one thing that stole Rebecca away from her life. She time-travelled, transported, floated in another era. Scout joined her, and purred near her ear just as Susannah tripped over a wagon wheel and twisted her ankle outside the slave's hut. The cat's sound had a rhythmic quality. The trip and the twist jolted Rebecca from the story. She thought of the pain in her own legs. That was the end of her concentration. Susannah's father was bound to kill her when he found out about her dalliance. Mitch was bound to kill her, too. And for what?

Don't think that way!

She took a notebook and pen from the nightstand and busied herself with a to-do list for the upcoming week. With so much to accomplish before Friday, she broke down each day into mini-lists. Her day off was a perfect baking day, so she added 'bake cookies' to Thursday. She could run errands before and after work, and added 'shop for presents' on Tuesday and Wednesday.

Mitch opened the door. "What are you doing?"

"I was reading, but decided to organize my week instead."

"I'm sure you'll get everything done. You always do," Mitch said. "Want to take a break and join us?"

How would she answer? What reply did he expect? What reply did he want?

"I was about to make fried ice-cream."

Mitch loved the dessert and never turned it down. "Okay."

While whisking the eggs the men's banter told her that Buffalo had created an even greater lead. She scooped six balls of ice-cream from her stash in the freezer and rolled them in the eggs. She slowed the preparation. Slowed as much as she could. Anything to avoid being with Mitch. Anything to avoid being subjected to Derek's looks.

"We're going into the fourth quarter now with a seventeen point lead," yelled Mitch.

She brought the plates out to the living room. Mitch grabbed her hand and pulled it downward. She followed his direction and sat beside him on the couch, watching Buffalo blow out the Dolphins.

When the game ended, Derek stretched and yawned. "Well I should get going. Thanks for everything, Mitch."

"Glad you came." Mitch walked Derek to the door.

Rebecca murmured goodbye and headed into the kitchen. She eyed the messy stovetop. After soaking a rag, she scrubbed it.

"Well, well, well, what are you doing now?"

"Cleaning. Making fried ice-cream is a messy job." She motioned to the grease splatter on the counter.

"I see." He tilted his head.

Anna wouldn't be proud of her. Anna would have wanted her to walk out, long before Susannah twisted her ankle.

Chapter 12

Rebecca sat at the dining room table organizing Christmas cards. She wrote addresses on the envelopes with a festive red pen, as her foot tapped to the holiday music playing softly in the background. Thirty cards to mail out this year. Mostly Mitch's acquaintances. Her small family didn't require many cards. Her father was an only child, and mother had one sister whom Rebecca barely knew. Two cousins she'd only met at weddings and funerals would receive the obligatory greeting, and her brother Michael.

Loud noises came from Mitch's office. The pen slipped in her hand and a red line appeared across an envelope. It wasn't a happy noise. He was fighting something. She jumped out of her chair, the legs squeaking on the wood, and rushed into the office.

"Mitch, what's wrong?"

"Did you shut the folder in the cabinet drawer like this?" Mitch yanked at the drawer, almost pulling the cabinet down.

"Please, stop! You're making it worse." She tried to move toward the cabinet, but Mitch shoved her to the side.

"This pisses me off. I'm trying to get some of the bills paid and you mess everything up."

"I know how to fix it, if you'd let me."

"Obviously because you've done this in the past. Do it then."

She moved in front of the drawer, stuck her hand deep inside, and pushed the jammed file down, then gingerly pulled on the drawer. It opened.

She straightened the file that had jammed, looking at the label. *New Homes.* Why did he have a file with that name? They were expanding this home, the one that was so dear to her. It had been Nan's. All of the memories she shared with her family lived here. It had been her father's childhood home, and she still felt his presence. She didn't want a new home.

Mitch grumbled, "If you weren't so lazy, this wouldn't have happened."

"Sorry, Mitch." She walked from the office. New homes? Why? When?

Rebeca sealed the card to her brother Michael. The sound of a beer top twisting came from the kitchen. Mitch walked around the corner into the dining room. She could feel his eyes watching her.

"What are you working on *now*?"

"Our Christmas cards. I also bought a thank you card for the Fields."

"You haven't mailed our cards yet?" He moved toward her.

"They'll go out tomorrow and arrive a few days before Christmas. Please don't worry."

He gripped the table and leaned toward her. "I'm worried about you, Rebecca. You just can't seem to get it together lately."

"I'm fine. It's been busy."

"Oh, I realize what's going on. You're so busy spending time on that quilt for your mother, you've forgotten about our cards."

He waved his hand over the table. "Clearly these aren't a high priority."

"The quilt is dear to me. It's just like my antique one." She put her pen down and took the antique quilt off the back of the sofa, hugging it against her. How could he say that? He had no idea how much time she'd put into the quilt. Most of the sewing was completed while he was at work, or studying, or at that bar playing pool with Melissa. He had nothing to complain about. The quilt did not adversely affect his life, his clean house, his meals, his ironed clothes. "I'll get them done today, I promise."

"Again, priorities." He stepped toward her.

She stepped back.

"Well, I guess if that's good enough for you." He turned and went into the kitchen.

A whimper escaped her lips. She sounded like a frightened puppy. Where did that come from? Her fear was audible. Her exhaustion was audible. Rebecca ran into the bathroom with the quilt. She locked the door behind her and fell to the ground. Sobbing, she hit the tile floor with her fists. A guttural scream escaped her lips. She threw herself backward and lay on the floor, tears flowing. Mucus ran down her face. Getting to her knees, she reached up to the counter and grabbed a ceramic toothbrush holder, then dumped the contents. She flung it at the wall. It shattered.

A knock at the door startled her.

"Rebecca, open the door!"

She picked up a jagged piece and examined it, running it along her wrist. A thought appeared.

If I push a little harder, a line would appear, just one long line. It would hurt a little, just a little. But all the pain would be gone. It would only take a minute or two. Yes, no more pain. Gone. Freedom. No more fear. No more hurt or pain. No more bruises. Sleep. Lots of blissful sleep.

She glanced down at the antique quilt. Her mother's was unfinished.

No. I'm not going to let Mitch ruin me. This isn't my fault.

She put the broken piece down.

Mitch shook the door handle. "I heard you scream and something broke in there. Open up now."

She rocked back and forth on the floor, hugging the quilt to herself.

The knocking turned into pounding. "Now, Rebecca!"

Fearful he would break down the door, she pulled herself to her knees and unlocked it, then slumped to the floor again.

He opened the door quickly and rushed in. He kicked a piece of the toothbrush holder and stared at her. "Did you break this?"

Rebecca didn't answer.

"What's wrong with you?"

Hiccupping, she shrugged.

"Is this because of what I said about the Christmas cards?" He knelt down beside her, and rubbed her back. Her skin crawled at the feel of his touch.

"Rebecca, what the hell is wrong with you? Answer me."

The truth wouldn't do. "It's not you. It's me."

"Go on."

"I got my period," she blurted, crying harder.

The tightness in his face eased. "Oh, Rebecca, now I understand. You wanted to be pregnant." He wrapped his legs around her, pulled her close, and rocked her in his arms. His strong arms threatened to strangle her. She couldn't breathe.

"You will be soon, hon."

"I know," she said. "I was so hopeful. Things felt different this time."

"We could go to your doctor and get a blood test to make sure everything is okay."

No! "I hate needles. And I don't think that's necessary. Let's wait a few months." She wiped her tears again, and added, "I'm just disappointed."

He pulled her back. "Are you sure?"

"Yes. Yes I'm sure."

"Okay. For now, we'll wait."

He helped her up, and Rebecca leaned on him for support as they walked down the hall. She collapsed onto the bed. Mitch pulled the comforter up to her chin, patted her belly, and told her to rest. Rebecca gazed at the ceiling. Why had he abused her? Why couldn't he stop? She took two calming breaths, trying to steady her heart rate, and thought about his question. The blood tests. It couldn't happen. It couldn't. If he found out about the pills ... there would be hell to pay. Worse than hell. She'd be dead. What would he create in his workshop for her then? Her coffin?

Time was running out.

A half hour later, Mitch came in and sat on the side of the bed.

"I know things have been tough these last few months. This damn test has had me all out of sorts. I've got to ace it. My promotion is riding on my results."

Rebecca looked into his face. Sincerity? Where did this come from? Was his violence really from the pressure of work and the exam? Really? Did she wear his bruises, suffer fear, all because his work was ... hard? Confused, she let him escort her out of the bedroom.

A lit candle and food covered the dining room table. The cards sat at the other end.

"Thank you. It smells delicious."

Mitch scooped a spoonful of baked ziti onto her plate and then loaded his. She took a slice of warm garlic bread and handed him the loaf.

As he uncorked a bottle of riesling and poured her a glass, he said, "I've been thinking. Maybe we should at least get you checked out by Doctor Epstein."

"Let's wait. Everything's okay."

He paused to think. "Fine. One more month. After vacation, I want tests run."

She nodded.

"Don't exhaust yourself shopping and planning for Christmas. Everything doesn't have to be perfect."

She silently disagreed. From experience, she knew that was exactly what Mitch expected. "I'll be fine." Setting the wine carefully on the table, she asked, "Are you going to stay at work tomorrow evening?"

"Yes, but only if you don't need me here. You took the news of the baby very hard. I'm worried about your mental state."

My mental state? "I'll be fine, but thanks for your concern."

"All right, if you don't need me."

Was that a trick comment? Was he looking to find another cause to be angry?

"It's not that I don't need you. When I get home from work we can talk on the phone then."

91

"I just want to make sure you're healthy. You'll be pregnant soon and the baby needs a strong mother, both physically and mentally, to carry her." He put his hand over hers. His touch weighed on her as much as his statement.

"I agree."

"Wait until you're pregnant. You'll see how well I take care of you." He gave her a crooked smile. "Just wait and see."

Chapter 13

*T*he newborn cooed while Scout purred and curled up by Rebecca's feet. A sense of peace flooded Rebecca and she savored the moment, rocking back and forth, eyes only on the baby. Motherhood suited her. Maddie filled a void inside her like nothing else.

When Maddie started to fuss, Rebecca placed her against her chest and rubbed her back, waiting for a burp. She became more agitated and Rebecca patted her back more quickly.

Maddie's nose crinkled, looking like the newborn that she was.

"Mommy, we need to leave. Now. We are in danger."

Thinking she imagined the words, Rebecca returned to rocking her, soon relaxing again.

The baby started to cry. Rebecca positioned her in her arms and unsnapped the maternity bra, exposing her breast. Maddie latched on and sucked for a moment. Stiffening in Rebecca's arms, she pulled away and looked into her mother's eyes.

Her lips parted and she whispered, "Now, Mother, we must leave. Daddy is coming and he's going to hurt you."

"No, he won't hurt me anymore. He promised."

"No, Mommy, you're wrong."

Rebecca stood and hurried to the bedroom to pack. She placed Maddie on the bed in between two pillows. As she threw clothes into a suitcase, Maddie repeated, "Hurry, Mommy, hurry. He's coming."

Rebecca rushed to the hope chest and pulled out her baby blanket, ignoring the wooden figurines, and raced back into the bedroom ready to take Maddie and the suitcase to the car.

The front door opened and then slammed shut. "Rebecca!"

Tears rolled down Maddie's chubby cheeks. "It's too late, Mommy. Goodbye."

*****

Rebecca hurried to let Anna in. The doorknob was cold and a swirl of white powder blasted through the open doorway.

"Brrr," Anna said.

"Come in quickly. It's not supposed to get over twenty degrees today. My mom is going to freeze when she visits. It's in the fifties right now in Savannah."

"It'll be a shock for her."

Rebecca put Anna's coat on the sofa. "Cute leggings and shirt. I used to have something like that a couple of years ago."

"It's a comfy outfit. You should try it again."

"I don't have to leave for work for another hour, so we have time to talk. Let me get you some coffee." She pulled the creamer from the refrigerator and poured a coffee for Anna.

"Thank you. You look exhausted."

"Gee thanks." Glad she'd put a scarf on over her sweater this morning, she felt confident Anna couldn't see the bruises.

"Let me rephrase. I mean you look stressed. Busy week with your mom coming?"

"Yeah." She plastered a smile on her face and forced her voice to sound happy. She didn't know how to approach the subject of the horrible weekend. "My mom and I are planning on cooking some of her famous southern dishes together. I'm excited," she lied.

"Sounds like fun. What else do you have planned?"

"We'll all go to Pine Meadow Garden and cut down our tree."

"Nice. That should be memorable."

Rebecca bit at her fingernail. The room swayed and she grabbed the table for support.

"What's wrong? You're pale." Anna set her mug down, dragging a chair next to her.

"I think I need to lie down."

Anna helped her to the couch. Rebecca pulled the quilt over herself.

"Can I get you something?"

She gripped Anna's arm. "No, just stay by my side."

Anna held her hand. Anna may have been her closest friend, but she didn't want to discuss the abuse. But she had to talk to someone about it. Someone safe. She said, "I have to talk to you about something, and figure it out as best I can."

"Take your time."

A few moments passed before Rebecca spoke. "I'm going to tell you about something terrible that happened, but I need you to promise not to react or do something without my permission."

Anna nodded. "I'm here for you. Whatever you need."

She slid herself to a seated position. "Where to begin?" Tears fell and she reached for a tissue on the dust-free end table.

"Was it the party?"

Rebecca blew her nose and nodded. "Yes, at first everything was fine, but then Mitch started being ... well, himself."

Rebecca detailed the evening, thoroughly, and included the incident involving Ben and Derek. Anna hugged her.

"Mitch is a monster, but Ben sounds like he wanted to help you. Maybe you should talk to him."

"I couldn't. Mitch would kill me. And there's more." She told Anna about her discussion with Mrs. Fields. "Derek told Mitch about my run in with Ben. Then Mitch overheard Barb talking about me being lonely and assumed I shared information with her. He was ready to explode. We left the party right afterward."

"Oh, God, I'm afraid of what you're going to tell me next."

Rebecca wiped her cheeks and whispered. "After we left, he drove like a madman. We almost hit a semi head on. He found an empty parking lot, and he attacked me. Anna, he strangled me. It was horrible. I was so scared."

"Unbelievable! You have to get away from him. Now!"

"You promised."

"Please—"

Rebecca put her hand up. "My parents had such a wonderful relationship. They rarely argued. Instead, they talked things out. Why can't I have that?"

Anna caressed her hair. "You'll get through this. We'll get through this. I'm with you."

Rebecca spoke through broken sobs. "My life isn't supposed to be like this. This shouldn't be happening to me." She buried her face in Anna's arms.

"He has to pay for what he did to you."

"It was awful."

"What a nightmare you're living." Pity flashed in Anna's eyes. "How are you feeling physically?"

Rebecca's fingers brushed the side of her neck. "My neck is tender. My body still aches and I have a headache that won't go away."

Anna stood and paced the room. "He's such a bastard. He has no right to touch you. I could just kill him."

"Anna, you promised."

"I'm sorry, Bec, I did. It's just that—"

"You promised," Rebecca pleaded.

"I'm being supportive, but you need to do something about this. Now."

Rebecca wiped her puffy eyes. "I want the impossible. I want things to get better."

"I know you do, and you deserve peace. But, I don't see that happening now or ever."

"At first I thought the abuse was my fault, but now I realize I didn't do anything wrong. I couldn't have stopped it. His jealousy and paranoia. It's the stress of the exam. If I can make it until his test, then his mood might improve." Rebecca bit her lip.

"I'm afraid it's not the case. He is who he is and nothing will change that," said Anna.

"I can't believe that. It's the stress he's under—"

"He's always under stress. His job is tough."

"I really thought I was screwing up. That's what Mitch kept telling me. I believed him. I know differently now. Maybe after the test, while on vacation things will get better."

"Oh, Rebecca. I'm glad you're seeing that it's not you that's causing the abuse, but the test is no excuse."

Rebecca's fists clenched. "I just hope …" She let the sentence trail off. She was tired, tired of hoping. "I'm going to keep taking the birth control pills. This isn't the time to be pregnant."

"Well, I'll take that as a small victory for you." Anna smiled. "Whatever your justification, it's definitely the right decision."

"I can stop taking the pills after his exam, if he changes. He's wondering why I'm not pregnant. Yesterday, he mentioned I should go to the doctor to figure out why, but I think I convinced him to wait."

Anna blew out a breath. "Thank God. You can decide about the pills later, but you'll see he's not going to change. Your next decision will be to leave him."

"No, not yet."

"Rebecca, he almost killed you. You have to get away. You can't wait until the next time. It might be too late."

"The test is coming up. I'll see how he is while on vacation and make a decision then."

Chapter 14

Joan called Rebecca into her office and closed the door. "I asked Margo if she'd cover for you for a few minutes."

"And she said yes?"

"Wonders never cease."

Rebecca smiled. She glanced at a picture on Joan's desk. Three young men stared back. "Are those your sons?"

"Yes." She pointed to each one. "Justin, Shane, and Tom."

"They're very handsome. And it's hard to believe you could have children that age."

"Well, thank you. That makes me smile! How have you been, Rebecca?"

"Good." Rebecca pulled the scarf tighter around her neck. "You?"

Joan sat and motioned for her to do the same. "Great. Getting ready for Christmas. The boys will all be in town. I'm very excited. We don't always get to be together for the holidays."

"My mother is visiting, too. I'm looking forward to it."

"Very nice." She pulled a piece of paper from a folder on her immaculate desk. "I have good news. I need you to fill out this application for the training program. They'll consider your application even though you don't have all of the qualifications."

"Really?" Rebecca leaned in.

She nodded.

"I'm lucky to have your support. You don't know how much this means to me."

"It helps that you've signed up for the class. It shows you're serious about your future at the bank." Joan jotted down a note. "As I've said, you're perfect for this job. Very professional, knowledgeable and personable."

Rebecca felt her face flush. "Thank you."

"This isn't a guarantee you'll get the job, but it's a good sign." Joan leaned in. "Do you mind if I ask you a personal question?"

Rebecca fidgeted. "Shouldn't I get back to work? Margo's waiting."

"She can wait. I wanted to ask you about your health. I've been concerned lately."

Rebecca put her hand over her heart. "Joan, thanks for the concern, but I'm fine. I've had some tension headaches lately, but I'll be seeing the doctor soon for them."

"I've noticed the headaches for a while now. They do seem to be getting more frequent and severe."

"They'll probably put me on some medication. Don't worry."

Joan stood, with Rebecca following. "Okay then, but I want you to know that if you ever need me, please call."

Rebecca followed Joan out of her office. Margo stood with her arms folded, pointing to the line after Joan passed her.

She moved to the line and started waiting on customers. Joan was a great support. Mitch would hate her.

Chapter 15

Rebecca walked alone on the beach gazing at the sunrise. She felt the glow of the warm sun on her skin, washing the pain and memories away. The warm salty breeze sank into her pores. She wrinkled her nose at the smell of the briny air. The waves rolled toward her, just nipping at her feet. She touched her toe to the water and saw a starfish. She picked it up, admiring its beauty. The creature moved in her hand and she jumped, dropping it. The starfish fell back into the water and disappeared.

*****

The ringing of the house phone roused Rebecca from sleep. She let it go and rolled over. Her cell blared. Someone wanted to speak to her. And now. Mitch. She sat up, turned her neck from side to side. Pain. But she had to answer. She gripped the door frame, and went straight for her purse.

"Hello?"

"Where are you?"

She eased onto the sofa next to Scout. "Mitch?"

"Of course it's me. What's going on?"

"I've been sleeping. I had a horrible headache so I left work early ... well, it was only a few minutes early."

"What are you talking about?"

"I asked Margo if I could go home, and she let me leave a half-hour early, but by the time I balanced the drawer it was only ten minutes before my shift ended."

"It's seven in the evening. I've been calling on and off for an hour. Are you telling me you slept through the ringing?"

"I guess so."

There was silence for a moment. "Should I check you out when I get home?"

"No, it's just a tension headache. I'll be fine."

"Are you going to stay in bed all night? Don't you have several tasks to do before this weekend?"

"I'll get started now that I'm awake."

There was more silence.

"Mitch? Are you still there?"

"Yeah, I'm here. I'm staying at work." He spoke to someone, and then said, "You need to take my suit to the cleaners tomorrow. The one I wore to the party. I'll also need my dark-blue dress shirt washed and pressed for Thursday. I have an important staff meeting at lunch."

"Okay."

He ended the call.

Rebecca rubbed her aching forehead. The phone rang again.

Her mother.

She sighed and answered the call.

"How are you, Mom?"

"Oh, I'm okay."

Not all was okay. Not with that tone.

"What's going on? Please tell me." She rubbed Scout's belly.

"It's work. They may have to cut my hours. I'll never be able to pay the mortgage if they do."

"Oh, Mom. Let me help—"

"The roof. I think it has a leak. I've got to call someone, but I'm afraid of what they'll tell me. Probably bad news. Costly."

"Mom."

"I should look for another job. I can't lose my health insurance. I just can't."

"Please, listen—"

"I'm sorry to complain, honey. How are you and that handsome husband of yours? Let me hear some good news."

Rebecca frowned. Scout rolled over and leapt off the sofa. The cat stopped and turned, looked to Rebecca and gave one slow blink, before settling on its rear and licking her paws.

"We're fine. Excited for you to visit. Let's talk about how I can help you when you're here."

"No help. I'll take care of myself. Talk soon. Love you."

"Love you, too."

Rebecca headed into the kitchen with Scout close behind, the cat's bell ringing as she trotted. She pulled the to-do list out of her purse. Raspberry coconut cookies. Her mother's favorite. She'd start with those.

Chapter 16

Rebecca walked down the aisle. Her flowing white gown sashayed as she moved. Mitch stood at the altar, smiling. The sight made her skin prickle. As she passed by family and friends, the air in the room grew colder. She shivered.

Nearing the altar, her teeth started to chatter, sounding like the ringing bell around Scout's neck. The guests started to put on their coats. Frost covered the pews.

The crucifix on the wall behind the altar caught her attention. Scarlet tears flowed from Jesus's eyes.

She looked at Mitch, needing to understand the phenomena. His hair formed icicles and his expression froze in place. Tears flowed down his face, mimicking Jesus's tears.

Mitch held something small in his hand. Rebecca couldn't make out what it was.

Her father appeared by her side. "Wake up, Reba. You need to wake up."

*****

Rebecca closed the drapes in the dining room and clicked on the Tiffany lamp on the end table in the adjoining living room so she had a dim light. As she nursed a cup of tea, her temples pounded. She was late for the morning shift at the bank. She couldn't call in sick. She needed to be punctual and reliable. She needed that job. She'd be isolated without it. And with the prospect of a new position, she could financially help her mother. Her mom could work part-time. Rebecca could rid herself of some of the guilt consuming her.

Her stomach turned and she rushed to the bathroom. Knees on the tiles, she vomited twice. She waited for more, but nothing further came. Her neck ached. Her legs ached. Everything ached.

She plucked her phone off the nightstand and called the bank. "Hello, it's Rebecca."

"Hi, what's up?"

"Joan, I'm sick to my stomach and my head is killing me. I'm not going to be able to work today."

"Oh, honey, I'm so sorry. I can't believe you still have that nasty headache. When can you see a doctor?"

"I'll try to get in today."

"Listen, Margo is in the back room right now. I'll tell her so you don't have to."

"Thanks. I don't think I could deal with her today." Rebecca didn't think she could deal with much at all that day.

*****

Rebecca scooped peanut butter dough into her hands, rolled it into a ball, and with a toothpick, dipped it into the chocolate melting on the stove. She glided the cookie off the toothpick and placed it onto the wax paper. She picked up more dough, and repeated the process. And again. And again.

The door slammed. She flinched. The last ball of dough sank into the chocolate. Shoes clicked on the hardwood floor. Mitch appeared. He sized her up from head to toe. She was dressed in pajama pants and an old sweatshirt, and her hair was pulled into a loose bun, with strands falling around her face.

"What's going on?"

"I'm making cookies." She pointed to the tray.

"I can see that." He cocked one eyebrow. "Why are you dressed like that?"

"I called in sick today. I still had that headache when I woke this morning. It didn't subside until the afternoon. Now I'm trying to get some of my baking done so we'll have desserts for Christmas."

He grabbed a chocolate mint square from a rack and popped it in his mouth. He spoke while chewing. "You look like a mutt."

Mitch went to the bedroom and closed the door. Rebecca figured he was going through his routine of showering, changing and putting on his comfortable clothes and slippers, but then he opened the door and called out to her. "Did you drop off my suit today like I told you to?"

The nausea from the morning returned. "No."

His footsteps grew louder. Her panic rose.

Rounding the doorway, he asked, "Why not? Are these cookies that much of a priority?" He didn't yell as she expected.

"No, I was dizzy and couldn't drive, plus I didn't want to risk going to the cleaners because it's next to the bank. I couldn't have Margo see me."

He motioned to the cookie spread. "Could you find time in your busy schedule tomorrow to take the suit to the cleaners or will you be too busy here?"

"Yes, I'll drop it off on my way to work."

"I suppose you didn't wash and iron the shirt that I need for Thursday either." Again, he didn't yell. It was posed as a simple question.

"It's all set for your meeting."

"So, are you cooking a meal or is this our dinner tonight?" He motioned to the cookie trays.

"I'll cook a meal."

Fettuccini alfredo and a warmed half loaf of Italian bread were served for dinner.

"I can't believe our vacation is in four weeks," Mitch said. "It's long overdue."

"It is."

"I've been working overtime for years now in preparation for this promotion. Few breaks when you're trying to prove you're the best."

Rebecca bit into a piece of bread.

"At least the decision will be made soon."

"It'll be nice to have that behind us," she said.

Mitch put down his fork. "Vacation should be relaxing."

"I'm glad we're going to St. Augustine. I want to visit Flagler College again. Will you go on the tour with me so you can see where I went to school? I'd like to show—"

"We'll see what else I'm doing. I'm sure I'll be busy."

"The campus is beautiful and historic."

"It's a boring tour, Rebecca. That's more your type of thing. I want to be active. Golf. Surf. You know, fun things."

"Don't you want to see the fort? The lighthouse?"

"Did you just hear me? We'll see."

Rebecca pushed the pasta around her plate.

"You're not hungry?"

"Not overly."

"Did you eat cookies while you were cooking?"

"No."

"Are you done baking cookies?"

"Not quite."

"Hon, I think you've got a problem. You're getting carried away with all of these desserts."

"I can drop a tray off at the volunteer fire department around the corner if we have too many. They'll appreciate the treats."

"You're certainly not visiting the fire department. We'll send the extra cookies home with your mother."

"But—"

"End of discussion. You should eat up. It's not bad."

Chapter 17

Cookies everywhere. Oh, God. What have I done? Trays of cookies filled the table. Dozens and dozens of different kinds of cookies. They spread into the living room, on the tables and floor, Mitch's suit wrinkled beneath them.

*****

Rebecca didn't want to supply Margo with any further ammunition. As the first employee to arrive, she turned off the security alarm, flicked on the lights, and started the coffee. She opened her bank drawer and waited for the computer to start up.

Joan arrived, holding a steaming cup of coffee. "How are you feeling today?"

"Better, thank you."

"What did the doctor say?"

"I wasn't able to go," she lied. "I couldn't get an appointment. Besides I don't think I could have driven myself there. I'll go soon."

"Oh, Rebecca, you need to get those headaches checked out. Chances are they're migraines and medicine could help. You'd get a lot of relief."

"I know. I'll get an appointment on my next day off. I promise."

"Good. By the way, Margo was fuming all day yesterday because you called in sick. Just thought I'd warn you."

"Oh, just great."

"Margo made a wise crack about demanding to see a doctor's note, but then said you'd probably have your husband write one. She's one nasty woman."

"Margo can think what she wants. I like this job and I'm not going to let her ruin it."

"Good attitude. She gives all of the tellers a hard time. I've talked to management several times about her attitude. It's not just you."

"I know. But I feel she's harder on me than others."

"That's because she's jealous of you. She knows you're going to move up within the bank. It's just a matter of time."

*****

Mitch wasn't home to decorate the house as planned, so Rebecca pulled the four tote boxes, filled to the brim with Christmas decorations, down from the attic and lugged them down the stairs. By the time she maneuvered the last box to the living room, she was breathing heavily. She checked the garage for the Lexus, but he still hadn't arrived. He'd be angry if she didn't get started. A handmade Christmas quilt draped over the sofa, a table runner and red and green candles on the table, garlands embellished with big red bows scattered through the living and dining room, and Frank Sinatra singing about a holly jolly Christmas, started the transformation well.

An hour had passed and still no Mitch. Rebecca grabbed her coat and hauled the outdoor Christmas lights to the front of the house. Snow blanketed the yard and roof. Rebecca donned her gloves, set a stepladder against the house, and with the rope of multi-colored lights over her shoulder, she headed upward. The lights were heavy and awkward. It wasn't easy to hang them over the hooks Mitch had screwed in all those years ago. Her gloves did little to warm her hands. Shaky fingers looped the strands around the rusty hooks.

She moved the ladder to the right and headed back up, with shrubs below her.

The last hook was just out of reach. The stupid hook taunted her. She couldn't move the ladder closer because of the lilac tree. A murder of crows cawed. They sounded mocking, like Mitch. They cawed again. She stretched further. No luck. She glanced at the roof. About a foot of snow threatened to slide down onto her. She pressed her lips together and stretched out her arm hoping for an impossible three inches.

The ladder swayed and she gasped, grabbed the gutter, and somehow steadied the ladder. She regained her footing, looked at that hook and decided to give it one last try. She didn't want a night of putdowns or ridicule. The task had to be completed. And completed to perfection. Taking off her gloves, she climbed to the ladder's top step. It wobbled. It wobbled again. The hook was almost in reach. Her feet and legs performed a dance of sorts, a juggle to get the ladder centered, and then she looped the strand over the hook. Done. Time to go back inside.

The microwave was heating up a cup of cocoa. She phoned Mitch.

"What's up?" he asked.

"Where are you?"

"I'm at Sunny's. Some of us decided to grab a bite."

"I thought we were going to decorate together tonight."

"I have more important things to do besides decorating the house, Rebecca."

"I finished putting most of the decorations up. At least we'll get the tree together."

"I'll see the decorations when I get home. I'm watching the Buffalo Sabres hockey game. Don't wait up for me."

Familiar noises came down the line, sounds she'd heard when Mitch answered his cell the night the water heater leaked. Clicking off the phone, she held her head in her hands, and remembered the comments made at the party by Melissa.

Chapter 18

Mitch stormed through the living room, pulling at the Christmas decorations. He grabbed a colorful, blown glass candleholder shaped like a wreath. He threw it against the fireplace and it shattered into pieces.

Rebecca covered her eyes.

The garland decorating the mantel was pulled from its place, sending the stocking hangers crashing to the floor.

In one swipe, all of the Precious Moments figurines landed on the hardwood.

"Don't I deserve a break from you once in a while?" demanded Mitch.

*****

Rebecca awoke the next morning to a bitter smell. Mitch lay next to her, reeking of alcohol. She rolled out of bed.

"Grab me a couple of ibuprofens and a glass of water before you shower."

Rebecca took two pills for herself hoping to stave off the impending headache, and then took him the pills and a glass of water.

"Don't take long," he ordered. "I need to get in."

"Why don't you go first? I don't have to shower right now."

"No, go ahead," he said, irritated. "But don't use all the hot water."

She was quick and didn't bother to dress and entered the bedroom wearing only a towel.

"So, when I get home tomorrow, Evelyn will be here, right?" Mitch asked.

"Yes." She faced him as she combed her hair. "I'm ... I'm hoping you and Mom can bond. It's important to me."

"Honey, I don't understand why you're so hostile. I just wanted to make sure that she has a ride home tomorrow."

Hostile? Hostile? What on earth did he pick from that comment that was hostile? She needed to alter her tone, guide him toward a friendly exchange. "That wasn't my intention. I must choose my words more carefully."

"That would be a good idea. So, the ride?"

"It's all set."

"Actually, I'm looking forward to seeing Evelyn."

"You are?"

"Sure. It'll be fun having her here for Christmas." He stood and slipped his arms around her.

She returned his hug. "I'm glad. I'm picking her up after work."

"We'll have a nice holiday together." Kissing her cheek and tugging at her towel, he pulled Rebecca down onto the bed. She complied, eager for her mother's visit to be smooth.

*****

Wow. It smells wonderful in here." Anna pulled off her hat and gloves and followed Rebecca into the kitchen, to the freshly baked cookies. "And these sure look delicious."

Rebecca made them both a cup of coffee and placed a sugar cookie on a plate for Anna.

"The house looks great."

"Thank you."

"It must have kept you guys busy all evening."

Rebecca hesitated with her reply, and then said, "It did. I don't know why I put such impossible demands on myself, trying to be perfect."

Anna smiled. "That's what you are. Perfect!"

Rebecca shook her head.

"You just want everyone in your life to be happy. There's nothing wrong with that, as long as you include yourself."

She turned away, tears in her eyes. "I guess I'm happy when Mitch is happy, and my mom."

"You're not in control of other people's emotions. You could drive yourself crazy trying to please everyone."

Rebecca wiped her face. "I'm not already crazy?"

Anna frowned. "No, you're not. But you're allowing yourself to live a crazy existence. I'm researching options. We'll work out the best way for you to leave Mitch. I'll find you a good lawyer."

"No. Don't. I can't even think about that right now."

"You don't have to. I'll do it. You're leaving Mitch one way or another."

"Anna, I'm going to fix this. We just have to get through—"

"Don't even say the words, Rebecca. I don't want to hear them. You're leaving Mitch. We'll just have to figure out how."

Rebecca walked away, putting her hand over her chest.

"Bec, come back here."

She slowly returned.

"We'll figure this out. I won't do anything rash. I promise."

"Thanks."

She pointed to the unwrapped boxes on the living room floor. "Can I help?"

"Sure." Rebecca retrieved the tape and scissors from the kitchen drawer.

"Go back to finishing your cookies, and I'll work on these."

Rebecca sipped her coffee and checked the oven. Just a couple more minutes. She readied another tray to put in when the others finished baking.

"What else is on your list? I'm sure you have your day all planned out," Anna said from the living room.

"Of course I do. I have lists, and lists for my lists." She moved around the corner so she didn't need to yell. "I'm going to bake, wrap the rest of the presents, and clean today."

"Sounds good." Anna played with one of the decorations. "This snowman is so cute. Are you excited to see your mom?"

"Yeah, I am. I just hope everything goes smoothly."

"Are you going to get a chance to talk to her alone? I mean, really talk to her?"

"About?"

"Everything."

"I'll see what I can do," she lied.

"You're talking to me, Rebecca. I know you like no one else does."

"I'll see what I can do. That's all I can promise."

"How will Mitch be with her around?"

"He said he was looking forward to her company."

"And you believed him?"

She didn't answer.

"I wonder what his motive is."

Rebecca was thinking the same thing.

Chapter 19

Joan handed Rebecca a gift box tied with a red ribbon. "This is for you. A delivery man dropped it off."

Rebecca was shocked. A delivery? For her? And at work?

"Well, aren't you going to open it?"

She untied the ribbon and opened the box. The scent of pine needles sprung from the box. Nestled inside was a winter floral arrangement of red roses, evergreen twigs, and baby's breath.

"What did Mitch do? Is he in the doghouse?" asked Joan.

"I don't know why he sent them."

Rebecca read the card. *To my beautiful Rebecca. Thank you for being such a wonderful wife. Always, Mitch.*

Joan gave a quick squeeze. "Probably because he's the perfect husband. Don't question, just enjoy."

Rebecca used the back office to call Mitch. It went to voice mail. "Hi, honey, it's me. Your flowers are beautiful. Thank you so much. I'll talk to you soon." That's what he would expect. An immediate acknowledgement. Immediate thanks.

Margo stared. Jealous, Rebecca thought. If she only knew. She clicked the phone off, tossed it in her purse, and quickly went back to work.

David stood in Rebecca's line. "Did I notice someone receiving flowers?"

"Yes, Mitch sent them."

"How nice. I used to take home flowers to my wife frequently. She loved yellow roses." His eyes were sad.

"I'm so sorry, David. Even though I was young when she passed, I remember her beautiful smile."

"Carolyn was a kind woman and wonderful mother."

"Yes, she was. Parties at your home were so much fun. I'll always remember our Fourth of July celebrations. Picnic in the afternoon, music and then fireworks at the amphitheater at night. I miss those days."

"Me too. Nan's German potato salad was so good. My mouth waters when I think of it."

"Oh, and Carolyn's cherry pies. Delicious. I've never tasted pies like them since."

"Mmm." He rubbed his belly. "I agree. She was a superb baker."

"And you're an excellent griller."

He laughed. "That's pretty easy compared to the pastries she whipped up with ease."

"True."

"How have you been?" he asked.

"Busy with the holidays."

He rubbed his chin. "Don't overdo it."

"I'll try not to."

"I'm off to the airport. Have a merry Christmas and take care of yourself."

"I will."

"We'll get together after the holidays, and share stories."

"Love to."

*****

Her mom's visits were always stressful. Two years ago, Mitch chose to ignore both Rebecca and her mother for the entire visit. Mitch assembled an excuse about missing his mother. It was an outright lie, but a feasible defense, and one her mother fell for. Mitch never mourned for the mother who drank herself to death.

"I'm sorry if I didn't get to spend as much time with you as I would have liked. It has been a difficult week. It's the anniversary of my mother's death and this time of year is a challenging time for me."

"Oh, Mitch. If I'd known I wouldn't have come. I'm so sorry." She hugged him for several moments.

Driving to the airport, snow drifted onto her windshield. Even if he was rude again this trip, life would get better after the exam. It just had to. The check-in area was busy. People hurried to security to get to their gate. Rebecca walked to the baggage area and sat down.

The loudspeaker boomed. *Please keep your luggage and personal items with you at all times. If you notice any suspicious activity, please contact a TSA Agent immediately.*

A couple who looked to be in their twenties sat across from Rebecca. The young gentleman took the woman's hand in his and brought it to his lips. He kissed each of her fingers gently. She snuggled into him, closing her eyes for a moment.

The couple whispered to each other. Rebecca stole another glance. The woman laughed at his words. They looked at something on her phone.

The woman said, "This picture shows the view from the condo perfectly."

"Look at this one. The color of the ocean is emerald. We should frame this for our apartment."

Rebecca wondered if this man hit his wife when they were at home. Was this woman now cringing at his touch, choosing her words carefully to keep him happy? Did her sleeves cover bruises? Did she wear a scarf to hide finger marks? They spoke of a vacation. She looked around at other couples. Did those men hit their women? Was the airport full of women cringing right at that moment, cringing because their husbands were pretending to be loving and caring and the best partner in the world? Did the husbands go out drinking with women from their office and lie about it? Or was she the only one who suffered what Mitch dealt? Surely there was happiness somewhere in the world. Hope?

Hawaii had been the only real vacation she and Mitch had taken together. They filled their days with sightseeing, beach days and lovemaking. Most of all, the vacation had been filled with love and respect. She wished she could go back in time. Find where things went wrong.

The woman reached into her backpack and pulled out a stuffed bear. Mitch had bought her a similar one while on their honeymoon.

As they played with it, she wondered if they were planning to have children. She hoped this sweet young woman wouldn't have the same fate as her. Birth control pills. Deceiving her husband. Were they happy? Would their relationship fall apart as quickly as her marriage?

She brushed her hair away from her shoulder and touched her neck as she watched the couple walk away.

"Bec?"

Rebecca's head snapped up.

"Honey, you look as if you're a million miles away." Her mother wore tan, suede boots, stylish jeans, and a Flagler College sweatshirt. She held a navy wool pea coat. Her blond hair fell around her shoulders.

As they hugged, Rebecca breathed in her mother's favorite floral perfume.

"How was the flight?"

"Fine. No problems." Her eyes swept Rebecca's face. "You look good, but a little tired. I hope you didn't kill yourself preparing for my arrival."

Rebecca's hand moved to the top of her turtleneck sweater. "No, I'm fine. I'm so excited you're here."

"Me too, Becky."

Rebecca took her arm, and they walked to the luggage carousel.

"Mom? I hate to mention this again, but could you call me Rebecca in front of Mitch? He prefers Rebecca and no nicknames."

"He's still like that?"

"Yes, Mom. Please just go with it."

"Oh, there's my bag." Her mom pointed to a red suitcase with a purple scarf wrapped around the handle.

Rebecca grabbed it off the conveyor belt and inspected the scarf. "What is this from?"

Her mother laughed. "You used to tie it in your hair when you cheered in high school. Remember the Purple Raiders?"

Rebecca didn't. She touched her temple.

"You didn't forget, did you?"

Her head spun.

"Bec, I mean Rebecca, are you okay? You look pale. Come sit." Her mom guided her to a nearby seat.

Chills ran through her body. "I'm fine. I'm overtired, that's all."

"It seems more than that. You can't remember when you were a cheerleader?"

"Of course I can. I'm fine now." Rebecca forced a reassuring smile. Why was her past a blur?

Her mother seemed to accept the lie, no less than the one about Mitch mourning his mother.

"Okay, but take your time. We'll walk slowly." And they did. "There was this sweet old lady sitting next to me on the flight. I gave her your whole life story."

"You did?"

"I'm so proud of you for moving up north and taking care of Nan in her final days."

Her mom put her arm around Rebecca as they walked. "I loved Nan. I enjoyed my time with her."

"I wish I could have been the one. It pained me when you gave up your dreams."

"Mom, you couldn't do it. You would have lost your job taking so much time off. No regrets."

"It meant so much to me, and it would have to your father."

In the parking lot, the biting wind nipped at Rebecca's cheeks. She pulled up the hood of her wool coat while her mom struggled into her own.

"I can't believe you told a stranger about our family."

"I told the lady the whole story about Mitch working as a new resident and how he was assigned to Nan."

"He took a special interest in Nan," Rebecca said.

Her mom grinned. "He took a special interest in you."

"He was so good back then."

"Yes, he was. Back then? What do you mean?"

"I mean he was good to Nan, that's all I'm saying."

"Anyway, I bragged about my beautiful daughter and her perfect life."

"Mom, please. My life isn't perfect."

"You have nothing to complain about. Mitch is a wonderful man, just like your father."

"Don't compare Mitch to Dad." Her tone was sharper than she'd meant. "Daddy was the best."

Her mother looked at her puzzled. "Mitch seems to be right up there, too. I'd think you of all people would agree."

"I just think Dad was in a class all by himself."

"With the way Mitch took care of Dad's mother and how he treats you, he's right up there for me."

"Mom, did you and dad ever fight?" The question came out with a little heat.

"Oh, we had our disagreements, honey. Like everyone else, I suppose. But that's marriage. It's not always smooth sailing. Once we argued and didn't talk for two days. We had forgotten what the argument was over, and laughed and laughed when we ... well, you know, made up."

"Mom!"

"Your father took me out to the finest restaurant that night. We had a little too much to drink, and—"

"Mom! I don't think I want to hear this."

"Oh, Rebecca. You and your brother bring me joy. Knowing both of you are happy helps to get me through the dark days."

Rebecca opened the trunk and heaved the suitcase in, forgetting about the box of flowers.

"No!" The suitcase landed squarely on the box.

"What happened?"

Rebecca snatched up the suitcase and put it on the asphalt. "Oh God, Mitch sent me flowers at work today, and I crushed them." She opened the box.

"They're salvageable. You've damaged the stems. We'll end up trimming them anyway. So don't worry."

Easy for you to say, Mom.

"Let's get these things in the trunk. It's freezing out here."

They inched along the highway, ice cracking under the tires.

"How have you been feeling, Mom?"

"The same, I guess. Stressed. There's still no word on my job. I'm hoping I'll be able to relax while I'm here."

"I hope so, too. I don't want you to worry while you're with us."

"It's hard, you know?"

"I know you're having a difficult time with money. I wish I could help you more. I'll find a way."

"We've been through this too many times. I'm not letting you or your brother support me."

"I'm sorry, Mom. There's going to come a time when you'll have no choice. We're fine with it. I'll do whatever I can."

After exiting the thruway, they pulled up to a red light. "Rebecca, look at me. I don't blame you for your father's death and you need to stop blaming yourself."

The light turned green.

"I don't know—" Rebecca accelerated too quickly onto the snowy street.

Her mother grabbed her arm. The car slid. She corrected the car.

"Don't grab my arm while I'm driving, Mom! That could have been—"

"I panicked. You put your foot down, and we—"

"But you don't—"

"Sorry, hon."

"Oh, I'm sorry, too, Mom." And she was. "I should have been more careful."

"Honey, don't do this to yourself anymore."

"Do what?"

"Blame yourself."

Rebecca would always blame herself, and with that, she had to take care of her mother. That's what her father would have wanted.

After several quiet moments, her mother said, "Michael and Abby send their love and gifts."

Rebecca's heart ached when thinking about her brother and his family. "That's sweet. Thanks for spending the weekend before Christmas with Mike and his family, so you could be here with us for Christmas."

"You're welcome, honey. I see Michael often. It's only fair to spend the real holiday with you."

Rebecca turned onto her street. "I'm glad you have them so close by."

"Me too. And when you have children, I'll have to visit more often."

"Please don't mention babies around Mitch. He's impatient enough."

"Aren't you, too?"

Her fingers gripped the wheel tighter. "I want Mitch to focus on the big exam he has coming up. He doesn't need anything else to worry about."

"All right, but I can't promise that I won't slip."

They carried the suitcase and roses into the house. Her mother arranged the flowers in a deep-red vase, putting them in the center of the dining room table.

"What do you think, hon?"

There was no evidence of them being damaged. "Great job, Mom."

Rebecca's phone rang. "Hello?"

"I'm on my way home, but the weather is terrible and the driving is slow."

She picked her fingers. "Just be careful. Did you get my message?"

"Yes, I'm glad you like them. Is your mom there?"

"Yes, she arrived just fine."

"Great! Can't wait to see her. Be there soon."

Rebecca poured herself a large glass of chardonnay. What was he playing at? Was he playing at all? She sipped her wine. Her mother was acting stronger than she had on the phone. Their conversation was light and easy and loving. Mitch seemed to be in a good mood. Fingers crossed, he really was looking forward to the evening.

Maybe we can have a nice Christmas weekend. Maybe things will change after he takes the test.

She took a sip of wine.

Just maybe.

Chapter 20

Rebecca placed the biscuits and butter on the dinner table.

"Wow, it smells great in here." Mitch removed his coat, hugged Evelyn and gave Rebecca a quick kiss on the cheek. He looked relaxed. Calm. Content. None of those looks could be trusted.

"How was your drive home?" asked Rebecca.

"The roads are pretty slick. But I'm here now and starving." Mitch sniffed the air. "Mmm, biscuits?"

"Yes, what else do you smell?"

He played along. "Let me think. Some sort of chicken dish."

Rebecca rested her hands on her hips. "Fried chicken with honey-pecan glaze and one more thing."

"I don't know. Tell me." He scooped Rebecca in his arms and twirled her around.

She squealed. "Put me down."

"Well?" He gave her a thoughtful look. "What else is there?"

Her mother brought the dishes from the kitchen. They all sat. Evelyn lifted the cover off a casserole dish.

"Sweet potato casserole. You know how much Mom loves sweet potatoes."

"I do. You got me there."

Rebecca saw what her mother saw. A perfect couple. Reciprocated love. Trust. An easy lie.

"You need to keep making the southern dishes you ate when growing up. It could be a tradition that our children continue, since the southern culture is part of who you are."

"But I ..."

"But you what?"

Rebecca read the warning in his words. His tone was full of innocence, but she knew otherwise. He'd mocked her cooking, calling it *barbecue* at the party.

"I agree," Mom said. "You'll want your family eating good southern cooking, as Michael and you did."

"Definitely," Mitch said. "And Rebecca is a wonderful cook. She takes after you."

"Why, thank you, Mitch." Her mother blushed.

Rebecca pasted a smile on her face and twirled a strand of hair around her finger.

Mitch said, "So, what have you been up to lately, Evelyn?"

"Well, of course working. And my work at One Love Animal Rescue. We organized a fundraiser which raised over fifteen thousand dollars. I was co-chair for the event. I spent almost all of my free time preparing for the event."

"I'm so glad it was a success," Mitch said.

"No wonder you've been so tired, Mom."

She laughed. "What really tired me out was my visit to Michael's family last week. My granddaughters are growing up so fast. They are so sweet, just like Rebecca." Her mother smiled at her. "I can't wait until you have chil ... I mean, the girls are so kind and cute."

Rebecca scooted back from the table. "Let's clear the dishes, Mom."

"I'm sorry. I slipped," her mom said in the kitchen.

Rebecca scrubbed a pan until it was spotless, then scraped plates and loaded them into the dishwasher. After drying her hands, she hung the hand towel on the rack and said, "Please don't mention it again."

"I said I was sorry. Why is it so important?"

Rebecca left the kitchen. "Do you want dessert?" she asked Mitch.

"First let's have some wine in the living room."

Mitch started a fire while Rebecca grabbed the glasses and another bottle of chardonnay.

"Mitch, would you mind handing me that quilt before you sit back down?" Mom flashed him a smile.

He laid it over her legs.

"Are you tired, Mom?"

"A little. Traveling always wears me out, but I'll stay up for dessert." Her eyes sparkled in the reflection of the flames. "I always have room for goodies."

Mitch rubbed Rebecca's legs. Christmas music played and the fire crackled. She closed her eyes. Mitch had been a gentleman all evening, charming her mother, and making her laugh. Mom glowed as Mitch spoke, just the way she'd done with Rebecca's father.

Anna wanted her to tell her mother the truth. How could she? How could she shatter this perfect image, shatter her mother's contentment? She couldn't ... wouldn't hurt her mother again. Hadn't she been the cause of enough trouble for her mom? The abuse would remain a secret.

"Rebecca?" Mitch's voice interrupted her thoughts.

Startled, she asked, "What?"

"What are you thinking about?"

"I–I was daydreaming about Christmas."

"I think you've had enough." He took her wine glass and glanced at her mother. "Rebecca has a low tolerance for alcohol."

"I'm fine. I know my limit."

Mitch scoffed. "She's certainly had enough. She's getting defensive and cranky."

Her mother laughed. "That's not cranky, Mitch. You should have seen her when she was a teen."

Her mother continued with stories from her past. Rebecca didn't listen. Her focus was on a cold stare boring into her. Mitch wanted her to argue, but she refused to oblige. There definitely was a chill in the air. She wrapped a fleece blanket around her legs.

"Oh, Evelyn," said Mitch. "I don't believe a word of it. Rebecca is absolutely ..."

Rebecca popped off the sofa and headed to the kitchen.

She put a few kinds of cookies on a festive tray and carried it back to the living room, along with napkins and plates. She enjoyed baking her loved ones' favorite treats. Loved ones? She almost laughed. She placed the tray on the coffee table, so everyone could reach the desserts from where they sat.

"Looks wonderful." Her mother filled her plate with one of each type.

Mitch's hand hovered over the cookies for a moment. He picked a gingerbread cookie and set it on his plate. "I have to watch my calories." He patted his sturdy stomach. "You've made enough desserts to feed an army. How many people are we having here this weekend?"

"I wanted to make both of your favorites."

"Well, I hope you like them, Evelyn, because you'll be taking many of them home with you. Knowing Rebecca, there will be a few more dozen in the kitchen. I'd have to work out several extra hours each day if I indulged in too many of these."

"How do you find the time to exercise?" Evelyn asked.

"There's an exceptional gym at the hospital for the employees. I use it either before or after my shift, or when I'm on call."

"I can't believe how much you do. I'm amazed you can find the time for everything, including studying for your exam. You must be exhausted."

"It's a grueling schedule," he admitted. "But I enjoy working under pressure."

Her mother reached for another chocolate mint and asked Mitch if he had any interesting patients or had been involved in any unique diagnoses lately. He told her the same story Rebecca had heard at length at the party. Her mother was fascinated. Rebecca was not. Mitch's chest puffed as he discussed the case.

"What an interesting case! I can't believe you figured that out. Brilliant."

"Thank you, Evelyn. It'll put me on top of the pile of candidates for the promotion."

"What great news. You continue to impress me. You're such a wonderful husband to my beautiful Rebecca and a remarkable doctor."

Rebecca forced a smile.

"Thank you. You did a great job raising her."

"Well, it's time for me to hit the sack. I'm tired," her mother announced.

Rebecca walked her to the guest bedroom.

At the doorway, her mother said, "I'm so happy for you, Rebecca. You have an amazing life with Mitch. You're truly blessed."

Chapter 21

Rebecca squirmed in his lap. She tried to tug at his long, white beard but her mother swatted her hand quickly.

"Bec, honey, try to sit still. Don't touch Santa's beard." Her mother straightened Michael's bowtie.

"Mom, stop fussing with me. Why do I have to get my picture taken? It's stupid."

Rebecca laughed at her brother.

He nudged her arm.

"Ouch. Mom ..."

"Everyone look at me." The photographer pressed the button. "Smile."

The flash startled Rebecca and she opened her eyes.

*****

Mitch drove Rebecca and her mom to Pine Meadow Garden late the next morning. Pick-up trucks and SUVs filled the parking lot. He grumbled when forced to circle the area to find an open parking spot. They were surrounded by the buzz of holiday activity. Children ran, dogs barked, and even Santa Claus took in the scene from his rocker on the porch of the Country Kitchen. The evergreens covered with fresh fallen snow were a perfect backdrop for their Christmas picture. Rebecca touched at her pocket. Her phone was there.

"I hope we'll get a nice tree." Rebecca looked into the forest and saw hundreds of evergreens, all different shapes and sizes. Sunlight struggled to peek through the dense woods. People milled about finding their own perfect tree.

Mitch whispered, "Seriously, Rebecca? It'll be up for a couple of weeks, shed its needles everywhere, and then be tossed to the curb."

They walked the path, snow crunching beneath their boots, and were handed a long, thin piece of cloth to write their name on. With that, they'd tag their tree, and then return for help with cutting and mounting it on the top of the car. Thirty minutes into their search for the right tree, her mother shivered.

"How about you go on to the restaurant for some cocoa, Mom? We'll take care of the tree."

"Yes go, Evelyn. No reason to wear yourself out. We'll be there soon."

"Okay, but make sure to get a nice picture of the tree coming down." She turned and marched off to the restaurant.

"How about this one?"

Rebecca studied it. "Too small."

"That's what you said about the last two, and the one before was too fat." Mitch's voice was even, but his face stern. "What kind of tree do you want?"

"I'd like one a little taller than you, and round. I really like the full trees. They look healthier. Perfect."

"There's no such thing as a perfect tree, Rebecca. Here. This one will do."

Rebecca's heart sank. Skinny. Shapeless. The bottom branches already browning.

Once the tree was cut down, Mitch said, "Go find your mother."

Rebecca's mother was in the gift shop that was attached to the Country Kitchen. She held a small container of maple syrup and a rustic looking picture frame. She lifted the frame and smiled. When she showed Rebecca the frame, Rebecca turned away.

Her mother asked, "Did you get some nice pictures?"

She twisted her hands together. "I forgot."

"Oh, Rebecca. How could you? I know how much you wanted a picture for your scrapbook."

"It's not a big deal, Mom."

Her mother's eyes flickered disbelief and she placed the frame back on the shelf. "Are you okay?"

Thoughts of slaps and punches swirled in her head. She kept her voice even. "Yes, of course."

She put her arm around Rebecca. "I'm worried. You keep everything in a scrapbook. Don't you want a memory of this Christmas?"

The words were like arrows aimed at Rebecca's heart. "Yes, of course I do."

"Rebecca?"

"Mom, I forgot to take a picture. That's all. We struggled with the tree and I forgot. End of discussion."

******

Mitch brought the tree in and set it up. "You can take it from here, Rebecca. I'm taking a break." He headed to the kitchen, grabbed a beer and went into his office.

It was midafternoon and she was exhausted. She didn't even want to think about preparing dinner. The evening would be long and they were going to midnight mass. Her mother looked tired as well, but rallied. "I'm up to the challenge. Are you?"

The tree seemed hardly worth the effort anymore. She wanted to lie down and go to sleep.

"Well, are you?"

She looked at the tree. "Sure, Mom."

The two women set to work, hanging lights on the tree. They split the pile of ornaments in two. Some of the baubles were cracked, others tarnished. They were beautiful when she bought them. Sparkling, mirror-like, soft and bright. And the tinsel. Small tears appeared on her cheeks. Her mother didn't seem to notice the marks, so Rebecca kept quiet. The women worked on separate sides of the tree.

"How is your latest scrapbook coming along?"

"Fine." Rebecca worked on looping a hook through the wire of an ornament.

"Good. I'd like to look through the other ones when we have a free moment, especially your wedding book. I can't get enough of that day. Is wonderful, wasn't it?"

"Yes, Mom." The contrast between her wedding day and today was like summer and winter, fur and sandpaper. The thought crushed her.

"You must be so excited about your vacation. Not long to go now. It'll be nice to get away from the cold."

"Yup."

Her mother laughed. "We're like Santa's elves. No rest when Christmas is hours away." Her cell phone rang. "Hello? Michael, how are you?"

Rebecca listened while continuing on the decorations.

"Yes, we had a wonderful day. We found a beautiful tree at such a quaint tree farm. Now we're decorating it ... we're going to midnight mass ... how about you guys? ... nice! ... that'll give the girls time to open presents before church ... tomorrow we'll open presents and relax during the day and then make a feast for dinner ... love you, too. Talk to you tomorrow!"

Her mother's discussion with Michael made Rebecca see the day through her eyes. It appeared perfect, except for Rebecca forgetting to take the picture.

Rebecca placed all of the presents under the tree. She stepped back to admire her handiwork and had to admit the results were beautiful. Everything looked picture perfect. Just like the ornaments; damaged, but noticeable by no one but her. She wiped at a tear and shook her head; wishing fate hadn't brought Mitch and her together.

Chapter 22

*R*ebecca ran out of her bedroom, clutching her favorite teddy bear. "Did Santa come?"

She rounded the dining room table, and squealed. Under the Christmas tree lay several wrapped gifts. Candy canes clung to the white cotton on her stocking.

"Mama! Daddy! Santa came!"

She rushed to Michael's bedroom and jumped on his bed.

"Get up so we can open the presents."

Michael sat and rubbed his eyes. He looked at the clock. "Bec, I thought we were waiting until six to get up. It's five-thirty."

"But you're up now, so let's go." She tugged at his arm.

"Okay already. I'm moving. Get Mom and Dad."

Standing next to his bed, she yelled, "Mama, Daddy, are you up?"

Michael covered his ears.

"Yes, we've started the coffee. Come out here so your brother can have a minute of peace," her mom said.

Rebecca gave Michael one last glance and hurried to the kitchen.

Her father scooped her up and swirled her around. "It's Christmas, Reba. Merry Christmas."

She threw her arms around his neck and planted a kiss.

He put her down, and she took his hand, pulling him toward the living room.

"I'll bring your coffee in, hon," her mother said.

"Okay, you can go through your stocking while we wait for Mom and Michael."

She dumped the contents of the stocking into her lap. One Barbie, five candy canes, a chocolate Santa, and colorful barrettes and headbands.

"Oh, I love all of these!"

Michael joined them, and slowly pulled out his presents.

"You got a chocolate Santa, too." The other presents didn't interest her.

Her mother walked in.

"Can I open my gifts now?"

She nodded as she sipped her coffee.

"Slow down, honey. Let me get some pictures." Her dad reached for the camera as she unwrapped the first gift.

"A Snoopy snow cone machine! Cool," she said.

Michael glanced over. "Let's make some when we're done opening our presents."

"After breakfast," her mom said.

Rebecca opened several more gifts. A perfume maker, a big brown teddy bear, and three books. She opened her last present. "Mommy, I can make you pot holders to match the kitchen."

"That would be nice. You can also send some to Nan."

"Oh, yes."

What are you going to do with another stuffed bear?" her dad said.

"They're called friends, Daddy. Not stuffed bears."

He laughed and snapped another picture.

She looked over at Michael's gifts. A board game, basketball, sneakers, a few cd's. Boring, she thought.

After more pictures were taken, her father said, "I can't wait to get this roll of film developed. I'll take it to the store tomorrow."

"I can't wait to see them," her mother said.

"Reba, come here. I have one more present for you."

She hurried to her father and he hoisted her up onto his lap. After handing her a little box, she opened it. A charm bracelet lay on a satin cloth.

"Pretty! Thank you, Daddy." She embraced him, wishing the moment could last forever.

*****

Christmas morning, Rebecca pulled on her yoga pants and Mitch's old sweatshirt and opened the bedroom door. She breathed in the smell of bacon. She heard whispers as she approached the kitchen. The word *exam* caught her ear.

"It's a practical exam. I have to show techniques I've learned so far in my residency," Mitch said.

"Are you worried about it?"

He laughed. "No. I've been doing these things for years."

Years? Mitch had told her too often those techniques were new to him. She noisily bumped into an end table. Mitch peeked around the corner. He pulled her into the bedroom and shut the door.

"What are you doing?" he asked.

"I thought ... I thought."

"Thought what?"

"Your studies. Your exams. Those techniques. They're not new?"

"Were you eavesdropping? Your mother was concerned about interrupting my studies." His voice was tight. "Of course I'm going to tell a white lie. Do you want me to make her feel uncomfortable about being here?"

Her heart pounded. "But—"

"I've already told you the test is difficult," he snapped. "I said that to her so she wouldn't feel guilty about taking time away from my studies."

She took slow, calming breaths.

"Rebecca, relax. The test is hard, dammit."

"I ... I believe you. It just made me confused." She gave a fake smile. "I didn't have a good night's sleep."

"You look tired. Merry Christmas, honey. Let's make this the perfect day." Taking her hand, he led her into the kitchen. "Look who I found."

"Merry Christmas, sweetie."

Breakfast eaten, they moved into the living room. Mitch lit the fire while Rebecca plugged in the tree lights. The presents looked beautiful wrapped in red, green and gold paper. There were more than she remembered. When Rebecca opened the drapes, a new layer of snow glistened in the sunlight. She set up the tripod so she could get a picture of the family with the presents and tree in the background. She homed in on Mitch and her mom, and then rushed to join them. Mitch held her close.

"Another picture for your scrapbook?" Mitch said.

Rebecca nodded.

Her mother smiled. "That's very special, Bec ... I mean Rebecca. You'll cherish those later on. So who wants to pick a present first?"

"You can be Mrs. Claus and hand out the gifts, honey." Mitch rubbed Rebecca's back.

Rebecca gave Mitch two big boxes. He struggled opening the larger, and went to the kitchen to retrieve a pair of scissors. He sliced open the tape and pulled out a large coat. He opened the other box, which contained heavy snow boots.

He tried on the navy down parka and matching boots, looking ready to brave the cold weather.

"You'll stay warm in this weather," her mom said.

Rebecca read the tag. "I hope so. The description says it will keep you warm down to five degrees."

"I hope it doesn't get that cold here anytime soon," Mitch said.

Rebecca took a rectangular box adorned with a giant golden bow and opened it. "Oh, Mom, I love it." Her hands shook as she paged through the old photo album.

"We can look over the pictures later. They date back to the early nineteen-hundreds and include some of your great-grandparents."

"Thank you, Mom." She hugged her tight.

Her mother wrestled with the paper on her own gift. Rebecca silently giggled, remembering how terrible she was at wrapping. Anna hadn't wrapped any of the presents Rebecca thought she had, so, in a rush Rebecca completed the job, and poorly.

After opening it, her mother flipped it over, examining it. Her puzzled expression made Rebecca laugh.

"Do you know what it is?"

"No, I'm trying to figure it out."

Rebecca laughed. "It's a Kindle."

She squealed with delight. "Wonderful. You'll have to show me how to use it."

"We loaded several books on it. I can show you how to buy more and download them later," said Mitch.

Her mother played with the buttons on the device.

Rebecca opened gifts from Mitch.

"Thank you! You really know my taste," she said, admiring the deep-purple silk scarf. She placed it between her new red terrycloth bathrobe and a Cuisinart stainless steel cookware set, making sure her spa gift certificate wasn't lost in the wrapping paper.

"Another gift from me." Her mother slid a box toward Rebecca.

Mitch's expression tightened when he saw matching cable knit sweaters. He disliked matching clothes. Her mother didn't notice a thing.

"Thanks, Mom. They're so warm." She hurried to pull a large gift bag from under the tree and handed it to her mother. "I hope you like this. I made it for you."

Her mother pulled the handmade quilt from the bag. Different shades of burgundy, navy, emerald, and tan colors covered the quilt.

"This is breathtaking, Rebecca. It must have taken you weeks." She fingered the binding and traced the log cabin pattern starting with a burgundy square and moving into bigger and bigger rectangles. She embraced Rebecca, squeezing her tightly.

"I'm glad you like it." Through tiny tears, she said, "I patterned it after grandmother's antique quilt." She pointed to the quilt lying on the sofa. "I thought about you all the time I sewed it."

"I'll cherish it forever, just like you treasure yours."

"I hope it fits in your suitcase, Evelyn."

"I'll make it fit. It's not going in the mail. I'll mail my clothes home if I have to."

"Well, that's it for the gifts. I'll start cleaning up this mess."

Mitch pulled Rebecca close. "Not so fast, Mrs. Claus. I'm not done with you."

"What do you mean? You bought me several gifts."

He reached far underneath the tree and pulled out two small boxes. Her hands shook as she opened the first box. Beautiful amethyst earrings shone from the sunlight streaming through the window, matching the necklace he gave her to wear to the party.

"Mitch—"

"Open the second box."

She did, and soon held a matching bracelet. "This is too much. You shouldn't have."

"You've put up with a lot from me these last few months. My studies will be over soon, and this time next year we'll have a baby." Mitch paused, then said, "You deserve the whole set."

She wanted to believe his words.

He nudged Rebecca. "Go get the necklace. Show your mother."

"Oh, Mitch," said her mother. "You're so good to her. I'm so happy you're part of the family."

Chapter 23

Her mother caressed Rebecca's cheek after taking off the warm washcloth. "Baby, it'll be okay. The medicine will help soon." She placed another cloth on Rebecca's forehead.

"No more. Too cold."

"Honey, the cool cloth will help you feel better."

"Don't care." Rebecca pushed it away. "No."

"Just a little longer. You're fever is still high."

Rebecca gave in, allowing the dampness to soak in, cooling her skin. Clutching her teddy bear tight, she dozed. When she woke, she felt for her mother.

"Mama?"

"I'm right here."

Rebecca touched her. "Can you stay and cuddle with me?"

"Sure. Scooch over just a little."

Rebecca nestled close to her mother's warm and inviting body, feeling her fever dissipate. A peaceful sensation took over her small body.

*****

Rebecca helped her mother pull the suitcase from the trunk. It was heavier than when she'd arrived, but the lap quilt she'd made fit into the case with little problem.

"I had a wonderful time, honey. The weekend was very special," her mother said.

Rebecca fingered her new earrings. "Thanks, Mom. It was great having you."

"You two have something special that many couples dream of."

Rebecca bit her lip and gave a half-smile, tears forming.

Her mom touched Rebecca's cheek. "Are you okay? You look upset."

Watching an airplane take off, she said, "I wish I could go with you."

"Honey, you're welcome to visit anytime. You know that."

Rebecca hadn't realized she'd spoken the words aloud. She let her mother's response hang in the air. "I can wait with you for a while."

"No, you need to get to work."

"Please don't go," Rebecca blurted.

Standing squarely in front of Rebecca, she asked, "What's the matter, honey?"

Rebecca took a deep breath. It was now or never. "It's Mitch ..."

"Mitch? What about him? Is he sick?"

"No." Now was her chance. "He sometimes ..." The words caught in her throat, then dislodged and came out quietly. "Sometimes gets angry."

"Oh, honey. Your husband is tired. He works all the time and has the exam to worry about. Plus, he wants a baby. Give him room to breathe. You should take a look at my life. I'm alone, money's tight—"

"I know, Mom, I'm sorry."

"You need to realize how lucky you are."

"I do." Rebecca held her mother's hand, gripping it tightly. "Forget I said anything. I just miss you."

"Me too, honey. Be thankful for what you have."

"I am."

"You'll visit me soon?" She leaned in and kissed Rebecca's cheek.

Rebecca touched her face. "As soon as I can." Watching her mother walk away, she whispered, "I hope to see you again, Mom."

Chapter 24

"How was Christmas? Your mom's visit?"

Rebecca motioned Anna to sit. "Mitch sent me flowers at work on Friday, was an angel to my mother all weekend, and bought me beautiful Christmas gifts." She held out her bracelet. "Including this. What more could a girl ask for?"

"Do you really want me to answer, or shall I buy into your fantasy world?"

Rebecca sat on the sofa. "Indulge my fantasy, please."

Anna crossed her legs. "Let me get this straight. Because you had one good weekend with Mitch, you think everything that has happened can be forgiven, and that things will get better."

Scout hopped onto Rebecca's lap. She busied her hands, rubbing her head, down her back and along her tail. "No. I don't."

"Really? I can't believe you said that."

"I've been doing a lot of thinking. Mitch seems to know when I'm at breaking point. He becomes the man I thought I'd married and pulls me back to him."

"But not for long."

"No. Not for long. I recognize it now."

"I'm so relieved to hear those words, Bec."

"I know."

"What brought you to this realization?"

"You and what you've said to me. I still think there's hope—"

"No, don't even say it. You're making progress, don't back up now. I mean it."

"I was just going to say that I want to get to vacation time and see how responsive he is to my ideas. If he really wants me to stay—"

"He wants to control you. He wants you under his thumb. Why wait? Leave him now."

"You know how complicated it is, Anna. My marriage is sacred to me. I love him. My mother ..."

"Your mom doesn't know the hell you're living in. She wants you to be happy."

"She won't believe me if I tell her the truth."

"Did you try?"

"She adores Mitch. You should have seen him around her. He acted like he did when we were first married."

"What if Mitch was nice to your mom on purpose?"

Rebecca opened her mouth to respond.

"Let me explain. If he acts like a loving husband around your mom, he gains her as an ally."

Rebecca nodded.

"So, if you complain about Mitch to your mom, she might think you're being petty."

"I hesitated telling her because Mitch was so loving in front of her."

"Exactly."

Rebecca pulled the quilt over her legs. Scout stayed nestled on her lap.

"He's manipulative. His *good husband* act was tactical. He wants you under his control, and he'll do whatever it takes."

Rebecca nodded again.

Anna wrinkled her brow. "I understand your commitment to your marriage and your fear of hurting your mother. But what else is keeping you here?"

Rebecca's cell rang. She jumped up, sending Scout fleeing, and answered it on the second ring.

"I'm glad you picked up," Mitch said.

"What's up?" Rebecca paced the living room, hitting her toe on the leg of an end table. She winced and grabbed her foot.

"I'm on call tonight and tomorrow night, so I'll be staying here. With all the studying I'll be doing, it's not worth driving home. I'll be home early Saturday afternoon."

"Well, we can have a quiet New Year's Eve together," Rebecca said.

"Regarding New Year's," Mitch said. "We have plans."

She dropped into a dining room chair, putting her hand to her forehead. "What plans?"

"Derek is hosting a party. He told me about it this morning."

"Oh? Well, have fun."

"Don't be ridiculous. He invited both of us. We'll meet his girlfriend. They're back together. Says he got sick of waiting to meet a sister of yours."

Rebecca couldn't think of a worse way to spend the evening. She pulled at a loose strand of hair. "Are you sure you don't want to stay home? You'll be exhausted from pulling an all-night shift."

"Don't be such a bore, Rebecca. Of course we don't want to stay in." He hung up.

"I take it you're going to be doing something you don't want to on New Year's Eve," said Anna.

"Of course."

*****

Rebecca strolled down the aisle, glancing at her list. She stopped in front of the bakery. It would be so much easier to buy baked goods. She frowned and shuffled past to the organic produce section. As she examined a red pepper, someone bumped the cart.

"Oh, sorry! Am I in your way?" She looked up and smiled. "Kelly! How are you?"

"Great! You?"

"Fine. Just running some errands. Did you work at the bank today? I can't keep our schedules straight in my head."

"I just finished. Margo was in her usual mood. Bad. I heard Joan saying nice things about you. I could see the veins on Margo's forehead ready to pop. It was classic."

"What did Joan say?" Rebecca asked.

They moved to a corner of the store to be out of the way of other shoppers.

"That you're amazing! Well, not in those words, but you are. She talked about how willing you are to learn new things and that you grasp them so quickly. And, of course, how much the customers like you."

Rebecca glowed. Appreciated. Treated with respect. At least she was valued somewhere.

"Are you looking forward to the employee party tonight?" Kelly asked.

"Yes, but I'll be avoiding Margo." She bit her fingernail.

"Don't worry about her. Remember last year? She was drunk within the first half-hour."

Rebecca laughed. "I remember. Then she was flirting with Steven."

"The guy from accounting?"

"Yup."

"I forgot about that."

"It was quite a spectacle."

"I'm sure. It's ironic we met today. I've been trying to get hold of you," Kelly said.

"Really?"

"Yes, do you want to go out to dinner next week?"

She thought about Mitch's schedule. He was on call Tuesday. "Um, sure. How about Tuesday?"

"Perfect. I thought you may not have wanted to get together."

"Why?"

"I've left two messages."

"Two messages? Really?"

"Yes."

Rebecca frowned.

"Is something wrong?"

"Do you remember when you called?"

"Last Sunday, I think. I thought you were probably hung over from the big party the night before. I also called Christmas Eve. I was afraid I'd interrupted a family celebration when no one answered."

Sunday, Rebecca had gone grocery shopping for Mitch and Derek. Christmas Eve they were out buying a tree. Mitch was the one who normally checked for messages. Rebecca gave her a puzzled expression.

"Didn't you get the messages? I left you my cell number."

She twisted her fingers. "That's weird. Maybe my answering machine isn't working. Come to think of it, I haven't received any messages lately."

Chapter 25

Rebecca stood in the bright kitchen light, running her finger over the engraved writing on a plaque. She held it up. Her heart had raced when the branch manager announced her name. *Employee of the Year.* Joan told her it was the first occasion a part-time employee had won.

The party had been held in a side room of Windgate Manor Country Club. An intimate setting. It was just big enough to hold the twenty branch employees. As Kelly predicted, Margo was tipsy within the first half-hour and by the time dinner was served, she was drunk and hanging onto Steven until he pushed her away.

Before dessert, Joan called her a taxi and Margo left without incident. Rebecca was glad Margo didn't witness her receiving the award. She probably would have booed.

Unfortunately, Rebecca had to leave after the award in case Mitch came home early from his shift. He hadn't.

Mitch barged into the living room. Rebecca scooted around the corner, with the plaque still in hand.

"I'm on call for Derek's party tonight, can you believe that?"

"What?"

"Remember Tim from the party? The dad of the twin girls. The pictures you couldn't turn away from."

She remembered all too well. "Of course I remember."

"Well, his father had a stroke and Tim's flying to Myrtle Beach to be with him."

And Mitch had not one ounce of sympathy? Not one thought for Tim, and how he was feeling?

"Oh, I hope he's going to be okay. I wouldn't wish losing a father on anyone."

"It's ludicrous. I was really looking forward to unwinding at Derek's."

"I know you need time to relax. The party won't be the same now."

"Exactly. Now I won't be able to drink."

"Would you like to hear some good news?" she asked.

"If you have any."

"I received the *Employee of the Year* award last night. It's based on the customer satisfaction surveys."

"Does that mean you'll get a raise?"

"No, I was awarded this wooden plaque which will stay up at the bank for a year and a nice gift basket with lots of goodies. It also means I'm doing a great job and the customers appreciate me."

"Well, it won't matter how much they appreciate you once you're pregnant. You'll be leaving." He put his hands on his hips. "Were there any men at this party?"

Thrown by his response, she asked, "Aren't you happy for me?"

"I asked you if there were any men at the party."

She bit her fingernail and mumbled, "Several, I suppose."

"Did you talk to them?"

"Yes, two from the accounting department, Steven and George. Only a brief hello, though."

"Good." Mitch headed to the bedroom.

While he showered and changed into his dark-brown khakis and a beige sweater, Rebecca tugged on a simple black dress. A short, red sweater covered her shoulders. They left for the party with their gift wrapped in Rebecca's hand sewn wine tote, tied with a silver ribbon.

Would this party be any different from the Fields' party? The mere thought made her hands tremble. She grasped the gift with two hands.

No valet. They pulled their car onto the snow-covered lawn. Rebecca studied the house. A two-story brick home with a nice sized front porch. Some jackets covered Adirondack chairs on the porch. Beer bottles littered the wooden table. A bachelor pad for sure, Rebecca thought.

The triple garage doors were open. Three cars. Derek stood near the middle vehicle, a Corvette with the license plate DRDC2.

To the right, a Ford F150, DRDC3, and to the left, a Mercedes Coupe, DRDC1.

"What do they stand for?"

"Doctor Derek Canton," Mitch explained.

Derek stumbled toward them. "Hey, glad you could make it." He shook Mitch's hand and gave Rebecca a too-familiar hug. He smelled of alcohol and body odor. He led them into the home.

"My girlfriend walked out on me today. Actually, she ran."

"No?" Mitch said. "Today?"

"Yes today. Can you believe the nerve? I had to finish preparing everything myself. I need to forget about her. Let's get drunk." Derek slapped Mitch on the back.

"I'd love to, but Tim had to go to Myrtle Beach. I have to cover his shift. I'm on call."

"What? No freaking way. Rebecca, tell me he's kidding."

She looked at Mitch.

Derek groaned.

"I'm disappointed, too," Mitch said. "I hope to make it until midnight without getting a call."

"Unbelievable." Derek frowned.

Derek excused himself to greet another guest. Mitch blended in with a group standing by the fireplace, leaving Rebecca to stroll through the home.

Dark, hardwood floors with a black leather sofa and chaise filled the living room. A large screen TV hung over the fireplace and football highlights were playing. Paintings of hunting scenes and pictures of mallard ducks covered the walls. She took a moment to view the hunting rifles positioned over the pictures. The house had an open floor plan. The dining room space was the only thing to divide the living room and kitchen. Scotch, vodka, wine and soda covered half of the table. Cheese and crackers, vegetables and fruit platters, pasta dishes, and shrimp covered the other half. Rebecca filled a plate with food and then sat on the sofa.

Guys laughed loudly while the women talked over the men. Alcohol flowed into glasses, and people lined up to do shots. Mitch nodded at her as if pleased she was sitting alone. Because Mitch couldn't drink, she hoped that meant he wouldn't lose his temper with her tonight. It was no guarantee. Alcohol wasn't his only trigger.

A nearby couple was in an animated discussion, taking in each other's words with respect. That was once she and Mitch. They used to have long, deep conversations. He'd listen to her ideas. No putdowns. She had been so taken with him, so in love.

Ben dropped into the seat beside her.

Her eyes went wide. "What do you want?"

"I just wanted to say hello."

Nervously, she searched for Mitch. His back was to her.

"How have you been? Your wrist looks better."

She fidgeted with her food, almost knocking her plate off her lap. "This really isn't a good time to talk."

"What's wrong? Can't you talk to me? Won't he let you?"

"I just don't want to right now. I was going to get more food."

"I'll join you. I need to eat, too."

"I've changed my mind. I'm going to the bathroom, and then I'll join Mitch. Please understand." She emphasized the last word.

"Okay, but I hope one day you'll see I'm not an enemy. He's actually standing over there."

In the bathroom Rebecca washed her hands. They trembled. She scrubbed until the hot water scalded her skin.

Why can't Ben stay out of my business? He's going to get me in more trouble. He needs to leave me alone.

Mitch was on the phone when she returned. He didn't look pleased. He hung up. "I have to get to the hospital. Paramedics are bringing in three victims from a car accident." Mitch rummaged through the pile of jackets.

"You're going?" Derek appeared beside them.

Mitch reached for their coats. "Looks like it."

"Do you have to drive Rebecca home first?" Derek's words slurred.

"Yes. We have to leave this minute."

"Rebecca, too? It's New Year's Eve."

Mitch zipped up his black, leather jacket. "I can't worry about that."

"I'll be fine," Rebecca said. "An early night won't hurt me."

Derek grinned. "You stay here. I'll drive you home when the party is over."

"I'm going with Mitch."

"Stay."

Mitch jumped in. "No, I'll take her."

Derek started to interject, but Rebecca quickly added, "How about this? I'll drive Mitch to the hospital and then drive myself home. I can pick Mitch up when he's done."

"Problem solved," said Mitch. "Let's go."

Rebecca pulled onto the road.

"No way would I have let you stay at the party without me. Derek is out of his mind."

"And I didn't want to stay," Rebecca said. "I wanted to leave with you."

"I can't believe him. The nerve of some people. They think they can control everything and everyone."

Chapter 26

They counted down watching the crystal ball on the television.

"Five, four, three, two, one. Happy New Year!"

Rebecca turned to kiss Mitch, but no one was there.

*****

For a Monday evening, Susie's Café was busy. Booths ringed the room. Tables were squeezed together in the middle. The wood floor and red-brick fireplace gave the restaurant a cozy feel. Rebecca waited for a server to take her order. It was then that she saw a familiar face. David Morris's silver hair was powdered with white snow.

Rebecca waved him over. She stood and opened her arms to him. "Are you meeting someone here?"

"Nope, I came right from the airport and thought I'd get a bite to eat before heading home."

"Perfect timing. Would you like to join me?" Rebecca motioned to the other side of the booth.

"I'd like that. We have to get back to our weekly dates." David struggled out of his bulky jacket and took a seat.

"How are you?" she asked.

"Tired, but happy to see your smiling face."

Was she smiling? "I'm glad to see you, too."

The server brought water for them both. Rebecca ordered her Susie's favorite: turkey with all the trimmings. David ordered chicken rice soup and a roast beef sandwich.

"I hope the soup will warm me. I'm chilled to the bone."

"Another frigid day."

"Aren't they all this time of year?"

"Absolutely. Oh, guess what? I won *Employee of the Year*!"

"That's wonderful, Rebecca. I'm not surprised. You deserve every bit of acknowledgment you receive. You're a great employee for the bank."

"Thank you. I appreciate that."

"Really, you have professionalism and class."

Rebecca felt her face flush. He'd complimented her more than Mitch did.

"How is Evelyn? I wish I could have seen her."

"Mom's good. She made Christmas very special. I'd like to see her more, but ..."

David arched his eyebrows. "Evelyn's too busy to visit, right?"

"Exactly," she lied. "I wish she didn't have to work so much. Even if I could visit her, she'd be working most of the time."

"That's how it is with Vicki. Between working and running the kids to their activities, when I visit I spend most of my time sitting alone in her house."

"What are their ages again?"

"Ten and twelve. They are getting more homework now and are so busy. Jason, the ten-year-old, had a big science project due at the end of break, so he was busy with that. Well, I should say Vicki and he were busy the last couple days of break."

Rebecca laughed. "I believe it. What about Lexy?"

"She had to read a book, which she did in the first couple of days over vacation. She's an avid reader, like her mother. It was something about a heroine named Lizzie."

"I wish I had more time to read. I'm in the middle of one and it's taking me forever to get through it. Susannah's my current heroine. Although I think she's about to come to know her father's wrath. She's not doing as she's supposed to."

"A woman suffering abuse from a male?"

Although she looked to David as he spoke, with that last comment she *really* looked. And he returned the look. The silver in his hair didn't appear so silver. He looked warmed, and the rice soup was yet to arrive.

"I thought a lot about you while I was away. When I saw my daughter, I realized how similar she is to you, Rebecca. She's a sweet woman, and a little naïve." He put his hand over hers indicating he meant no harm.

Her hand felt trapped beneath his, though there was no real hold.

"She has a much better understanding of life now than she did before."

David didn't immediately explain *before*, but Rebecca knew she was expected to ask, and she did. "Before?"

"Did I ever tell you Vicki's story? Maybe it's time I did."

"I'd like to hear it," she lied. She anticipated Vicki's life to resemble hers way too much.

"When Vicki was twenty-four she married Craig. You were just a child at the time. Soon after they married, she landed a job as an accountant at a large company in Chicago. Pretty prestigious actually. She worked her way up to a management position. Perfect, wouldn't you say?"

"Yes, I suppose." Rebecca's eyes left David's. Where was their food? Where was a distraction? An interruption? Something to stall and maybe prevent the telling?

"Well-liked and respected at work, her home life was a different story."

She didn't respond. She didn't want to hear any more.

"Craig went to grad school at the University of Chicago. During the first couple of years of their marriage, Vicki supported him financially. She was a good wife." He wrung his hands together as if wringing a neck. "But, he was a real bastard," he spat with malice. "Repaid her kindness and support with tongue lashings. As she built him up, he tore my little girl down. I knew nothing about it, because I never saw them, and she never said a word. She somehow felt she was to blame."

Rebecca felt her face flush.

"Years later, when she told me how it all started, I was shocked. I had no idea this could happen to my daughter. She was in an abusive marriage for years, and I wasn't even aware of it."

"She mustn't have wanted you to know. So how could you?"

"Twenty-five years as a police officer should have taught me to recognize abuse in my own daughter's home. I obviously had a lot to learn about people. But I can still pick it out, in some people." He stared into her eyes. "Victims can try to hide the abuse from others. No one should be treated disrespectfully. No one should be abused. Ever."

Rebecca squirmed in her seat.

"What do you think?"

"I ... I don't know what to say."

"Now when we discuss it, she tells me she didn't want to upset me. Upset me?" He looked up at the ceiling as if searching for answers. "I'm her father. It was my job to protect my baby."

"I'm sure she didn't want to hurt you. She probably thought she could handle it on her own."

"All abuse needs to be stopped immediately."

The server came over and refilled David's water.

"Thank you," said Rebecca, and looked to the server. How could she ask him to stay? How could she ask him to save her from the conversation? He walked away.

"It only gets worse over time. Three years into their marriage, he got a lucrative job working for an international company. Vicki hoped he'd be busier with more responsibilities. She thought Craig would get better."

"Did he?" Rebecca asked, and felt herself suddenly interested to hear a reply.

"Worse. Abuse only gets worse."

Rebecca sat back in her seat, wanting to cover her ears.

"The abuse turned physical. She didn't know what to do. Her circle of friends kept her somewhat sane, but she didn't even tell them." He put his hand on his chest, and took one deep breath.

Rebecca found her fork twirling beneath her fingers. She stopped, and placed her hands in her lap. "That's a sad story."

"Then Vicki became pregnant. She hoped the baby would make Craig treat her better. It didn't. It made it worse."

"That's terrible." Her tone lacked conviction. She looked for the server. Where were their meals?

"Two children, and several more years of marriage. She finally told me. But not before that jerk started abusing the kids."

"What? He hurt the kids? His own kids?" Her tone exploded with emotion.

"When she finally asked for help, it was almost too late. My happy girl had vanished somewhere deep into herself, and it took years for her to return."

"How did she get out?"

"A victim advocacy organization in conjunction with a women's shelter, and the police. All of these organizations worked secretly to get her away from that monster."

"But the kids. Why didn't she just get up and go?"

"If she had only thought that way. But now, the emotional scars are subsiding because the three of them see a psychologist frequently. I fear they'll live with the memories forever." He pounded the table.

Rebecca jumped and the silverware clanked on the table.

"Dammit. It should never have gone on so long."

People at neighboring tables looked over.

"Sorry. It makes me so angry to think about the bastard."

"Your daughter is lucky to have you. You're supportive and understand her. That's what she needs."

Their meals arrived. David stirred his soup. Rebecca didn't feel like eating.

"We've got a great relationship now, and I treasure that." He sipped from his spoon. "I'm glad we were finally able to talk about this. I've wanted to tell you about Vicki for quite some time now."

"I'm glad you did." Did she lie?

"I want you to know you can talk to me about anything." David's eyes appeared to read her mind. His focus seemed to travel through her and stop at her soul. "I've become a good listener. You can trust me."

Chapter 27

Rebecca stood on the bank of Lake Ontario. She whipped a small rock into the water. It cut and bounced. The devastation in her mother, followed by her brother, David and ending with her friends appeared as each new ripple developed. Each ripple brought more pain. The results magnified. Their lives would change forever.

She breathed in, but couldn't fill her lungs. Inhaling sharply, her breath caught in her throat. Panicked, she searched her pockets for an inhaler. There wasn't one.

She looked at the lake to calm her, but it mocked her, the ripples starting to churn.

*****

"I'm so excited we're hanging out. How long have we been trying to get together?"

Rebecca and Kelly walked across Sunny's parking lot. Rebecca's stomach was in knots.

"Too long."

"What's Mitch doing?" Kelly pulled her hair into a ponytail, applied a coat of apricot-colored lipstick and smacked her lips together.

"He's working. I didn't tell him about us hanging out."

"Really? Why not?"

"He always ruins our plans." As the words tumbled out of her mouth, she immediately regretted them. Would Kelly pick up on the meaning? "Not on purpose, of course."

Rebecca searched for familiar cars, finding none. It was like her visits to the doctor. The knots loosened. She tugged at her coat, and followed Kelly inside, her long, black skirt settling, now out of the breeze.

The hostess greeted them. "We have a fifteen minute wait. You can sit at the bar and we'll call you when your table is ready."

Kelly declined.

Rebecca let out a breath she didn't know she was holding. "Thanks."

"You're not comfortable sitting at the bar. So no problem."

People moved about in the entranceway and spilled into the bar. Their voices competed with each other. She could see the bar from where she stood. It had a tropical theme. Two palm trees and tiki lights, and raised tables with pineapples for candle holders. The restaurant was similar. Painted oceans and palm trees on the sky-blue walls.

"Aren't you glad Margo's on vacation?"

"Absolutely," said Rebecca. "It's nice not to have her nitpicking at every detail, and I'm enjoying the extra hours, too."

"I know. She makes me crazy. She's always telling me to put a smile on my face, and be extra nice to Mrs. Rucker'."

"Ugh, our favorite wealthy client."

"Exactly, and she always comes into my lane," Kelly said, giggling. "Then Margo says 'make sure your shoulders are straight, Kelly'." She pushed her shoulders as far back as she could. They danced in a marching motion.

Rebecca laughed. "That's great."

"I've had a lot of practice."

"What are your plans after graduation?"

"A friend who works at an advertising company in North Carolina is searching for marketing executives. I applied and got a great position."

"Congratulations."

"Thanks. I'm super excited."

Kelly would be moving.

"It's a shame we didn't get to go out before this, though." Rebecca liked Kelly. She only had Anna to talk to, and another friend would have been nice. But, she also knew the dangers of inviting someone too close. She'd never regret Anna walking into her life, but Anna made her confront things she'd rather ignore.

"I know. I don't know why we haven't."

The hostess called Kelly's name and she said, "Let's get those Buffalo wings I've been craving."

They made a wide loop around the bar. They ordered and Kelly chatted about her new job. She couldn't wait until graduation. She'd be looking for an apartment over spring break. Kelly's excitement was contagious and Rebecca couldn't help but feel encouraged about the possibilities of having her own career. It seemed Mitch's interference was totally forgotten.

Their food came. The wings were hot.

Kelly said, "Enough about me. I could talk all night. What about that promotion? You'd be happy to be away from Margo's watchful eye."

Rebecca sipped her raspberry tea. "If I get it. And yes, you have no idea."

Kelly laughed.

"I'm also going back to school part-time."

"Really? That's great. What are you going to take?"

"Accounting. I started on my business degree a few years ago down in Florida, but had to drop out."

"I didn't know. Why did you drop out?"

"My grandmother needed home care, and I decided to move here and take care of her."

"That's so thoughtful of you. What a sacrifice."

"She meant the world to me."

"Well, I'm glad you're able to start up again."

Rebecca bit into another wing and fanned her mouth. "I need a refill on my iced tea. These wings are hot. Do you see our server?" Rebecca's search got no further than the bar.

Kelly pointed in the other direction, murmuring something, then said, "What's wrong?"

Rebecca blinked. The vision remained. Mitch and Derek, beer in their hands, with two women, one with black, spiked hair. It had to be Melissa.

"Bec?" Kelly touched Rebecca's arm.

Rebecca tore her gaze away. "I'm sorry?"

"I said our server is over there." She pointed in the other direction again. "What's wrong?"

Rebecca leaned back in her seat to avoid Mitch's line of sight. "It's nothing. I'll wait until she's closer."

"You're upset about something. What is it?"

Rebecca did the unthinkable—she confided. "Don't look, but I see Mitch sitting at the bar. I thought he was working."

Kelly swiveled.

"Don't look!"

"I won't. But what's wrong with that? Does he come here often?"

"He must."

"Maybe he called you and you couldn't hear the ring over the noise."

Rebecca checked her cell. One message. She strained to hear.

"What is it? What did it say?" Kelly asked.

She stared at the phone. "He left me a message saying not to wait up. He'd be studying for a few hours."

Kelly turned again. "Oh boy. How recent was it?"

"A half-hour ago." Her eyes watered. "He must have called on his way out of work."

"Why would he tell you he's working?"

"Studying," Rebecca corrected. "He always says he's studying."

"Rebecca?"

"I don't know."

The unfamiliar scents Mitch had carried on his breath and clothes. The noises in the background when he called. The comments made at the Fields' party.

He's been lying.

"You look pale. Are you okay?"

Rebecca held the table for support. "Just give me a minute."

"Here. Take a sip of water."

After she sipped, she felt the dizziness pass. "I'm okay now. Thanks."

"Do you want to go?"

"I don't think I could stand."

"What do you think is going on?"

"I don't know. Maybe he was asked out after he left the message."

Kelly scrunched her face. "Then he would have called you back and left another one."

Rebecca turned away.

"Sorry, but I think he's got a lot of explaining to do when he gets home tonight." Kelly straightened in her seat. "Or you could walk over there right now. Ask him in front of his friends."

Rebecca's eyes widened. "No. He'd freak."

"Well, he's the one with the women, lying about where he is."

She didn't respond.

"Rebecca?"

"With Mitch, that's not the best strategy."

"Why?"

"I've got to get out of here." Perspiration formed on her forehead.

"Are you okay? You look like you're going to be sick."

"I might be."

Kelly paid the bill with cash.

Rebecca passed a blue Ford F150 in the car park. DRDC3. Derek Canton. Mitch had ruined another night without even laying a hand on her.

Chapter 28

Facing Mitch, she wrapped her arms around his shoulders and massaged his back muscles. Her nimble hands moved toward his neck, pressing into his shoulders.

"Mmm." Mitch pulled her closer and took a deep breath, inhaling her perfume.

She could smell the perfume, too, but it wasn't hers.

She worked her fingers down his back and stopped above his pants. Digging into flesh, she asked, "How does that feel?"

He responded with a kiss. He ran his hands through her hair, stopping at the base of the skull and pressed her mouth with more force.

She slipped the belt through the buckle and released, his pants loosening.

He moaned.

He responded by unbuttoning her blouse. His eyes met hers. She stared back at him. It was Melissa.

Chapter 29

The clock on the beige wall of the hospital cafeteria read 5:50 pm. Mitch was almost an hour late. Rebecca walked around, called Mitch, and got his voice mail yet again. She pulled out a chair. It screeched on the tile floor. A tall, blond man entered from a side door. *Ben.* Her breath hitched and she prayed he hadn't seen her. Pretending to talk on her cell, she looked out the main door.

A hand touched her shoulder.

"Hi, Rebecca. What brings you here?"

She pretended to click off the phone and slid it into her pocket.

"May I sit?" He pulled out a chair.

"No," Rebecca blurted. "Mitch will be here shortly."

He shook his head. "I don't think so."

She squirmed in her seat. "Why do you say that?"

Twisting the cap off his bottled water, he said, "He's in the middle of a procedure. He might be busy for another hour."

"I'll wait."

"So be it." Ben fiddled with his gold watch. "Did you hear about Tim's dad?"

"I did. How's he doing?"

"He's in pretty bad shape. It was a stroke, but they're hoping for a good recovery."

"I feel terrible for Tim and his family."

"Yeah, we shouldn't take life for granted."

Rebecca looked around.

"He's not coming, Rebecca."

"So you've said."

"How have you been? I've been thinking about you."

"Me? Why?"

"How are you?"

"Fine and you?"

He ran his fingers through his short hair. "How are you really?"

"Mitch is probably on his way. No need for you to be here. I'm sure you have some studying to do."

"What studying?"

"Aren't you taking the exam with Mitch?"

His forehead creased. "The test coming up? You can't study for that."

"What do you mean?"

"The test is simply a practical exam on procedures that we've been perfecting for the last couple of years. It'll be easy."

Rebecca couldn't speak. She turned away, a lone tear trickling down her cheek. She tried to ignore it and hoped Ben didn't notice.

He did. He handed her a napkin. "What has Mitch told you?"

She refused to make eye contact.

"Look, if Mitch has told you these are anything other than perfunctory exams, he's exaggerating. I'll review the proper procedures, but I won't waste an exorbitant amount of time. There's no reason to. Mitch knows that."

"Maybe Mitch needs to. Maybe he ... he ..." She stood on wobbly legs. She couldn't breathe. Her body felt heavy with doubt pulling her under.

Ben rushed to catch her, guiding her into the chair. He gave her sips of water until her dizziness passed.

"What's wrong? Talk to me." He stroked her back and talked quietly.

"I'm so embarrassed. I didn't eat lunch. Low blood sugar."

"I think it's much more than that. You're crying."

"I haven't eaten in a while. That's all."

"Then let me get you some food."

"No, I have to leave." She stood, this time holding her balance. "I'll go straight home and have dinner."

He insisted on walking her to her car.

When Rebecca pulled into the driveway, she saw Anna standing outside. Rebecca did a double take. Anna wore one of the matching cable-knit sweaters Rebecca's mother had given to her and Mitch for Christmas.

Rebecca motioned for her to come in through the garage. They sat at the dining room table.

"Bec, what's going on?"

Rebecca looked out the window.

"Don't worry. I'll sneak out the front door when he gets home."

"I'm so confused," she said while she tugged at a loose thread on her sweatshirt.

"Tell me everything."

Rebecca bit her lip. "I went to Sunny's last night with Kelly. Mitch was there, but he'd left me a message saying he'd be studying and not to wait up."

"He lied. Nothing you shouldn't have expected. What did you do?"

"I was so upset. I left Sunny's immediately. He didn't mention anything about it this morning."

"So now you don't know what he was doing when he said he was studying."

"Exactly. He asked me to meet him at the hospital tonight for dinner, but didn't say anything about what he did last night."

"I've told you before. He's manipulative. No surprise if he's having an affair."

"I don't know that. *You* don't know that."

"Come on, Rebecca."

"Well, there's more. You're not going to believe it."

"More than lying about his whereabouts?"

"While waiting for Mitch, I saw Ben. He said something."

"What?"

"He said you can't study for the test that they are going to take."

"So Mitch is lying again. Didn't he tell your mom the same thing?"

"Yes, I thought that Mitch had been studying for weeks. I thought that was the source of his stress."

"You mean his abuse. Nothing excuses that, Bec."

"It doesn't matter anyways, if what Ben is saying is true."

"Because Mitch is lying about everything."

Rebecca stood from the table and spun around. "Ben has to be lying."

"What? Bec, really? You're kidding me, right?"

"No, I'm not."

"What motive would Ben have to lie?"

Rebecca cried into her hands. "I don't know. I can't figure all this out. It just can't be true. But I think it is."

"You need to consider that Ben is telling you the truth and Mitch hasn't been honest this whole time."

She shook her head.

"You know what this would mean, don't you?"

Rebecca put her head up, looked directly at Anna, and admitted, "Yes, it means Mitch is not going to change."

Chapter 30

The door burst open. Rebecca looked for Anna, but she was gone. As Mitch entered the living room, he scowled. He walked past her without a word and went straight to the bedroom. He called her in.

"How was work?" She bit at her fingernails.

He glared until she put her hands in her sweatshirt pocket.

He changed out of his work clothes. His chest muscles looked flexed, rippling with barely contained rage. "Fine. I got Branden to cover for me, so I could come home early." He grabbed a t-shirt and jeans and slipped them on.

He headed into the kitchen, opened the refrigerator and pulled out a beer, downing it.

"Can I fix you something for dinner?"

"Did *you* eat?"

"I had a bite to eat when I came home."

"Home from where?"

"The hospital. I waited for you for dinner and left you messages."

"I was in the middle of something."

"I understand," she said.

"Well, that's good." He slammed his empty bottle down.

The hairs on her arms prickled. "I'm going to do some laundry. Let me know if you need anything."

As she turned, he gripped her arm and spun her around.

"So, what did *you* do at the hospital?" He dug his fingers into her flesh.

She winced in pain. "I waited. I called."

"And?"

"And I kept waiting and ..." She swallowed hard.

"And?"

He must know about Ben.

He spoke to her as if she was a child. "Rebecca, aren't you leaving something out?"

She nodded, afraid to speak.

"Good girl. Tell me what you did at the hospital." He caressed her cheek.

"I ... I, well, Ben ... Ben ..." She wrinkled her nose.

"Go on," he said, the caress moving to her temple.

"I didn't want to talk to him. I told him to go away."

He gripped her hair. "Fascinating. And did he?"

His hold on her prevented her from backing away. She remained as still as possible, terrified of his next move.

Thoughts scattering like leaves in the wind, she scrambled to collect words. "No ... no. He kept talking to me."

Mitch released her hair. He taunted her by pouting. "Oh, so he wouldn't listen? Poor Rebecca. Nobody listens to you, do they?"

"Mitch—"

"What were you doing with him?"

"We talked for a few minutes, that's all."

"Really?"

"Yes."

He rubbed his chin. "Hmm. Interesting."

She shook her head. It was a movement pleading for a reprieve from what she knew was to come.

He pulled her toward him. "Well, I beg to differ. I found the scene *very* interesting. Ben with his arm around you and all ..."

Mitch was there.

"It's not what it looked like. I got dizzy and he walked me to the car. That's all."

His grip tightened. "I don't care what the reason is. I don't want Ben or any other man near you."

She nodded, and then blinked her tear-filled eyes. She twisted her throbbing arm in a futile attempt to loosen his grip.

"I don't think you understand, so I'll make it clear."

"It's just a misunderstanding. I got dizzy—"

"You must have forgotten what I've said to you in the past about talking to Ben. You know I hate him. Really, Rebecca, of all people?" He reached for her throat.

A voice in her head yelled, *Run*. It was the jolt she needed. She wrenched her arm free and dodged his hand.

He lunged.

She scooted through the hallway, grabbing her keys from the end table and rushed to the door.

He trailed her. "Little bitch! Wait until I'm done with you. No man will ever want you."

She pushed over a lamp, sending it behind her steps. He tripped and fell. She dashed to open the door to the garage. She could taste her escape. Mere seconds away.

Where would she go? David? Kelly? Joan? Anna? She had resources now. People she could depend on.

"You'll be sorry!"

She started to shut the door when a hand appeared. Mitch pulled from the inside. She pulled with incredible strength, screaming. Her life depended on it.

"Don't you ever betray me," he roared.

He threw open the door and grabbed her arm, pulling. She writhed, but couldn't break free. He dragged her into the living room.

"Mitch, please. I didn't do anything wrong. We talked, and then I got dizzy and—"

"Shut up!"

Tears streamed down her face as she begged, "Please listen."

"What you need is a lesson and that's what you're going to get." He released her arm, pushing her to the floor.

Scurrying backward out of his reach, she said, "Please, I'm sorry. Forgive me."

"When will you learn that you belong to me?" Mitch towered over her, pinning her stomach with his foot.

When she stared at the monster she called her husband, a picture of her parents flashed in her mind. She had to fight. Fight for her mother. She couldn't survive without her daughter.

I will survive this.

"What am I going to do with you? What do you think I should do?" He pushed her stomach down harder.

"I'm sorry," she cried, begging for mercy.

Taking his foot off, he kicked her leg, then pulled her up by her shoulders. She felt like a ball being tossed around. He overpowered her in every way: strength, size, and stamina.

He gave her a violent shake then slapped her.

She cried out in pain, reaching for her stinging cheek, and stumbled backwards into the wall. The *Water Lilies* crashed to the floor.

He pointed to the picture. "Don't you remember the promise you made when we were engaged? You promised to be with me, Rebecca. No one else. When we married, you said you'd be with me *until death do us part*."

"I am faithful to you." Using a dining room chair as leverage, she stood.

He stepped closer. "You can't outrun me. Ever. You have nowhere to hide."

She slid along the wall into the living room. He followed.

"You'll never leave me. You're mine forever. That's what we promised each other. If you try, I'll find you. Do you understand me?"

She couldn't answer.

He backhanded her jaw.

Weeping, she nodded. "I'd never leave you."

"What did you talk about with Ben?"

Her body shook and pain seared through every limb.

He stepped closer. "Answer me!"

She put her hands up. "Okay, I'll tell you." She paused, thinking of what to say. "He told me about the upcoming test."

Mitch scowled. "What did that weasel say?"

She choked back tears and lied. "He said the test was hard, but he'd ace it."

His lips parted. "He's worried about the exam?"

She nodded.

"Hmm." His face relaxed.

She'd made the right choice. He moved in closer and kissed her cheek.

His lips on her skin made her cringe. Fear mixed with disgust, and she turned away.

He made a fist. She squeezed her eyes shut and waited for the blow. Instead, the drywall next to her face exploded. Chalky dust filled the air around her nose and she coughed.

He pulled his fist out of the wallboard and shook it. "I could've broken your face, but I didn't."

Rebecca wished he'd broken his hand.

When she sidestepped away from him, he clasped her neck, and then banged her head against the wall. *Fight! Fight! Fight!* Words inside her head. Her fear turned to anger.

"Leave me alone! Stop hurting me!"

He loosened his grip.

"*You* talk about betrayal. Why were *you* at Sunny's last night?"

"What?"

Stay strong and brave, just like Anna would. She lifted her chin. "You told me you were at the hospital."

He tilted his head. "How can you be sure I wasn't?"

She looked him directly in the eye. "Because I saw you there."

His voice came out in a low growl. "So, what are you telling me, Rebecca?"

"I saw you there."

They stood a foot apart.

"Let me make sure I understand you correctly. *You* were at Sunny's and saw *me*."

"That's right."

Mitch closed the gap between them quickly. "What in the hell were you doing at Sunny's?"

"I went with a work friend."

"Who?"

"Kelly."

"How often do you go?"

"Just this once."

"Really? And how am I supposed to believe you? You probably go there all the time while I'm working my ass off to support you." His forehead pressed against hers.

She turned away. "It was my first time. I saw you and Derek. I thought you were ..."

"Were what, Rebecca? Studying?"

She nodded.

"Don't I deserve a little time off from studying? I needed a break. You wouldn't understand. Damn, Rebecca. I should *break* something of yours."

He elbowed her in the ribs. The force of the blow knocked her off balance. She fell, face first to the floor.

She cried, "I do. I understand."

"That doesn't explain why you were there without my permission."

She crawled backwards, desperate to get away. "We ate dinner. That's all. I swear."

He scooped her up into his arms. He grabbed onto her as she cried. He didn't let go, just held her.

She could feel his heart beating and his rapid breathing. He pushed her away.

She crumpled to the floor in a heap.

He stood over her. "You've had a busy couple of days. Sunny's and then talking to Ben. Do you think you can stay out of trouble until the exam or do I need to come home every night to study here and watch you?"

"I'll be good. I promise." She clasped her hands together as if praying.

Chapter 31

A cold breeze blew across Rebecca, rousing her as she lay on the hardwood floor. Where was the cold coming from? Only one eye opened. Her left eye had swollen shut.

"Bec? Are you okay?" Anna's muffled voice sounded far away.

Rebecca moaned and rolled over, and saw Anna through her good eye.

"Oh, Rebecca. What did that monster do to you?" Anna lifted Rebecca's head and cradled it in her arms. "Oh, your face is swollen. Bastard! I'm calling the police."

"No, don't. Please promise you won't."

"I have to. Look at you. I can see marks on your arm from his grasp. Your jaw is bruised, too. And your eye. Damn it! I am calling the police."

"No. He'd kill me for sure. Please. Don't make my life harder than it already is."

"Something might be broken. You need help."

"No, I don't. Mitch doesn't break bones."

"It's only a matter of time. Or he'll do something worse. I'm not allowing this to happen anymore."

Rebecca shook her head. "Please, give me until after the exam and vacation. That's my chance to talk to him. It's my last chance."

"It might be the last of you. You need help. There are domestic violence organizations in town."

"I can't take the risk right now. He threatened to kill me. I just have to make it til the exam."

"The exam is easy, remember? You've heard that."

"Give me until after vacation."

"No."

"I'm begging you."

Anna looked away. "That's all, Bec. Then you're getting help. Promise?"

"I promise."

"Let me get you some ice for your eye. Stay here."

"I'll go with you. I need to make sure I can stand."

Anna eased her up. Rebecca sat waiting for the dizziness to pass. Her legs trembled as she balanced on her good leg and slowly put pressure on her injured one. She cried out when a sharp, stabbing pain sliced through every part of her. Rebecca used Anna and the wall for support before hobbling the short distance to the kitchen. They stopped several times.

Anna pulled ice packs from the freezer, grabbed the pill bottle, and Rebecca choked down two ibuprofen.

Anna guided her back to the sofa. Rebecca reclined and placed the packs on the most painful parts of her body. Pulling her grandmother's antique quilt over her, she hoped to stop the shaking.

"Everything hurts. My face especially."

Anna propped Rebecca's head up on a pillow. "Oh, Rebecca, I can't stand to see you in such pain. What else can I do?"

"Stay with me, please, until Mitch comes home."

"I'm here for you, as always."

She lay on her side. Anna rubbed her back.

"It's so hard seeing you like this."

Rebecca's chin trembled. "I know," she whispered. The bleeding had stopped, but her skin was still swollen and bruised.

"Did you confront Mitch about Sunny's?" Anna asked.

Rebecca moaned.

"Sorry, don't try to talk right now. You can tell me another time."

"He saw me," she whispered.

"Saw you where? At Sunny's?"

"No, when I talked to Ben."

"What? Mitch is the one who has lied about everything, and you're beaten because he saw you with Ben?"

Rebecca nodded.

"Disgusting." Anna stroked Rebecca's hair. "Rest."

*****

Rebecca waded into the cool water, careful not to step on any sharp shells. The sand felt like it was disintegrating under her feet. She moved deeper. When she was waist high, she started to do the breast stroke, moving out to sea. Soon she couldn't touch the sand, and she floated on her back.

The sun warmed her face and her body swayed to the rhythm of the waves.

She closed her eyes.

The wind picked up. When she opened her eyes, she noticed the sky had turned dark. A flash of lightning, with thunder rumbling. She straightened and looked around. No land was in sight.

She was in danger. Always in danger.

*****

Rebecca's eyes popped open. The house was dark and Anna was gone. The ice packs were now room temperature. A dreadful thought crossed her mind. If Mitch was in the house, would he start hurting her again? Her head felt like it had been pounded with a baseball bat, and her face burned. Her leg screamed in pain as she slid into an upright position. She attempted to stand. She was unsteady and she took small steps. Rebecca moved to the doorway of the master bedroom. Mitch lay in their bed, taking over her part as well, snoring away in a deep, untroubled sleep.

Using the walls as a support, she made her way into the kitchen, taking more pain meds before crawling into bed in the guest room. Twirling the ends of her hair as she'd done as a child, she willed herself to calm down. Drifting off to sleep, her body throbbed in pain. She hoped to find a happy dream.

*****

The sky darkened and the wind thrashed as Rebecca stood on the beach. Sand blew, whipping at her naked body. A tornado in the distance destroyed everything in its path. She tried to run, but her legs were immobile, sinking into the wet sand. As the beast approached, she screamed, but no sound came out. Who would have heard her anyway?

"Susannah," she heard. "That's it. No more. You lay with the man, that ... that black man. You chose your path. Be gone."

"I'm not Susannah. I'm Rebecca."

"You both chose. Now go."

Directly overhead, the funnel threatened to consume her. Prepared to be swept out to sea, she said goodbye to her family, her life.

Her arms reached into the tornado, waiting to be pulled away. Debris flew all around her, barely missing her exposed skin. A starfish circled her body. She tried to take hold of it, before it disappeared in the wind. Another and another. Starfish filled the air. She couldn't grasp them. Couldn't save them.

Chapter 32

Rebecca woke and looked around the room. She saw her childhood dresser across from the bed with Betsy staring at her. Antique rocking chair in the corner. She remembered that she was in the guest room.

She lay in bed and listened to the sounds of the house. Freezing rain tapped against the windows and coffee brewed in the kitchen.

Mitch whistled in the background. Pulling the comforter over her face, she prayed for the monster to stay away. Why had she stuck up for herself? Why did she think she could be Anna?

Lots of hot tears spilled from her eyes and she sank deeper into bed. She couldn't face Mitch today. This abuse was too much.

The garage door rumbled, and then closed. Relief washed over her. She was safe for the moment. Pulling herself up on her elbows, she squinted her eyes, her cheek throbbing, and stole a glance at the clock across the room. Two hours until work. She touched her jaw, ready for pain. Not as bad as other times. Slowly, she sat up in bed and swung her legs around to the side.

She pulled up the leg of her sweatpants. Bruises and swollen skin. It would be difficult to walk.

Is he ever going to stop? She'd done nothing wrong. He had. The bruise on her arm looked like she'd expected. Finger marks. How bad were the bruises on her face? She limped to the bathroom and steeled herself before looking at the reflection in the mirror.

Damn!

No way could they be covered up. The swelling, too. Why wasn't she shocked? What she saw was an atrocity. Nothing less. Why did she not feel anger or the need for revenge? But then ... this was her normal.

Rebecca dialed the bank.

"Kelly?"

"Hey, Rebecca? I've wanted to call you. How'd it go when you talked to Mitch?"

Rebecca sniffled.

"Did you bust him?"

Silence.

"What's wrong?"

Through a stifled cry, she said, "It's complicated."

"It seems pretty clear cut to me. He lied."

"I know he did, but—"

"What?"

"We got into an argument. It was pretty intense."

"Are you okay?"

"Yeah," she said, trying to stop the tears. "I just want to forget about the whole thing."

"Now I'm worried about you."

"I'm fine. Don't worry."

"Aren't you coming in soon? We can take our break together and you can tell me about it."

"Well, actually, I can't. I've been sick to my stomach all morning."

"Oh, no. Is it the fight?"

"Maybe. But I think it's the stomach bug going around."

"I've heard that it's brutal."

Rebecca hated betraying the trust of a friend. "It is."

"Well, I hope you get better soon. I'm bummed we won't be working together, but another time."

Rebecca moved to the sofa and pulled up the quilt. A sob broke free.

What a pitiful life!

Chapter 33

The next morning, Mitch sat at the dining room table reading *The New York Times* while sipping his coffee. Rebecca nibbled on toast.

"You need to keep ice on your face. Are you taking the Diflunisal I prescribed?" He didn't look up from the paper.

"Yes."

"You'll be fine by Monday, ready to get back to work."

She took her plate into the kitchen. It was a slow feat. She wobbled and cringed with the pain each step brought. Coffee mug in one hand and a bag of ice in the other, she retreated to the bedroom, away from Mitch. As best she could, she completed the household chores. Mitch had instructed that her face be iced every twenty minutes.

"Are you icing?" he would yell.

"Yes," she replied each time. And she did.

Lunchtime came. Rebecca served a grilled chicken salad and steaming vegetable soup. She touched the *Water Lilies*. She'd rehung the picture, but it sat slightly to the right. It was from the past. From long ago.

Mitch came into the dining room, his hand hidden behind his back. His expression was unreadable. She turned from it.

They sat. A small wooden figurine sat next to her plate. A dolphin, eyes carved out, and a face that smiled back at her.

"Did you just make this? It's nice," she said dutifully.

"Yes. I thought it would be a reminder of our upcoming vacation." He spooned his soup into a bowl. "I'm glad you like it. It took me a bit of time. Those eyes were difficult to capture."

Those eyes. They looked like holes. No soul. Pits. Black. Nothingness. She fiddled with the dolphin and rested it on the table between them. "I do," she lied.

He blew on his soup. "The exam will be over soon. I'll be so relieved to not have that hanging over my head like a guillotine."

A guillotine. Over whose head?

She nibbled on her chicken. It was tasteless.

Mitch played with the bottles of salad dressing. "Where's the ranch dressing?"

"We don't have any."

He picked the blue cheese dressing, put some on his salad, and slammed the bottle back down on the table. "Well, put it on your list and buy it tomorrow."

Rebecca picked through her meal. Nothing was appetizing. Not to her, anyway. It was like dust in her mouth. But Mitch didn't complain. The ranch dressing was the only hurdle. Dessert should prove to be smooth sailing. She'd made a cherry cheesecake. He'd asked for a cheesecake a few days earlier.

She served up a large piece for Mitch, and a smaller piece for herself, then refilled his glass of riesling.

"You know I wanted blueberry cheesecake. I told you that."

"Did you? I'm awfully—"

Mitch pushed the plate away, picked up the dolphin and threw it at the wall, barely missing the *Water Lilies*. The dolphin's tail broke off.

*****

Rebecca outlined the hope chest with her finger. Beautiful, intricate carvings, each one representing her family. A heart, a rose, a tree of life, intertwined. She opened the box, the hinge creaking. Inside lay her most beloved treasure. It was her pale-pink baby blanket. A pair of booties and a christening gown were hidden underneath the blanket alongside her charm bracelet.

The wooden figurines on the base of the chest beckoned to be held. Mitch's gifts. She picked them up one at a time. A Christmas tree representing their first holiday. A heart for giving him hers. The baby lamb in anticipation of a child. The tailless dolphin to remind her of the life-changing vacation soon to come.

The dolphin wiggled in her hand and bit her finger.

Blood gushed.

She grabbed her blanket to stop the bleeding.

The blood soaked into the baby blanket, turning it crimson.

The blanket bled.

Her hand bled.

So much blood.

*****

The next morning, Rebecca picked the dolphin up off the floor and brought the pieces into the living room. She opened the cedar chest and put them in with the other carved figurines.

She touched the bruise on the side of her face, then reached for the blanket and rubbed the fleece against her cheek. Even though a musty smell drowned the material, she imagined a fresh baby scent. How badly she wanted children, but she had a feeling that it wasn't going to happen.

Chapter 34

Monday, Rebecca hurried through the bank's door. She'd applied and reapplied make-up, but no amount could conceal the bruise on her cheek. She tried a bandage, but it was too obvious. Her long hair might keep some stares away, but it was doubtful.

Margo was back. She stood at the customer service desk assisting a client, but the woman had eyes everywhere.

She pulled Rebecca into her office. "What the hell happened to you?"

"Mitch opened the door and I was just going out and it whacked me in the face."

She wrinkled her brow. "Really? That's strange." She touched the bruise.

Rebecca winced.

"How'd it happen again? Slower this time."

"I wasn't paying attention—"

"As usual."

"I wasn't paying attention and I walked to the door, looked away, and when I looked back, it slammed into my face." She motioned with her hands a door hitting her cheek. "Mitch felt horrible. I was already sick with a stomach virus and he couldn't believe what happened."

"Did he take you to the hospital?"

"No, I insisted I was fine. I've had ice on it since the accident."

"What day did you say this happened?"

Had she told her? "It was Saturday."

"So you were sick on Friday and got whacked in the face Saturday?"

"Yes, that's right. I've been unlucky. It'll be better soon."

"Well, you won't be working in the open today. You're on drive-up window duty until your face heals." Margo turned on her heel and marched away.

*****

Rebecca lit the kindling in the fireplace, and added a log. She curled up on the sofa with her grandmother's masterpiece, throwing one end over Anna's legs.

"Your face is healing," said Anna.

Rebecca touched her cheek. "I still need concealer to cover it up. Mitch reminds me every chance he gets to ice and ice and ice some more."

"Like it's your fault." Anna frowned.

"Margo put me in the drive-up window so customers wouldn't notice my face. I hope this doesn't ruin my chance for that promotion."

"It had better not. You're finally getting to where you want to be. You can't let anything get in your way like—"

"Mitch." Rebecca stirred her cocoa, mixing in a handful of mini-marshmallows.

Anna huffed. "Exactly. You've got to get out of this marriage, and now."

Rebecca put the mug on the coffee table and threw the quilt off her lap. She poked the fire, hoping to drown out Anna's words.

Anna moved to the edge of her seat. "Come on, talk to me."

Rebecca watched the flames.

"Snap out of it. This isn't your fault. You need to help yourself if you won't let anyone else."

Rebecca stared at her without staring. How? How was she to leave? Anna made it sound easy. Nothing was easy anymore. With no money? Leave this house? If she got the promotion—

"Bec," Anna coaxed. "Please, don't pull away." She wrapped the quilt over Rebecca's shoulders.

"I don't know what to do. I've got to get through to him during vacation."

"You aren't going on vacation with him. Get that out of your head."

Anna's next words were muffled to Rebecca. Nothing was easy anymore. With no money? Leave this house?

Anna waved her hands in front of Rebecca's face. "Earth to Rebecca. Come back to me. We'll solve this problem together."

"How are we going to fix this? Mitch will never let me leave."

"I wish you could see what's right in front of you," Anna said.

Rebecca stared into the fire. It was too late.

Chapter 35

Rebecca's face had almost healed. Well enough to allow concealer to do a good job. With a little blush, nobody knew. She contacted David and met him at Susie's Café.

"I assume Mitch is working late?"

She took a quick glance at the menu, and set it down. "Overnight."

"That many hours must be hard on you and your marriage."

Rebecca shrugged. "I guess."

Their plates were heaped with food. David squeezed ketchup onto his plate and talked about the 'A' his grandson Jason received for his science project. His eyes shone with pride.

"Vicki had more good news for me. She's dating. Nothing serious, but they go out occasionally. It's good for her. She's taking it slowly, cautiously."

"That *is* news."

"Of course, the kids are her first priority. They always will be." With a serious tone, he added, "As we talked about before, it gets more complicated and dangerous for a woman in an abusive relationship when she has children. Not only is all of their safety at stake, but they also have more trouble leaving. Having children doesn't make abusers stop abusing even if that's what he promised. And what does it teach the kids? That it's okay to knock someone around? Are you okay?" David asked.

Rebecca snapped her head up. "Sorry, I was just thinking about something."

"Please, Rebecca, trust me." His eyes locked on hers.

She turned away quickly. "I do."

He took her hand. "I made a promise to myself after finding out about my little girl that I'd speak up if I ever suspected another woman was being abused."

Rebecca pulled her hand away.

"I see the pain in your eyes. The same pain that was in Vicki's."

She touched her cheek, unable to form words of protest, words of denial.

"You don't have to say anything. I just want you to know I care for your well-being and I'm here for you."

Rebecca burst into tears. She wiped at her face before the tears could wash away the concealer and blush. "Sorry, I didn't mean to cry."

"Don't apologize. I didn't want to upset you."

She blew her nose. Her hands trembled. "Mitch and I have problems, but we're working on them." Oh, the measure of relief with that tiny, minute confession. To talk about it! But then, just as quickly, the lies and cover-ups came. "Remember the exam I told you about that Mitch has to take? It's the Monday before vacation. I'm hoping I can get through to him when we're alone. He'll have less on his mind then." She didn't believe a word she uttered. She tried. She believed it all before, but now, lying was simply an addictive behavior.

"Remember, people don't change overnight, if at all. Be careful." Compassion shone through his pale-blue eyes.

"I will." She wiped her eyes. "I understand." She felt like a prisoner. Trapped.

"How does Evelyn feel about your situation? She must be devastated."

"Well ..." Rebecca cut into her turkey.

"She doesn't know, does she?"

She chewed her food for a long moment. "I don't want to upset Mom. She went through so much with Dad's death."

"She needs to know the truth. She deserves to know. Your mother should be in your real life, not an imaginary one."

"No." She filled her mouth again.

"You need protection."

"I don't want her to worry," she said with her mouth full.

"Your mother is stronger than you think. Give her a chance to prove it to you."

"It's so hard to think about hurting her."

"She'll hurt more when she finds out you felt you couldn't confide in her. I'm speaking from my own experience."

She swallowed. "I'll consider it."

Chapter 36

Mitch's voice message had sounded urgent. Rebecca rushed through the glass doors of the hospital. She spotted him sitting on a beige sofa. He rose and squeezed her tight enough to lift her off her feet. He laughed, set her back down, and took her by the hand. They took the elevator to the second floor, found a quiet waiting room and sat.

"You're beautiful."

"Your message sounded urgent."

"I've been thinking about how much fun our vacation will be. I bet you'll be pregnant by the time we leave Florida."

"Oh?"

"I talked to Doctor Epstein today. He said if we need him, he'll get us in right away. Even though he's booked solid, he'll make time for me."

Time? Time was not on her side. Time was evil. Time was running out.

"One way or another, we'll have my child." He squeezed her hand until it hurt.

She nodded.

"The forecast for St. Augustine Beach is amazing. They're going to have record highs. Sunny and mid-seventies for the beginning of our vacation week, much warmer than normal."

Taking a deep breath, she said, "We'll have so much fun together."

"Have you looked online at the resort yet? It's impressive."

He pulled out his smartphone, tapped the internet icon, and pulled up the resort's website.

Rebecca leaned over. The cottage where they would be staying was secluded. It was one of ten cottages, all on stilts, located close to the ocean, and separate from the main hotel. It was only steps from the dunes, leading right to the ocean.

She said, "I can't believe this is our first vacation since our honeymoon."

"It's been too long. I'm looking forward to driving to the World Golf Village and playing on the famous *King and Bear* course. I booked my tee times months ago."

"Will you golf alone?"

"It's a busy place. They'll match me up with others." He clicked and brought up another website. "I also want to check out the World Golf Hall Of Fame while I'm there."

"How nice. I can't wait to relax at the beach."

"Ah, that's not what I have planned for you. I've picked out lots of tourist activities."

Rebecca opened her mouth to speak, but was cut off.

"You can go on a scenic cruise around Matanzas Bay, and then visit Castillo de San Marcos. It's the oldest masonry fort in the U.S."

"I've already been there when I was at Flagler. It was just a short walk away. What if I give you a tour of the local places?"

"I've got other plans."

"Don't you want to see where I went to college?"

"You mean until you dropped out?"

She sat back. "Mitch, I did that for my family. I wanted to stay and work on my career, but it just—"

"Whatever. Anyway, I'll be golfing and jet skiing."

"You're jet skiing, too?"

"Sure. The waterway is a great place to ski. I can check out downtown and the fort by taking the inlet."

"I'd love to try that, too."

"Hon, you're hardly coordinated enough. Besides, you'll be busy touring."

"I don't need to tour. I'm looking forward to lying out in the sun."

He grew serious. "I don't want guys hitting on you at the resort or on the beach, especially if I'm not there."

Rebecca bit her nails. "I guess I'll sightsee a little, but can we go for walks in the evening?"

"Stop biting your fingers."

She placed her hands by her sides. Dr. Fields popped his head into the room. Mitch stood to greet him.

"Sit back down, Mitch. Hello, Rebecca. I'm glad you're both here," Jonathon said, sitting in the recliner next to them. "What are you two doing Saturday night?"

"I'm working until five, but I can stay longer if you need me to."

He laughed. "No, Mitch. Barb and I would like to take both of you to dinner, if you're available."

Mitch raised his eyebrows. "Rebecca, your mother isn't coming up this weekend, is she?"

"What? No, she's not."

"Nothing is going on?"

Rebecca gave him a questioning look. "Do you need to study? The exam is Monday."

Mitch squeezed her hand. She winced.

"Study?" said Jonathon. "The exam is nothing to be concerned with, Mitch. Can you meet us at Vincent's Restaurant at seven?"

"That sounds perfect," said Mitch.

"Barb will be pleased. It's her idea. See you then."

Mitch paced the small room. "Jon doesn't know what he's talking about. He probably took the exam decades ago and doesn't remember."

She gave a tight smile. "I'm sure that's it."

"I've got to get back to my patients. I'll walk you to the elevator."

"So why did I need to rush here? Your message—"

"What? You aren't excited to spend a little time with your husband?"

"Of course," she said.

Mitch stabbed at the elevator button. Ben headed their way. Mitch couldn't see him but Rebecca could. She wanted to pull her eyes away. They wouldn't budge. Her hand touched her cheek. It didn't seem to be a voluntary movement. Ben watched for a second, and then shook his head before turning away.

Chapter 37

Rebecca's heart raced as she opened the office door. The consequences would be severe if Mitch caught her, but determination to find the truth about the test overrode self-preservation.

Where to begin? The computer. While waiting for it to boot up, she scanned the top of the desk. Pens, notepads and tissues sat in perfect order. The cat rubbed against her leg. She jumped out of the chair.

"Scout, you scared me."

Rebecca sat back down. Her fingers hovered over the keyboard. The bite marks and chewed down nails caught her attention and she grimaced. Long, slender and well-manicured nails were in her past. She wished she could control that habit. Disgusting.

Back to the task at hand. She reasoned Mitch should have a file on the computer organizing his notes. She opened the documents. *Recent Documents*. Nothing resembled test information. She tried the folders. Nothing. Why wouldn't he have an exam file? She ran her hands through her hair, thinking about where an exam test bank would be. The icons? She checked. None for a test bank. His email? It asked for a password.

Mitch.

Incorrect Password.

Rebecca.

Incorrect Password.

Scout meowed.

Scout.

The inbox popped open.

She didn't know exactly what she was looking for. She searched the messages.

Melissa.

She scanned the inbox again and noticed emails from Derek and Branden, too. She clicked on Melissa's name and read the email.

Hey, what's up? Are we going to Sunny's again tomorrow night? It's my turn to buy the drinks, don't forget!

M.

She moved over to the filing cabinet, yanked it open. After searching through files, looking for anything relating to a test, she finally found something labeled Certification Exam. She pulled it out.

Empty.

Frustration tempered with a piece of anger boiled inside.

What is going on?

A noise in the distance caught her attention.

The garage door.

She looked around the office. The filing cabinet was open, with folders on top, and the computer was still running.

213

She shoved the folders into the cabinet haphazardly, causing it to jam.

No!

She pushed on the drawer, but it didn't budge. She pulled on the right side of the drawer and it screeched shut, metal scratching on metal. She rushed to the laptop.

Footsteps approached.

Pressing the button, the computer abruptly shut down.

"What are you doing in here?"

The computer screen went blank, and she held a tissue. "Dusting."

"Since when do you dust with a tissue?"

"Um, Scout was missing and I found her in here. Then I noticed dust. You know me. So I just started wiping."

He walked toward the filing cabinet. Rebecca silently begged God to make sure he didn't open it.

"You know how I feel about you being in here. My office doesn't need cleaning. You did it the other day."

"Did what?"

"Cleaned in here."

She nodded.

"Well, you found her, so let's get out of here."

Mitch changed his clothes and plopped on the sofa.

"Get me a beer, hon."

She brought it to him and asked, "Do you want me to make dinner?"

"No. Let's sit here and talk." He moved over so she could sit next to him. "I visited the children's wing today. There are so many terminal cases. It breaks my heart."

"That's so sad."

"Every once in a while I like to keep things in perspective."

"Mitch, I'm so sorry about your sister. Cancer is evil. It doesn't discriminate."

He took a swig of beer. "I know I shouldn't visit, but sometimes I can't help it."

"Those memories must be very painful for you."

He stared down at the floor. "Maddie was an amazing little sister." Looking away, he said, "I wish she'd responded to chemo better, but she didn't."

"Oh, Mitch, I'm so sorry." She squeezed his hand.

"At least my dad waited to leave until after Maddie's death." Mitch was silent for several seconds. "Do you want a glass of wine?"

"No, thank you. Do you want to talk about him?"

He shook his head as he finished the beer. Setting the bottle down hard on the table, he said, "Tomorrow I'll have just enough time to shower and shave before we leave for the restaurant." As he motioned her to get another bottle, he said, "Doctor Fields could have picked a better night. I have so much going on right now, and he knows it."

"We're busy right now." She thought, hesitated, but went on. "And of course the test."

A muscle ticked in his jaw. "Exactly. I don't know what he's thinking."

She waited for him to continue.

"He'll probably mention the exam again. Say something like I don't need to study for it."

She considered her next comment. "You need to spend the amount of time studying that you feel comfortable with."

He squeezed her hand a little too hard. "You're wonderful. You know that, don't you?"

Rebecca smiled.

"What are you going to wear to dinner?"

"Probably my green wool suit."

"That's a work suit. It's too conservative and old-fashioned. Go out tomorrow and buy something different. Don't worry about the money. I'll pay for it."

"Are you sure?"

"It's important we make a good impression. My upcoming promotion will be a turning point in my career."

Chapter 38

Spinning. Swirling. Out of control thoughts. Words floating through her mind, bombarding her senses.

She reached in the air and grabbed one as it flew by. It felt like cardboard.

After she threw it back, she reached for another one.

She read it and gasped.

Run.

Her stomach lurched and she took another one.

Danger.

She covered her head with her arms and screamed. The words kept flying, flying at her, trying to make her see, see something. No!

The words abruptly stopped spinning and fell to the ground. Slowly, she uncovered her head. All around her lay the words. She read them, but they didn't make sense. Just random words.

Mitch, are, in, out, soon, get, run, will, you, know, danger, now.

*****

Rebecca reached for the words she had seen, but they were like icicles melting away in her memory.

Later, she drove to the mall. Mitch had set his credit card on the kitchen counter before he'd left for work.

Pawing through the racks, she dismissed each outfit. They were either too sexy or too rigid. She didn't want Mitch to be angry if she brought home clothes that were too formal, like her wool suit. It was difficult. Nothing seemed to fit the occasion. She grabbed a number of items that were her size and found the dressing room. Perhaps they would look different on.

The last piece she tried fit the occasion best. Long, black, sleeveless dress with a short, sequined, silver jacket embodied the elegant look she hoped to achieve. She walked into the main dressing room to get a full-length view. Turning back and forth, she noticed she'd caught the eye of another customer.

"That dress looks beautiful on you," the woman said.

"Thank you."

"That's a great look for a confident woman. The jacket has a lively flair to it, for a fun-loving girl."

Rebecca scrutinized herself in the mirror. Did she look confident and fun? She gave a hesitant nod and tugged at the clothes.

"Enjoy." She gave Rebecca a departing smile.

Rebecca returned to the fitting room. She wanted to picture herself as the stranger had. Reality was the opposite. What got her to this place in her life? Why was everything so messed up?

Trying to think back to a time when she was happy forced Rebecca to recall life before Mitch. She tried to remember, but her thoughts were muddled. Foggy and scrambled in her mind, the memories wouldn't surface. She closed her eyes and rubbed her forehead, but nothing came. Except for her father's death, the past was a blank slate. At the airport, her mother had mentioned her cheerleading days. They were vague moments slipping away.

Hurrying to change back into her clothes, she tried to piece together flashing images. They spun through her head as fast as shooting stars. Flashes of her father surfaced, followed by a cheerleading routine from school, but she couldn't hold onto the pictures. She left the dressing room in a hurry. The department store layout overwhelmed her and she started to shake. She searched for a nearby register, but couldn't find one. She dropped the jacket, bent down to pick it up. Tears spilled from her eyes. She wiped them away before they could hit the shop floor.

"Calm down and pull yourself together," a familiar voice said.

She looked around, but no one was there. Taking a few steps, she saw a register in the distance. She rushed over to it and flung the items on the counter, fumbling with Mitch's credit card as she checked out. Walking to the car, she ignored the ice pelting her face.

She sat for several moments, the flashes of memories resurfacing. Still not able to make sense of them, she rocked back and forth in her seat, crying. She tried to trick her mind into thinking of something else.

Then the realization hit her. The past was returning. It mocked her. She'd lost the woman she once was.

*****

The garage door slammed. Mitch stormed through the house.

"Rebecca, where are you?"

"What is it?"

"I'm late. Is there an ironed shirt ready?" He ripped off his parka and tossed it on the sofa.

She hung it up. "Yes, I picked up all your suits from the dry cleaner this morning and ironed some of your shirts. You have a few outfits to choose from. Everything's laid out on the bed."

He walked into the bedroom and she followed. "Help me pick one out."

Several outfits sat neatly on the bed, arranged as though they were part of a shop window display. Matching ties and shirts. Suits. Shoes. Socks. Mitch discarded all of them and chose a sweater and cords. Rebecca returned the shirts and pants to their hangers.

Mitch came back in with a scotch, sat down, and watched her.

"What's wrong?"

His sipped his drink. "Rough day." He pointed to his upper back.

She massaged his shoulders. "What happened?"

"A disagreement with Ben regarding a patient diagnosis. He's a total prick." He took one of her hands and rubbed it against the stubble on his cheek. Kissing her hand, he said, "I don't want to get into the specifics."

He let go and she kneaded his shoulders harder.

He blew out a frustrated breath. "I hope Doctor Fields doesn't mention the disagreement tonight."

"Does he even know about it?"

Mitch shrugged.

"Try not to dwell on it. Let's enjoy this evening as a celebration of your success."

"I intend to. I have much more than Ben ever will."

Rebecca forced a smile. "We should get ready to go."

Mitch stood, pulling her into an embrace, and then whispered, "Let's share a shower."

"I've already showered and dried my hair."

He pushed her out of the way, walked into the bathroom, slamming the door behind him.

She dressed in her sophisticated new clothes and applied make-up and rose-colored lipstick. The pale-purple color of the eye shadow made her blue eyes look vibrant. She studied herself in the mirror. She'd successfully hid the last of the bruise with concealer. Maybe they could peacefully get through a night with the Fields.

Showered and shaved, Mitch entered the bedroom wearing only a towel.

"Your dress is stunning. It shows off all your curves, but it's still classy."

"Thanks."

As Mitch dressed, Rebecca pulled her hair into a bun, leaving a few strands to dangle around her face.

"Rebecca, your hair. You know I prefer it down."

She turned her head left and right, obtaining side angles in the mirror. She liked what she saw. Mitch obviously didn't, and she'd taken too long in her deliberations.

"Fix it or I'll do it and you won't enjoy the process. You have five minutes. And wear the new jewelry I bought you."

She took out the clip and let her hair fall around her shoulders, put on her new jewelry, slipped on her heels and joined Mitch in the living room. "Ready."

He looked her up and down. "Turn."

She did. He grabbed his coat.

They drove in silence. Rebecca stared out the window. When Mitch pulled up to the valet, he clenched her arm. His fingers dug into her skin.

"This will be a perfect evening. Make sure of it."

The Fields greeted Mitch and Rebecca as they entered Vincent's Restaurant.

"Hello, Doctor Fields." Mitch reached for Jonathon's hand.

"Please call us Jon and Barb. No formalities tonight, Mitch."

Barb hugged Rebecca, and Mitch extended a hand. They seated themselves at a table near the cobblestone fireplace.

She shivered.

"Rebecca, are you cold?" asked Jonathon. "Would you like to sit closer to the fire?"

"No, thanks. I just caught a chill."

Mitch gently rubbed her arm. "Are you okay, honey?"

"Fine, thank you."

The server arrived, scribbled quickly on a notepad, repeated the orders and disappeared to the kitchen.

"We're excited about the construction starting on the new children's wing this spring. Or should I say Evan's Home?" Jonathon said.

Rebecca said, "Exciting."

"Do you know how the wing got its name?"

Rebecca shook her head. "No, I don't."

"It's a success story, really. Richard Swanson's grandson, Evan, spent several weeks in the hospital after birth due to a condition called gastroschisis. They were able to perform successful surgeries to fix his intestines and abdomen."

"Marvelous."

"It was a severe case," Mitch chimed in.

Barb smiled. Her lips wore a beautiful shade of red. "As soon as we get to the spring thaw, we'll break ground."

"Mr. Swanson came through big with the donation. What a win for the hospital." Jonathon shook Mitch's shoulder.

"Absolutely. He's been one of our most generous supporters," Mitch said.

"He certainly is showing his appreciation," Barb agreed.

The wine and appetizers arrived.

Jonathon speared a meatball. "Did you hear the news about Tim?"

"I heard his father is going to need physical therapy and home care," Mitch said.

"Yes, true, but there's more," Jonathon said.

"What's that?" Mitch picked up a piece of bruschetta.

"His wife Emily is expecting again."

"Really?" Rebecca asked.

"Yes, she's due this summer." Jonathon laughed. "Between the baby and twins, she'll have her hands full for sure."

Barb looked to Rebecca. "She'll manage. Her mother lives nearby and will give her a hand with the kids."

"Good," Rebecca said.

"Yeah, just great," said Mitch.

The meals arrived. Rebecca pushed her baked ziti around with her fork.

"Can you believe the Bills made the playoffs?" Jonathon asked Mitch.

"I'm pleasantly surprised. Are you a Bills or Browns fan?" Mitch cut into his prime rib.

"Coming from Cleveland, I was a Browns fan, but I feel I should root for the home team."

Barb savored her mashed potatoes. She wiped her mouth with her napkin, then leaned over and whispered to Rebecca. "These men could talk about football all night. What have you been up to lately?"

"Just work and home life keeping me busy for now, but we're going on vacation next week."

"How exciting. Where to?"

"St. Augustine. I went to college there and love the area. We're staying at the beach." She sneaked a peek at Mitch.

"That sounds wonderful. I'm jealous. You get to leave this cold and snowy weather."

"Yes, and for nine days!"

"Now I'm really jealous."

Rebecca laughed.

"And what has kept you busy?"

Barb straightened. "Well, I've been working on the volunteer program. As the Director, I have a lot of coordinating to do."

"What does that job entail?" Rebecca sipped her riesling.

"Volunteers acting on behalf of the hospital have started almost a dozen organizations to help with the needs of the community. I oversee all of the groups."

"Wow that must be demanding of your time."

"It is, but I enjoy it. I get to work with the hospital employees and members of the community. I'm the liaison between each committee and the hospital. If there are special resources a group needs, such as money, food or clothing, I see if we can come up with them." She cut into her prime rib. "Just the other day the soup kitchen needed winter jackets for some of their patrons because the temperature dropped into the twenties. The clothing organization donated coats."

Rebecca caught a few words of the men's conversation. *Running back. Wide receiver.*

"The leaders of each volunteer group are hospital employees, but many other people from the community are active on the committees."

"I might like to join one."

"I hoped you would. That was one reason I wanted you to join us tonight. You mentioned you'd like to do some volunteer work when we first met at our party."

"Oh, yes, I did."

"You can volunteer alone or with Mitch if you want to. There are so many groups needing help, it'll be hard to choose."

"Do any involve children?"

"Of course. There's one run by a nurse in the pediatric wing which might interest you. Volunteers read books to the sick children. The group is called *Healing Words, Healing Hearts.*"

"That sounds perfect."

"Give me your email address and phone number. I'll give you a list of organizations with their contact information. I'll call you after you've had a chance to review it all."

Rebecca pulled out a scratch pad from her purse, jotted down the information, and handed the paper to Barb.

"Expect an email from me."

Wine arrived with dessert. Rebecca and Mitch shared a slice of triple chocolate mousse. It melted in her mouth.

Jonathon tried his crème caramel cheesecake, spooning the caramel drizzle on his plate while Barb sipped her hazelnut coffee.

Leaning over, Jonathon looked Mitch in the eye. "You'll be moving up in the ranks. You're a fantastic doctor."

"I appreciate the vote of confidence."

Rebecca eyed Mitch, but he didn't meet her gaze. Jonathon paid the check and everyone rose from the table.

"Thank you so much for an enjoyable evening and for dinner," Mitch said.

The two couples parted ways after saying goodbye.

Once they were on the road, Mitch spoke. "Everything is finally falling into place. Life is how I planned it. Except for the children."

Rebecca tensed. "In time, Mitch. Try to be patient."

"Damn that Tim." Mitch hit the steering wheel with his palm. "He has everything. If you're not pregnant when we get back from the vacation, you'll need to be examined by Doctor Epstein. A full examination. Understand?"

"Okay."

"I wonder if your infertility has anything to do with those headaches you've been getting. They've gotten worse haven't they?"

She was surprised he'd noticed. "Aren't they migraines?"

They pulled into the garage and he said, "We'll get you checked out, just to be sure." He shot her a suspicious look when they parked the car. "Immediately after vacation."

Chapter 39

Rebecca gazed at the young woman sitting across from her. About nine months pregnant she guessed. She pictured the woman going into labor at any moment.

A teen shifted in her squeaky chair a few seats over. She, too, was expecting.

A baby whimpered in her mother's arms next to Rebecca. She tried to peek at the baby's face, but a delicate blanket blocked her line of sight.

She stood and circled the room. Pregnant women and newborns surrounded her.

Slowly, her eyes traveled to her own stomach. Gasping, she stared down at a large belly.

No.

It couldn't be.

Trapped.

*****

Sunday afternoon, Mitch left the house. He'd said he was going to review his notes one last time. She didn't question him.

She booted up the computer and opened a message from Barb. A file was attached. She skipped most of the message and printed the two-page list. The list was impressive. A wide range of services, mostly local, but a few abroad. One group offered free medical care while another obtained information on helping children gain access to health insurance. Another focused on financial planning and support.

Healing Words, Healing Hearts. She circled it.

One organization ran a homeless shelter. She marveled at the amount of work and dedication it must take. The name of the president sounded familiar. Amy. The woman Jonathon was so taken with at his party. Interesting.

The last organization listed was *The VIEW*, and the president was Ben Larson. Ben? What was he involved with? Residents weren't expected to join these organizations, let alone lead them. She typed in the website listed next to Ben's name. The page loaded and Rebecca sat back in her seat, stunned.

Welcome to The VIEW: The Voice Inside Every Woman. If you are in an abusive relationship, whether physical, emotional or verbal, there is help for you. The first step is for you to ask for assistance. Everything remains confidential.

Oh no! What if Mitch checked her webpage history? And he would. She was certain. She hit the escape button. Could Ben see through her? Read her mind? Did she walk around with a flashing light above her head warning the world that an abused woman was approaching? David surely knew. And it seemed, so too, did Ben.

The cell phone rang and she jumped. "Hello?" she asked in a rushed voice.

"What's going on?" Mitch asked.

Words tumbled out of her mouth as she tried to sound nonchalant.

"What?" he asked.

"Sorry, I was just cleaning and I'm out of breath."

"You did sound strange, like you were hiding something."

Rebecca forced a chuckle. "No."

"Checking in on you, that's all."

They finished their short conversation. Mitch was still at work. She turned off the computer and shredded the list.

Why was Ben involved in an organization to help victims of domestic violence? She wanted to find out more information from Mrs. Fields. There had to be a personal reason. Is that why he had reached out?

Hours later, Barb called.

"I enjoyed dinner with you. Did you get a chance to look at the list of volunteer organizations?"

"Yes, it's amazing how much work has gone into these groups. I'm so impressed."

"The volunteers do an incredible amount of work."

"I was interested to see some residents are involved."

"True. Volunteers make up the majority of the groups, but Branden spends a lot of time at the soup kitchen. Ben runs *The VIEW.*"

"Wow."

"He's done a great job with his organization. I think he must spend all of his free time working on it."

"Do you know why he formed it?"

"No. He never talks about his motivation. I suspect it's personal."

"I wonder if he grew up in an abusive home."

"I don't think so. He raves about his parents and loves visiting them. No, I think this is something more recent. Maybe a former girlfriend had been abused in her past. I'm not sure."

Rebecca wasn't going to learn any more about Ben from Barb. "I'm amazed by the whole list."

"Are you still interested in joining the *Healing Words, Healing Hearts* group?"

"Yes, sign me up. Oh, well, I'll have to talk to Mitch about it."

"I thought you already did. He was the one to tell me about your interest."

"Um, of course. Yes. Just let me double check with him."

"I'll call you after your vacation. Rebecca, I don't want to overstep our friendship, but I wanted to let you know something."

"What's that?"

Barb hesitated then said, "If you ever want to talk ... about anything, please call me."

Rebecca almost touched her head. Was there truly a flashing light sitting on top?

Chapter 40

The instructor dipped the fountain pen into the inkwell.

Rebecca looked closely. It was a Mickey Mouse mug.

He dabbed the pen on the blotter and examined it.

Satisfied, he leaned the nib onto the paper and using Roundhand Script, wrote the letter 'F' in red.

"No!" Rebecca's body shook. "You can't do this to us, to me."

He scowled, but didn't speak.

"Please, you don't understand. This is my life we're talking about."

She rushed to him, putting her hands on his shoulders. Shaking him, she cried and begged him to change Mitch's exam score.

"Anna! Help me! Anna!"

*****

Rebecca woke as Mitch shook her.

"You're shouting, Rebecca. Wake up, you're having a nightmare."

Mitch held her, but Rebecca pulled away, gasping for breath.

"Geez, Rebecca, I'm just trying to calm you."

"What's going on? What time is it?"

"Honey, relax. It's morning, but I've got to get going to the exam."

"You haven't taken it yet?"

Mitch frowned. "No. It's today."

Rebecca rose from bed, peeking at the clock.

"What's up with you? You're shaking."

"Just a bad dream. I don't even know what it was about."

"All right then. Wish me luck."

She stood. "I know you'll do great."

"I'll be home right after the exam. It ends at five."

The dream lingered in her mind. What if he didn't do well? She hadn't considered the possibility of him not passing. It was the only chance she had of expecting some change. It was the milestone in their life.

Her body swayed. She collapsed onto the bed, shaking. Her head spun with dark thoughts. The yelling, hitting, pushing. Choking, demands, bruises. Lies, suspicions, deceit. More bruises, concealer, bandages. Pills. It had to stop. She couldn't take it any longer. Wouldn't.

No, he'll do fine. Pull yourself together and be strong. It was all she could think of to keep sane.

She arrived at work right on time. Joan popped out of her office and ushered Rebecca in, motioning her to take a seat. Rebecca took in Joan's demeanor. Classy. Professional. Confident. Being in her presence made her feel that way, too.

"I've got great news! You've got the promotion."

"Yes!" Rebecca squeezed her fists together, pumping her arms by her side.

"It's great to see you so happy. Even though you haven't completed your degree, between your hard work, winning the award, and the letters of recommendation, they've decided to hire you for the new position."

"I don't know what to say."

Joan smiled. "Say nothing, just sign the paperwork. Here's a contract and information on the training program."

She slid the papers toward Rebecca and put down a pen. "You excited?"

"Yes. Thank you so much for this opportunity."

"You've earned it."

Rebecca read the contract. *Full-time employee. Salaried position. Training program dates.* She refused to think of Mitch's reaction. She needed this. They needed this. She'd hold off telling him. She grabbed the pen and quickly signed the papers.

"Stay here," said Joan. "I'll make a copy for you."

Mitch's face flashed in Rebecca's mind, but she pushed the image away.

This is for me. Finally something for me. Who spoke?

Chapter 41

As Rebecca drove home, the cell phone rang.

"How was the test?" she asked.

Silence.

She cleared her throat. "Mitch?"

"Hello. Is this Rebecca?" an unfamiliar voice asked.

"I'm sorry, yes it is."

"This is Ben Larson. Remember me?"

Dropping the phone in her lap, she pulled into a parking lot and put the car into park.

She recovered and picked up the phone. Ben was still speaking.

"Is Mitch okay?"

"He's fine, I assume. I called to talk to you. I got your number from Barb Fields."

"Barb?" *How dare she.*

"Yes. I hope you don't mind."

"Well, I—"

"Can I talk to you?"

"No. No I can't."

"Please."

She hesitated. "If you're quick."

"Okay. Well, first of all, how are you?"

"And second?" Her thumb nail flicked at her middle finger, over and over.

"I've heard you've learned about *The VIEW*."

"I did."

"I'm glad. I wondered if you were interested in learning more about the organization."

"To volunteer?"

"Possibly, or something else." Ben's voice was so quiet.

Rebecca pressed the phone to her ear. "Like what?"

"Could I talk to you in person sometime soon?"

"I don't think so."

"Rebecca, we both know the reason why you can't talk to me *is* the problem."

"I think you've said—"

"I want to help you. My organization can help you."

"Please stop."

"I'm not trying to upset you."

"I need to get home."

Ben sighed. "Please, let me talk to you."

She looked at the dashboard. 3:45 pm. "Why aren't you still taking the exam?"

"It finished more than an hour ago."

"What are you talking about?"

"The exam. We all finished ages ago."

"Your concern is misplaced. Everything is fine with me."

"Mitch is a loose cannon."

Her head throbbed.

"Remember, guys like him don't change."

Rebecca hung up. She put the car into drive and hurried home.

Mitch's car wasn't in the garage. Why wasn't he back yet? What if the exam wasn't going well for him?

Tension built like a rocket waiting to take off, and Rebecca exploded.

"Stupid test. Stupid," she shouted, as she paced around the house. "You've ruined my life." She stormed into the bedroom, threw a pillow and knocked a trophy off Mitch's dresser.

The thud quieted her rants. Setting the trophy upright, she made sure it hadn't dented the wooden dresser. Moments later, the garage door opened.

Rebecca walked to the entranceway, preparing herself for the unknown. Mitch came bursting through the door holding a brown paper bag in his arms.

Her chest tightened as she moved to greet her husband.

"How was your exam?"

"It went well. Quite easy and straight forward. No tricky questions."

Her chest seemed to deflate, as if a giant balloon untied. Pressure gone. "Thank goodness. I'm so happy." And for a moment, she was. This was it! This was the time she'd been waiting for. Things were going to be fine. Fine! A smile grew on her face. She giggled. She giggled some more.

"Have you been drinking?"

"No." She laughed some more. "I'm just so happy for you. For us." She took the bag, freeing his hands so he could remove his coat.

"Have you started dinner?"

"No, I just got home."

"I'll pour some wine."

She spun in a circle. She felt like a child again. Free to have fun. Free to dance as if no one was watching.

"Are you sure you haven't been drinking?"

"I'm sure. I'm just happy."

He removed two glasses from the hutch as she took the wine opener from a kitchen drawer and handed it to him. He leaned over and kissed her. "Good. That's the way it should be."

Rigatoni and Rebecca's homemade sauce bubbled away on the stove. Mitch chatted about the exam and his upcoming promotion. He lit the rose-scented candles sitting on the dining room table as she brought in the plates of food. After dimming the lights, he handed her a glass filled to the rim with riesling.

Mitch extended his glass toward Rebecca. "To a new beginning."

Their glasses clinked. These were the words she'd longed to hear. She sat and took a deep breath. The floral scent filled her with more hope. Taking a sip of wine, Rebecca closed her eyes savoring the flavor. Woody, rich and delicious. As they ate, Mitch talked further about the exam. She hung on his every word.

"I know things have been difficult, but the exam is over. Life will go back to the way it used to be. You're crying?"

"Happy tears. They're happy tears." It didn't matter what he'd been doing. Lying. Drinking at Sunny's. The violence. It was now all over. The stress was now over.

He reached across the table, taking her hand. "I love you, Rebecca."

More tears spilled from her eyes and she tried to wipe them away.

Mitch moved behind her, massaging her shoulders. He leaned over, kissing her tears.

"Stay seated." He cleared the dishes.

Stretching her muscles, she welcomed the new sense of calmness she felt. Delicious. Vibrant. Warm.

He peeked into the dining room from the kitchen. "Be back in a couple minutes," he said. He went to the garage and came back with another package. "Don't move."

"What are you up to?" she laughed.

"Just you wait." He walked into their bedroom.

She heard movement. As she waited, she twirled her long hair. Life was good again. The wine relaxed her, and she leaned back in the wooden chair.

Mitch smiled when he returned to the table. "More?"

Rebecca put her hand up too late. The bottle emptied into her glass, filling it completely.

She giggled. "Mitch, you know I can't drink that much."

He blew out the candles, and led Rebecca by the hand to the bedroom, glasses and a second bottle in tow.

Rebecca gasped when she entered the room. Mitch had turned their bedroom into a showcase of candlelight. Tea lights lined the dressers and nightstands. Tiny flames flickered throughout the bedroom. The faint lights cast a beautiful glow. Scattered rose petals were strewn over the comforter. The sensual fragrance evoked a yearning deep within Rebecca.

Mitch sat on the bed, pulling her between his legs. He hugged her and looked up into her face. "I love you so much."

Desire grew inside her. Real desire. Desire for his body. Desire for his touch. "I love you, too."

He held her tight as they made love. He told her how much he loved her over and over again. She longed for the night to last forever.

Lying in bed together, he caressed her hair. She traced the outline of his face. Her fingers prickled when they moved over the stubble on his chin. Looking into his deep brown eyes, she saw the old Mitch becoming new again.

He turned to his side, facing her. "Every night with you should be like tonight."

Her voice quivered as she spoke. "I need more of them."

He rubbed her cheek with the palm of his hand. "Things are better now, Rebecca. The test is behind me."

*****

Frank Sinatra floated on his back. The pond was full of water lilies. He kicked gently. A small splash. Rebecca laughed. It wasn't the first time. He was so alive with their lovemaking. He made her feel whole, loved, wanted, adored.

A bell sounded. Scout must have been playing close by, chasing birds.

Frank turned. He looked past Rebecca. She followed his gaze. The pond turned into a lake. Mitch stood at the edge, Scout in his hands.

Frank started singing. Mitch joined him. They harmonized well. Mitch plunged Scout under the water. The cat thrashed. Thrashed some more. Their singing grew louder.

"No," Rebecca screamed. She tried to move through the water, get to Scout, but her movements were slow, awkward. "No," she screamed again.

*****

Rebecca awoke to Mitch's lips gently pressing on hers.

"Good morning, sleepy," he said.

She stretched. "Mmm, morning."

"I wish we could stay in bed together all day."

"Me too."

"But work is calling." Mitch kissed her quickly, headed for the bathroom.

The dream was just a dream. That's no longer your reality. Rebecca summoned the feelings from last night. The tenderness. The love. The talking. The touching. *The dream was just a dream.*

Mitch came back to the bedroom and started dressing for work. She eyed the strong arms that had held her so close the night before. They excited her now. Yesterday she had feared their strength. He pulled on his dress pants. Distinguished. She was proud of him. Not afraid. He buttoned his dark blue dress shirt and started to put on his tie. His hands. They'd touched her gently the night before unlike so many other times.

"We'll want to buy a new house soon."

"What?" Rebecca sat up. Was he talking about that folder she'd seen?

He held his arms wide. "You didn't think we'd live in your house forever."

"But it's my grandmother's home. I adore every square inch of it. You said we'd stay."

"Rebecca, it's not practical. It's not near the hospital and doesn't have enough room for children."

"But—"

"Besides, we'll be joining the country club soon."

"I don't understand."

"The homes at Windgate Manor are spacious. Some back right up to the golf course."

"Have you looked at those homes already?"

"Not on the inside."

Mitch had promised they'd remodel and expand when they had children, not move to some fancy development. This was her family home. This is what she'd inherited. So many memories she cherished had happened right here. How could she leave? Why would he change his mind now?

"I like this mature yard, the tire swing from my childhood, and the flower garden grandma established. How can I leave?"

"We're starting a new life, remember? It'll be great. I promise."

*****

The water grew cold, icy. Mitch took her by the hand and walked toward the ocean's edge. She'd never seen this place before. Everything was new. New trees, new bench seats, new pier.

Mitch urged her to come with him, but she couldn't take the chilly temperature.

His eyes turned darker than the usual mud brown and she turned away, looking out toward the horizon.

The waves calmed and the water turned clear. Ice. The ice stopped at their feet and Mitch pulled her onto it.

Her feet screamed in pain from the temperature. He tugged at her arm. She slipped on the ice, but he caught her.

After walking out into the ocean for a distance, he turned to her and said, "Goodbye."

The ice cracked, sending her falling into the cold, dark water.

Screaming, she reached her hand out to him, but he was gone.

She sunk under the surface and disappeared.

*****

"Rebecca, what did you do with my reading glasses?"

Shaking off the strange dream, she searched her mind, but couldn't remember seeing them. "Umm, I don't think I've noticed them around lately."

"They're supposed to be right here on my nightstand. They clearly aren't. I've checked in my office, too. Where did you put them?"

"Really, I haven't seen them." She jumped out of bed. "I'll look for them."

She checked the bedroom and office, once, and then twice, thinking both she and Mitch may have missed them on their first run through. She headed to the living room.

"I need them for work. I have to leave now."

"I'm sure they're here somewhere. I'll keep looking."

She looked under the quilt and by the magazines on the coffee table.

He moved *The New York Times* at the end of the dining room table, uncovering the missing glasses.

He walked toward her, putting the glasses in his shirt pocket. She met his gaze. Mitch extended his hands toward her. Those hands. So close to her throat. No!

Everything about that moment was so thick, like someone had sucked all the air from the room with a vacuum cleaner. Rebecca step backward, too quickly. She hit a chair. It tumbled. Mitch grabbed her wrist before she fell onto the ground.

"Watch yourself, hon. You're getting clumsy."

There was no fist. No yelling. No screaming. No pain.

"Are you okay?"

"Yes. I must have just slipped."

"I'm off to work. I'll see you tonight. I love you."

"I love you, too."

Chapter 42

The rain pelted the windshield. Rebecca pulled into the bank's parking lot. Kelly's car pulled in beside her.

"What are you doing here today?" Rebecca asked.

"Margo's mother is sick. She's taking the day off, so I'm filling in."

"I'm happy to hear—" Rebecca covered her mouth and giggled. "I mean I'm sad about Margo's mother, but excited we'll be working together today."

"Hey, we're both early. Do you want to grab a quick coffee?"

"Sure."

"Let's walk to Starbucks."

Rebecca zipped up her coat. They avoided the puddles in their high-heeled shoes.

Kelly pulled her wallet out of her Vera Bradley bag. They ordered and paid.

"Nice bag."

"Thanks. One of my favorite purchases."

They moved over to the pick-up line.

"I can't make it through the day without my caramel frappuccino. I'm so excited for you. You must be thrilled to get that promotion."

"I'm certainly grateful to Joan for giving me the opportunity."

"Bec, you've earned it. How pumped are you that you're not going to be working for Margo anymore?"

Their names were called. They took their drinks to a tall table with stools.

A wide smile crossed Rebecca's lips. "Thrilled."

"Great to see you smiling."

"Isn't it? I feel great."

"So, things ... the bar the other night ... all sorted out?"

"Oh yes. Mitch was under so much stress with his studying. He needed time out. That's all."

"Glad to hear. And that means the exam went well?"

"Very well. He's looking at a promotion, too."

"Wow! You're a power couple."

"Is he as excited about your news?"

"My news?"

"Your promotion."

"I haven't told him yet. I will while we're on vacation."

"Why?"

"Why what?"

"Why not tell him immediately?"

Kelly had a point. Why not? Why not call him right now? Something held Rebecca back. "I want to keep it as a surprise," she lied.

"What's going on?"

"What do you mean?"

"I saw your happiness slip."

"What?"

"I'm sorry, I shouldn't pry. I have a habit of doing that with friends."

"Don't apologize. All is good. It's just that Mitch is talking about moving to a new house."

"A fresh start. Sounds good. No?"

"I like my home. It was my grandmother's."

"Ah, that paints a different story."

"Mitch has been a difficult person to please. The exam and all that stress, you know? He expected everything to be just so and the same rules didn't apply to him, if that makes sense."

"I dated a loser once. He yelled and threw things. I feared being around him, but I was also afraid to break up with him."

"Oh, that's not—"

"I didn't trust him. He treated me more like a piece of property than a girlfriend. I thought when he realized his possession was leaving him, he'd freak out and do something crazy."

"What did you do?"

"When we were out at a restaurant, I told him we were breaking up. If he did anything stupid, there'd be witnesses. Then I cut him off cold turkey. Blocked his calls and texts."

"And?"

"Eventually, he found another girl. Guys like that don't change. They only get worse."

Rebecca pulled her jacket around her tighter.

Kelly looked at her watch. "Oh, it's time for work. We don't want to be late. How about we plan to get together after you're back from vacation and we'll have a conversation somewhere more private?"

"I would love that. Can't wait."

Chapter 43

David met Rebecca in the entranceway of Susie's Café. They hugged for a moment before following the server to a booth.

"I can't believe it's already Wednesday," Rebecca said.

"The weeks fly by so quickly. You're looking well."

"I'm feeling well."

The server brought over water and took their orders.

"Mitch working again?"

"Yes, he's getting in some extra hours before we leave for vacation on Friday. I can't wait to get to the warmer weather. This endless snow is killing me."

"Winter drags on forever here. Will you be staying at a beach?"

"Yes, right on the ocean. The pictures of the resort are beautiful."

"Rebecca, would you like to leave the address and contact details with me, just in case?"

She touched David's hand. "Everything's fine, David. I promise. Everything's looking up."

"So Mitch's exam is done?"

"He thinks he aced it. The promotion should be his."

"You must be relieved."

Rebecca's eyes did not meet his. "I am."

"I'm sensing something is troubling you."

"Nothing for you to worry about. It's just that he wants to move to Windgate Manor."

"Why?"

"He says the homes are spacious and they back up to a golf course."

"But he knows how much your house means to you and the family."

"You'd think so. When we were first married he promised we'd expand our home instead of moving."

The way David's eyebrows crinkled showed his worry lines. Her father's forehead looked the same way when he was upset. "David, it's okay. If a house move is the worst thing on my plate, I can't complain too much."

"Have you thought about our conversation from last week? Are you going to tell your mom?"

"There's nothing to tell."

"Rebecca—"

"There's nothing to tell. The exam is over and Mitch is relaxed. He's the husband he used to be."

The food arrived and she picked at the mashed potatoes. "I'm getting the promotion at the bank."

"That's good news."

"It's great news. I'm fulfilling a dream I've had for several years."

"What did Mitch say?"

Rebecca busied herself cutting her turkey.

"You haven't told him yet?"

She shook her head. "Not yet. I'm going to discuss some things with him over vacation."

"You're fearful of what he'll say."

"No I'm not," she lied.

"Men like him don't change."

"David."

"You'll always be in danger. You don't have to live like this. He'll feel like he's losing control, and you know what will happen."

"David!"

"Remember, I've seen your bruises. Rebecca, is divorce an option for you?"

Her eyes widened and she gave him a questioning look.

"Sometimes in an especially difficult marriage like yours, divorce is not an option."

"I don't understand."

"Sometimes the abused wants to leave, but feels as if her life is in danger. The abuser may have threatened her." He leaned in closer. "You can get help, Rebecca. There are support groups that can assist you. There's even one here in town. You can stay in a safe place until you figure everything out."

"I have nothing to escape from, David."

"The organization is very helpful for abused women."

Did he even hear her? "I'm not one of them, David. All my marital problems are behind me. They're over."

"Okay. Okay." David pursed his lips, and held his hands up like he was surrendering. "Just play along with me. Hear me out. Let's just say ... let's just say that the worst happened, and nothing changed. Can you do that?" He wasn't surrendering.

"Yes, but—"

"For an old family friend?"

"Okay."

"Good. Most of the time the organizations can be instrumental in getting the victim away from her abuser. For some people, the process doesn't work."

"So they stay?"

"Some do. Sometimes women try to go through the court system and obtain an order of protection."

"An order of protection is just a piece of paper." Rebecca knew full well if she had ever sought one of those, it would do nothing to stop Mitch. In fact, it would infuriate him more. Divulging their private life to a courtroom full of people? He'd be madder than furious.

"It doesn't work for everyone. Some people think they're above the law. Others feel entitled to harass the victim in spite of the order. It's not real protection, but it can help."

"So then what do the others do?"

"Vanish."

"What?"

"You can vanish."

"Me?"

"They can vanish."

"How?"

"There are ways. There are places to go where Mitch won't ever find you. Leave town. Change your name. Don't contact old friends or family. It's very hard, but you'd be safe. That's what is most important."

Rebecca shook her head back and forth. "I could never do that. Mom would be devastated. I'd never see her again. I couldn't be there for her, to help her."

"So are we talking about anyone or you now? It would kill her if something happened to you. Rebecca, I've been there. A parent wants their child to be safe."

"I can't hurt my mom."

Chapter 44

Rebecca lit a scented candle, picked up her phone, and settled down in the bedroom. Scout snuggled next to her. Rebecca pet her, smoothing the cat's soft fur. Scout thanked her by lifting her face and rubbing noses with Rebecca and purring that rhythmic sound.

Rebecca breathed in the vanilla scent as it filled the room. As a child, the family spent the first two weeks of July at her grandparents' home. She and Nan's tradition was to bake her birthday cake on July 5th, her special day. Vanilla cake with chocolate frosting. Every year. Rebecca would ready the ingredients using stainless steel measuring cups and spoons, and place it all out on the Formica counter. The Formica, too low-class for Mitch, had since been replaced with granite. Rebecca missed the original kitchen.

She'd pull a metal chair with its plastic seat cover close to her grandmother. Nan would guide Rebecca's hand as she poured the ingredients into the old mixer. The beaters rumbled around in the bowl. That ancient mixer now sat in the back of her cabinet. It still worked. Why didn't she use it? Mitch. He had laughed at her and bought a shiny new KitchenAid mixer.

She dismissed the negative thought. Making the frosting was her favorite part. Grandpa always found a reason to be in the kitchen when they scraped the chocolate frosting off the beaters. He'd make a puppy-dog face and Rebecca would hand him a beater. For her generosity, he'd thank her with a big kiss, his whiskers scratching her cheek, and he would dot her nose with frosting.

"Chocolate is my weakness," he would say.

"All sweets are your weakness, especially your sweet Rebecca," her grandmother would respond.

Rebecca touched her cheek. Even though the home had been remodeled, she could still feel their presence. How she missed her grandparents. And her father.

She plugged in the phone number. She was about to hang up when her mother answered.

"Just wanted to talk to you before Mitch and I leave tomorrow."

"I'm excited for you. You'll have lots of fun."

"I hope so."

"I'm sure you'll spend your days together at the beach and doing lots of sightseeing."

There was none of that in Mitch's plans.

"I'm looking forward to spending time with him. We haven't taken a real vacation since our honeymoon."

Rebecca picked up the small teddy bear Mitch had purchased for her on their honeymoon. She hugged it and smiled at its adorable Hawaiian shirt and hula skirt. A perfect vacation, a perfect husband.

They'd hiked the 'Akaka Falls State Park trail toward the waterfall, swatting pesky mosquitos on the way. The lush foliage was like nothing she'd ever seen. Mitch held her so tight when they reached the overlook spot for 'Akaka Falls.

"The waterfall is almost as mesmerizing and beautiful as you," he had said.

A friendly body-boarding competition in the ocean led to Rebecca winning a half-hour massage by Mitch, who'd lost. He'd carried her out of the water after she beat him five times in a row in their race to the sand. Placing her on their towels, he covered her with kisses. They barely made it back to their hotel suite where desire set in.

The evenings were spent taking in the local culture. Rebecca could see passion in his eyes as Mitch watched her learn how to hula at a luau. Pride had filled her. She was classy, talented, clever. The first years of their marriage.

Had he been deceiving her all along? No. No, surely not. He couldn't have. But ....

"Well, I guess that goes with Mitch's job," her mother said breaking Rebecca's trance.

"Oh, and the exam?"

"Finished, Mom. He thinks he did really well."

"That's wonderful. All the sacrifices he's made to ensure a sound future for both of you."

"I've made sacrifices, too." The words slipped out unintentionally.

"Honey, you know Mitch works constantly."

"I'm getting a promotion."

Silence.

"Mom, are you there?"

"I'm nervous, Rebecca. Mitch wants to have children. You don't even need to work."

"I want kids, too, but not right now. I'd like to have a life outside the home first, pursue my dreams. I want to take care of you."

"I don't need help. I'll survive. I want you to make Mitch happy."

"What about how I feel? What I want?"

"I know you want to become a career woman, but you've always longed for children, haven't you?"

"Someday. But for now, I want a career to be able to support myself." *And you.*

"Don't you know how lucky you are? You'll be able to stay home with your children."

"Home? He wants to move out of here."

"Out of where?"

"Out of here. Out of Grandma's house."

"And go where?"

"Some new development by the golf course."

More silence. Rebecca could almost hear the cogs in her mother's head. Forward. Back. Around. Slow. Fast.

"Listen, honey, I know your marriage isn't perfect. Mitch can be a lot to take at times. But overall, you have many things going for you that a lot of women would kill for."

"Mom, what are you saying?" Rebecca clenched her fists. Her father would never have said those words.

"Hon, Mitch is intense. He wants things done his way. I've seen how he is."

"No you haven't."

"Of course I have."

Something deep inside Rebecca snapped. "And that's okay with you? That he treats me so badly?" *Daddy treated Mom like an equal. They were respectful and compassionate to each other. How can Mom admit to knowing about Mitch and find his behavior acceptable?*

"I didn't say he doesn't treat you well. Where is all of this coming from?"

She tossed the bear aside. "Never mind, Mom. Just forget I said anything."

"No. Listen to me. I'm stronger than you think and I want to know what you're talking about."

"He hurts me sometimes. He *used* to hurt me."

"What? Does he yell at you?"

She plunged forward, her father's face in her mind. "He abuses me, Mom. He hits me. Sometimes he leaves bruises. I get so scared."

"Oh, my God. Are you hurt? Can I come see you?"

"No, I'm fine right now."

"What are you going to do? You have to leave him. You have to leave him now!"

She grabbed a tissue and wiped her nose. "It's all behind me, Mom."

"What crap! How ... how long has this been going on?"

Rebecca tiptoed through the house and peeked into the garage. No Lexus. "I don't remember when it started, not exactly. It doesn't matter." She walked back to the bedroom.

"Rebecca, why didn't you tell me? I knew he was hard to deal with. Oh, I can't believe I said those things. I didn't mean you have to take the good with *that*."

"I know, Mom."

"I had no idea things were that bad." Her broken voice softened with each word. "Your father is rolling over in his grave right now."

"It's okay. It's my fault you didn't know. I didn't want to disappoint you."

"Don't say that. Don't you *ever* say that. You could never disappoint me. You've never been to blame." The line went quiet for a moment. "Not for your father's death either. You have to let go of the guilt and start taking care of yourself. Get away from him."

"Mom, it's all stopped. The exam was his trigger. There's no more abuse and I'm starting a career."

"He's pushing you out of your family home."

The grandfather clock chimed. Rebecca jumped. What had she done by telling her mom? Anger and worry? This is exactly what she wanted to avoid. And all for what, if things had changed? And they had changed. She should have just shut up.

"Rebecca? What are you going to do?"

"Nothing right now. David is mentoring me."

"God bless that man. I want to help, too. Tell me what I can do."

"Nothing. I'll talk to Mitch while we're away and everything will be fine."

"I don't like the sound of this. People don't change."

Chapter 45

"Are you packed?" Anna asked.

"Yes."

"And the pills? You're still going to take the pills, aren't you?"

"Yes, Anna. For a while. Look where I hid them."

Anna peeked at the aspirin bottle hidden in a compartment in the suitcase. "Please, Rebecca. Please reconsider going on vacation."

"I'll be fine. You'll see."

"I have a bad feeling. I don't think you should go."

"Everything has been great since the exam finished. He'll get a promotion. I got a promotion. There's no turning back now."

Doubt clouded Anna's face.

"Say you're happy for me."

"How can I possibly? Mitch will explode at the news."

"You think he will. I don't."

"You're not sure though, are you?"

"Of course I'm sure," she lied. Rebecca turned her friend around, and marched her toward the door. "I've got to finish packing. He'll be home soon."

They hugged for a long moment. When they pulled away, Rebecca noticed Anna's tears.

Rebecca forced a confident smile. "Don't worry about me. By the time you see me again, my life will have completely changed. Just you wait and see."

*****

Anna sat quietly in a stark, white room. Four Water Lilies prints hung crookedly on the walls. The plastic seat squeaked when she shifted her weight.

She dabbed at her swollen eyes, catching tears in her fingers as they fell.

Rebecca called to her through the window, but Anna didn't respond, didn't even flinch.

Chills ripped through Rebecca and she warmed her bare arms with her hands. Her naked body shivered. She had to get to Anna, but her legs wouldn't move. She looked down at them.

When she turned back to look at Anna, she was dotting her wet eyes with a purple scarf. Her pale face seemed to be growing whiter.

That scarf. It looked so familiar. She searched her mind, but couldn't pull up the significance. Wanting to touch it, hold it, she tried to reach out to knock on the window. Her arms wouldn't move.

"Anna! It's me, Rebecca. Help me!"

Anna leaned over and sobbed into the scarf.

Drowning

Rebecca's body slowly became transparent.

Eventually she was gone.

She was swallowed up in the pain and the truth.

Chapter 46

Mitch was late. Rebecca decided to fill the dead time, and dragged the suitcase and Mitch's golf clubs to her car, heaving them into the trunk.

A moment later, Mitch barged through the door. "I'm going to the bathroom. I assume you have everything packed."

"Yes."

"Good girl."

Mitch went to the bathroom and quickly returned. He looked around the entranceway.

"Where's the luggage?"

"We're all set. I packed it."

"Already? In my car?"

"I packed it into mine."

"We're taking my car, Rebecca, so the luggage needs to be in my car, not yours."

"But mine is gassed, packed, and ready to go."

"My car, Rebecca."

He shoved past her, opened both trunks and started moving luggage from her car to his. That ever-present knot in her stomach grew.

*****

Turbulence didn't seem to bother Mitch. His seat was back with his head tipped away from Rebecca. His book lay open on his lap. Rebecca continued with hers.

Susannah's ankle started to swell. Pain shot through every part of her as she gingerly tried to take another step. A gasp escaped her lips and she covered her mouth. Being caught here would prove deadly.

Away. She needed to be away. Crawling back to the plantation was her only option. The blanketed sky would provide some concealment, but the dew—her clothes would be damp.

The door to the hut creaked open. "Susy? That you? What's wrong?" Grafton whispered.

She turned, her face growing hot from pain and fear. "Shh."

"What is it? Are you in danger?" He approached, and she could smell him. His skin clean from the river.

She motioned him backward. "I strained my ankle, but I have to leave. Father will be looking for me."

"You're hurt. Can you walk?" He crouched down beside her.

The warmth of his body comforted her. She leaned in toward him, until common sense prevailed.

"Please, go. You're risking both of our lives."

She stood and put weight on her ankle. "Oh, it hurts."

Silently, Grafton examined her injury, first with two fingers, then four, then ten. His touch was gentle, tender. Her own fingers felt the need to touch, just as he was. She rubbed his back, first with two fingers, then four, then ten, following his lead. He glanced up. Those wide eyes held a river of longing.

"I'll carry you home." He scooped her up in his arms and walked down the path.

She wanted to resist, but couldn't deny herself his nurturing spirit. She rested her head on his shoulders. To be close to him, if only for a few minutes more ...

The flight attendant stood in the aisle with the beverage cart. Rebecca motioned the attendant away, not wanting Mitch's sleep disturbed.

Rebecca put her book down and closed her eyes.

"There are rumors, Mr. Wethersfield. About your daughter," Mitch said. He looked around the room. Dark timber walls and furniture made the large room appear smaller. He gazed at a family painting and smirked.

The gentleman put his hand up, and called to a servant. "Whiskey, for both of us. Now."

The servant obliged and the gentlemen sipped their drinks.

Mr. Wethersfield waved the servant away and set the glass on the side table. "Which one?"

"Susannah."

His face grew ashen.

The favorite, Mitch knew. His baby.

"What is this rumor?"

Mitch leaned forward in his chair. "Grafton."

Mr. Wethersfield closed his eyes and massaged his temples. "No! How is this true?"

"They've been seen together, her leaving his hut. The way they look at each other."

"*The help is talking about this?*"

"*Yes.*"

Mr. Wethersfield stood and paced the great room, the floor squeaking under his feet. He stopped to poke the fire. "*You understand what this means, don't you? This news you bring to me?*"

"*Yes, it means death—death to Annah.*"

Rebecca's eyes shot wide open.

Chapter 47

It was dark. The shuttle driver dropped them off at the pathway to their cottage. The briny air evoked a distant memory. Tybee Island. Michael. Building forts in the sand. Running to meet the waves as they sprinted to the shore and crashed on the beach. Her father with his fishing pole.

She skipped toward the sound of the waves. "Oh, Mitch, this is heaven. Can we go down to the beach?"

"It's midnight and pitch black out here. We don't even know the way. Besides, we've got an early start tomorrow morning. I have a lot of things planned."

"But, the moon—"

"No, Rebecca. Not tonight."

They walked up the steep, wooden stairs leading to the cottage door. Rebecca stopped at the top. A wide porch running the distance of the cottage held a wrought iron bistro table with two chairs, a grill and a porch swing. Sipping coffee with Mitch in the mornings as they watched the sunrise would be magical. They could have productive, undisturbed discussions. This was her chance. Life was going to be wonderful.

He slid the keycard into the door and searched for a light switch. The room burst to life.

Rebecca gasped. "Oh, it's more beautiful than the resort pictures online."

Moving across the tile floor and into the living area, three seahorse statues held a circular, glass table in place. A ceramic dolphin and *Coastal Living* magazines rested on the table. Full beach pillows on the sand-colored sofa beckoned her company and she sat. They felt like clouds, soft enveloping clouds. A canvas painting of a sun rising over the ocean drew her in. They could capture a picture of their own in the morning and hang it by their beloved *Water Lilies* print. Two pictures side by side reminding them of wonderful moments together.

She touched a starfish sitting on a weathered table. Her hand jerked back as snippets of dreams returned. A tornado. Starfish circling her. They'd been out of reach. But then in another dream, she'd picked one up. It moved in her hand. Frightened, she dropped it. Gone. But they were dreams. Just dreams. This was their vacation. Their new reality. Her new life had begun. There was no need to be jumpy.

She walked into the galley kitchen, opening cabinets. "The plates have sandpipers on them. I love those birds. I hope we see some at the beach." She turned to show Mitch, but he wasn't there.

She found him in the bedroom. Sea-green furniture, potpourri in a large clamshell, palm tree bedding. And clean, very clean. It even smelled clean. Very tropical. Very quaint. She rubbed the clamshell, dipped her fingers into the potpourri and brought some to her nose. Rose. The night with Mitch. Sensual and passionate.

She turned away. "I love the bedding. So nice. I like everything about this place. Don't you, Mitch? Mitch?"

"It's nice. Upscale. Good thing or I'd be angry. It cost a fortune for the week." Mitch unpacked his clothes and hung his polo shirts and golf pants neatly in the closet.

"Well, I think it's worth it. I couldn't have picked a better place for vacation. I'm relaxed already."

"Aren't you going to get ready for bed?" Mitch upended his toiletry bag, and grabbed a toothbrush and paste.

"Yes, I was just looking at everything."

"If you're tired tomorrow morning," he said with the brush busy in his mouth. 'Don't be cranky." He spat.

"Oh, how could I be cranky in a place like this? Just you and me, Mitch. It's pure bliss." She joined Mitch at the bathroom sink. He unpacked the rest of his things and headed to the bed, and pulled the comforter over himself.

Following Mitch's actions, she soon lay beside him. He rolled over, undressing her. His movements were quick, passionless. So unlike their romantic evening just days ago.

He turned, facing away from her. She thought about fishing out her book from her bag to read in bed. But she'd need light, and that would disturb Mitch. She stared into the darkness. Tomorrow was the beginning of a new life.

Chapter 48

Her father holding a child, nuzzling her in the curves of his chest.

A five-year-old being taught to ride a bike by her father.

A tenth birthday. Michael, her parents and Nan crowding around a table waiting for the little girl to blow out the candles. The wasted wish.

Michael playing 'go fish' with a little girl.

A softball game. A thin, but muscular blond girl pitching a no hitter, making her parents beam with pride.

The head cheerleader. Her hair pulled back with a purple scarf.

Straight 'A' student.

Homecoming queen smiling proudly in a beautiful pale-blue dress, a dress to match her eyes.

A group of teenagers gathered around a bonfire, discussing the upcoming graduation.

Anna. The pictures were of Anna.

Rebecca woke, bewildered. It wasn't Anna, it was her. Wasn't that what Mitch had seen in her? She could be all those things again. Would be.

*****

The sun was breaking over the horizon when Mitch and Rebecca left the cottage. She lingered on the porch watching the orange glow rise. Pelicans flew over their heads toward the water. Mitch shot her a look and she followed him down the stairs to the Sea Shells Café.

Large windows and sky-blue paint rendered the room a constant brightness. White wood furniture and tan table cloths with blue sea creatures added a beach feeling. Serving trays of breakfast food lined the far wall of the restaurant.

"Let's head over to the buffet. I'm starving." Mitch held her hand as they walked through the cozy restaurant.

"Wow, look at all the choices. An omelet station, breakfast casserole, bacon, sausage, grits, French toast. Coffee and juices. I had no idea."

"Don't go crazy. You have dresses to fit into."

Rebecca fought a frown. Did he really have to say that? But she complied, and scooped a selection of mixed fruit onto her plate. She started to walk away from the buffet, and when Mitch turned his back she took a piece of French toast and bit into it. Not so compliant.

Once seated, Mitch said, "I'm pretty familiar with the course layout that I'll be playing on today."

"That's great. I'm sure you'll play well. I think I'm going to hang around here today. Explore the resort and walk on the beach. I've brought some books, too." Her book. *Death to Annah.* The warm air seemed to disappear for a moment.

"Rebecca?"

"Yes?"

"Re-bec-ca."

"What?"

Mitch stared, but there was no obvious emotion behind his eyes. No impatience, no anger, no humor. He was ... bland. Well, it was better than the old Mitch.

"I told you I've already made plans for you to visit the historic district."

"But, I've seen it before, remember? Flagler College is located right downtown. The beach would be relaxing. Besides I'm tired from the trip."

He shook his head. "You've got other plans."

"I have?"

"Yes." He chewed on his second piece of bacon.

Even staying at the cottage would have better suited her. She pictured the ocean view from the porch. The way the sun peeked through the clouds. The pelicans flying as if they didn't have a care in the world. Free. She'd been drawn to the water. She longed to be there. It was as if touching a toe into the sea water would mark the beginning of the vacation, the start of a new chapter, a revelry to herald beginnings. And why did he care where she spent her day? He had his plans. She'd heard them all before.

"Let's at least walk on the beach together after we eat." She bit into a piece of cantaloupe.

"No time," Mitch said. Still bland.

"Why not?" She almost stopped herself. Questioning Mitch? It was something had she dared not do in a long time. So subservient. So controlled. So tethered. And now, she was so ... Rebecca.

"You overslept."

She tried again. "But, you only gave me fifteen minutes to get ready. You could have woken me up earlier."

"You needed your sleep. You just said so yourself."

"But I—"

"I wonder what caliber of golfer I'll get matched with today." He finished the last of his coffee. "Should be interesting. I hope he's a challenge. I want to bring my game up a notch." He stood. "Are you ready to go?"

She glanced down at her half-eaten food. "Can you stay until I'm finished eating?"

"The shuttle for the World Golf Village picks up at a quarter past the hour. Why are you so argumentative? This is meant to be a vacation. Peaceful."

"I wanted to talk to you."

"Is it worth me missing my tee off time?"

Rebecca's fingers wanted to crawl to her mouth. She wanted to chew at her nails. Why? Did she recognize something in Mitch's stance? He was a tree looming over a garden. A garden called Rebecca. So much shade. She gripped the side of her chair to keep them down. "No." Those fingers wanted to climb to her mouth. "Maybe we'll talk before dinner?"

"Sure, I promise. Your Red Train Trolley will be here at nine-thirty." He pulled the ticket from his wallet.

She smirked and mumbled, "Try to say that five times fast."

"What?"

"Red Train Trolley."

"That's childish Rebecca."

Why couldn't he laugh? She turned away. Was there no pleasing him today?

"Get me a chunk of chocolate mint fudge from your favorite candy store."

Whetstone Chocolates. "When will I see you?"

"This afternoon." He shoved his chair in, hitting the table spilling coffee. "And I've made dinner reservations for six."

This was meant to be a vacation. Peaceful.

She dabbed at the mess with a napkin. Why was he so against spending time with her? Why didn't he enjoy her company? She had no intention of hopping on the Red Train Trolley.

*****

Rebecca strolled through the resort's main building. She spotted a fitness center and salon. She touched her hair, and pulled a strand up to her eyes. Her fingers. Little bite marks speckled the area around her nails. She shoved them into her pockets, away, to be ignored. And then she came across a spa. The list of services was extensive and the descriptions included so many adjectives, Rebecca wanted them all. Tropical-blend facial, with sea-fresh steam, and luxuriant massage. Salt and sand exfoliation with fertile-rich mud mask and ripe citrus tonic. Sensory seaweed scrub, with creamy oceanic moisture bath. Lavender and sea salts manicure. An idea popped into her head. If she got a manicure, Mitch would be pleased. Different types of massages were listed as well. Deep tissue massage, hot stone massage. She rolled her shoulders.

I've got to treat myself to one of these.

She smiled and breathed in deeply. An image flashed in her mind. Another man touching her. A massage was out of the question. Even if she could get a female, Mitch might doubt her. She'd better stay away from the spa completely. Just in case. She gave her ugly fingers one last look before hiding them behind her back.

After she left the main building, she followed the stone trail to the edge of the beach. The rumbling of the waves called to her. She wiggled her toes in the sand. Bending down, she spooned the sand with her palm and watched it filter through her hands.

This is where she wanted to be today, not traveling around a town she was already familiar with. Her vacation. Her choice.

But the damn fudge. She didn't dare ignore that request. Why? Why did she still need to bow to his demands? *Call it compromise, Rebecca. All good marriages need compromise.* She'd get the trolley to downtown and buy the fudge, and then head back to the resort. Then she could spend the day at the beach. Rebecca felt like a rebellious school girl. It felt good. It felt natural and real.

After riding the Red Train Trolley and buying the fudge, she made it back to the cottage. Mitch wasn't there as expected, so the rest of the day was hers to enjoy. She slipped on her bathing suit and cover-up. A cool breeze skipped along the beach, blowing strands of hair into her face. She tucked them behind her ears.

She strolled along the sandy beach, closer and closer to the water. She walked to the water's edge and dipped her toes once, twice and a third time before she could leave them in for a period. It was cold. Very cold. She let the water lap over her ankles.

The sun's rays glistened across the water. A flock of sandpipers landed on the beach nearby and sang a high-pitched, harmonious tune, like a soprano singing in an opera. She listened to their song until they flew away, giving them a parting wave.

Walkers and joggers moved along the beach, watching the ocean and chatting with each other. She waved and said hello to her fellow beachgoers as they passed on the clear, warm morning. Her arms swinging wide and her steps quick, she hummed her father's favorite tune, *When Irish Eyes Are Smiling*.

She kicked the sand and stepped on the hollow bumps. In the distance she saw a few dolphins swimming. Her heart skipped a beat. She blinked her eyes twice. Were they missing their tails like the figurine Mitch broke? No. Her eyes were playing tricks.

As they moved down the beach, she followed and tried to keep up with the beautiful creatures.

Waves hurried past her feet, pushing up the dry sand. White bubbles played peek-a-boo with her toes. With one toe, she wrote her name on the sand, and then wrote Mitch's. She brushed away his name. A wave rolled in and erased her name as well. No trace remained, but in its place lay new, smooth sand, like a newly placed fleece blanket.

She laughed and jogged at the edge of the waves, kicking the water as the tide rolled in. She giggled at her own childlike behavior. The wave returned home. Sand caught between her toes. She refused to wipe it away. She embraced the feel, the sand sticking to her feet, messy. So different from the regimented life she was used to leading, with everything in its place, everything orderly, chores, work, and reading Mitch's moods.

Another wave glided onto the shore. It stole the sand from her feet. Another came, then another, then another, never ceasing, cycling, never ending. All endless and ordinary, but beautiful and unique. The immensity of the ocean was too incredible, too miraculous. She was a grain, admiring its home.

She walked toward the direction of the resort. Beach chairs were visible in the distance. She made her way to the chairs, showed the attendant her keycard, and took one sitting next to an umbrella. She covered herself with the resort towel to keep the sun from tanning her fair skin. Mitch would be suspicious of a tan or burn marks. She laid back and let the sound of the waves and the warm breeze lull her.

Chapter 49

She stood and walked to the water's edge. Ten starfish lay in the sand in the shape of a heart while the water lapped close, barely caressing them.

She reached down and cautiously picked one up. Memory told her the starfish had once been out of reach. Strange. When? Now she held onto one. It nuzzled into her palm, seeming to welcome her touch.

Her eyes watered and she blinked them dry, spotting two dolphins swimming north. They were missing tails.

When she turned her attention back to the starfish, they'd encircled her feet, wanting her, needing her. They stood one by one and used two of their limbs to move toward her. Their other limbs appeared to be reaching up to her, waving in a frantic motion. They needed to be saved.

One by one, she placed them in the water, hoping they'd survive. They floated away quickly. She gave a little wave and blew a kiss.

She had saved them all.

"Ma'am," the attendant said, "You asked me to tell you when it was four o'clock."

Rebecca shielded her eyes from the lowering sun.

"It's a little after."

"Thank you." she said, smiling. She now saw life as never before.

Freedom.

Choices.

Pride.

She was telling him tonight. And he would listen. They would celebrate. The new Mitch would be so pleased.

*****

"Rebecca, are you ready?"

She stepped out of the bathroom with her hair wrapped in a towel. Mitch had just returned to their room and stood over their suitcase. He wore a casual button-down shirt and shorts, different from the golf clothes he'd had on this morning. He looked refreshed from a shower.

"When did you change?"

"This afternoon. I was in a hurry to get to the bar."

"You've already been back here? After your golf?"

"Yes. Is there a problem?"

"Why didn't you let me know? You promised we'd talk."

"You were out touring."

It wasn't a question. It didn't need a response.

"So ... where have you been?"

He sat on the bed. "I met some businessmen at the golf course. They're staying here, too, and we had a couple of drinks."

"But Mitch—"

"Re-bec-ca, we're here for a week. The guys are only here until Wednesday."

"We need to talk, Mitch. I'd really like to discuss our future."

"Really? It's all planned out. So get ready. The guys are waiting."

"What guys?"

Without answering, Mitch pointed to his Bulova. "Time is ticking. And wear something sexy."

"Sexy?" He hadn't asked her to dress that way for some time.

"I'm sure you heard me the first time. Look wonderful for me."

She changed into a floral, strapless sheath dress. "Do you like?" said asked, twirling.

"What about your hair?"

"I'll let it air dry. You said we were in a hurry."

"Style it. For me, hon. I want you looking fantastic."

"But, I thought—"

"Your thinking is making us late."

Rebecca wanted to tell Mitch she'd bought him some fudge. But she hesitated. It wasn't the mint chocolate he'd requested. It was peanut and caramel. She'd wait until he asked about it. She dried and curled her hair, put her sandals on and headed for the door. Her heel slipped across the floor. She caught herself before she fell.

"Are you okay?"

"Yes, I think so," she said, stretching her ankle left and right.

"They shouldn't have this type of tile on the floor." Mitch kicked at the floor, his shoe scuffing along the tiles. "Too slippery, way too slippery." He didn't check her ankle as a doctor might. He didn't inspect her ankle as Grafton did for Susannah in her story.

But he did take her hand and they left the cottage. The perfect couple.

*****

The oak bar complemented the bamboo floor. Bright-colored liquor bottles lined a mirrored wall at the back of the bar. Exotic named drinks on a menu caught her eye. Blue Hurricane, Tropical Thunder, Pomegranate Margarita, Coconut Rum Mojito. It was as impressive as the menu at the spa. Her mouth watered.

She caught her reflection in the mirror as she walked by. The worry lines and dark circles had disappeared and her eyes gleamed. People were sipping drinks from coconut shells and from glasses with salt encrusted on the rims. She heard laughter and glasses clinking. People smiled as they walked by.

A pretty, young woman with a necklace fashioned from a sand dollar flirted with the easy-going bartender. The hostess seated Rebecca and Mitch at a table near the bar. When the server came over, she brought ice water and menus.

"The specials this evening are top sirloin covered with peppercorn sauce and seared Mahi Mahi with mango sauce. Any questions?"

Mitch shook his head.

"I'll be back to take your orders." She smiled and left.

"Collin suggested I try the Mahi or the yellow tuna. He also recommended either the escargot or the sautéed calamari."

Rebecca peered over her menu. "Who is Collin?"

"He and I were hooked up together as part of a foursome today. Those are the guys I told you about."

Mitch ordered the escargot for an appetizer, the Mahi Mahi dinner, and a bottle of the house chardonnay.

"No appetizer for me. I'll have prime rib, medium-well, with rice pilaf and black-eyed peas for my dinner."

"You can try some of my appetizer," said Mitch.

"No thanks."

"It would broaden your sense of class, Rebecca."

Once again, she fought a frown. There was no need for that comment. She played with the fabric at her cleavage. "You didn't say if you liked my dress. Do you like the style?"

"Looks great. Vacation is great. Tomorrow I'm going to play golf again with the guys. Don't forget you have the scenic cruise booked for the morning, and then lunch reservations in the Café Cordova at the Casa Monica Hotel. Wear the royal blue dress I bought you. We'll be fishing Monday, and we might try surfing on Tuesday. The Surf Station down the road is known for their lessons. I'll rent a wet suit and board."

"I don't know how to surf."

"Not *we* as in you and me. *We*. The guys and I. You don't mind do you?"

"I suppose not," she lied.

"Don't you worry your pretty little head about spending time with me. We'll meet every evening for dinner and spend the rest of the night working on our future."

The appetizer and wine arrived and Mitch held up a forkful of escargot. She refused it.

"Your stubborn streak is showing, Rebecca."

He tried again.

"Please," she said.

"Try it."

"No, Mitch."

"Eat it." He placed the fork at her lips.

She had no choice. It tasted like someone else's spit and she grabbed her water and chugged. "That's ... terrible."

He threw an escargot into his mouth and smiled.

She took another large gulp of water and then said, "How was golf?"

"Relaxing. I broke a one hundred, close to my personal best. Tomorrow will be even better. And the course, unbelievable. Manicured to perfection."

She hid her nails under the table.

"How was your day?"

"It was fun and relax—" She wasn't supposed to lie on the beach. Touring the historic district was his plan for her. But this was the new Mitch. "It was nice. I bought you fudge."

"Thanks. Did you go into some of the art galleries?"

She hesitated. Tell the truth? "Um, no. But I'll go tomorrow. There's one right in the Casa Monica."

Mitch's Mahi Mahi dish and Rebecca's prime rib arrived.

"I'm sure you'll see some fine art. Maybe in a few years we'll be shopping for our own pieces."

"That would be nice."

"Look around tomorrow. See what your style is. I know you love the *Water Lilies* print."

She nibbled on a piece of prime rib. Delicious. Cooked to perfection. Attentive and respectful, this was the right time.

"I've got to tell you something."

"What is it?"

"I've been offered a promotion at the bank. I'm going to take it."

He took a long drink of his wine and placed the empty glass on the table.

"Have you?" There was no celebration to his tone. Only contrived control.

"Yes."

"You could become pregnant any day now."

"I know, and hopefully I will, and soon. But in the meantime I'm going to work on my career."

"You'll soon be quitting that job. That was short-term. Now that we're buying a new house you'll be getting it set up."

"The promotion is something I've dreamed of. I can help my—"

"We've talked about this before. No more discussion."

"I'm taking the position."

"Like hell, you are," he spat.

"Mitch, you said things would change after your test. It's done now. Now it's time for—"

"Mitch?" A voice shouted from across the room.

"Collin. Join us," Mitch yelled back.

Rebecca put a hand on Mitch's arm. "Mitch, we need to finish this conversation. Can't he wait?"

He grabbed her hand and squeezed hard. "I'll kill you if you take that promotion—and I'll get away with it. Don't you ever, *ever,* betray my trust. Do you hear me?"

She clenched and unclenched her hand. It hurt. His grip tightened.

"I said, do you hear me?"

"Yes."

No, this can't be happening. Mitch changed. Her mind darted to snippets of conversations she'd had with others. *He's not going to change. He's not going to change.*

They were right.

A heavy weight in her chest threatened to overtake her. She put her hand over her breast, trying to squash the pain. Her dreams shattered before her eyes.

No, I don't believe it.

She looked at Mitch, hoping for some sign of regret. Nothing. He stared at her with the same cold eyes she'd seen countless times.

She bit her fingers hard. Her eyes darted around the room, but focused on nothing. Blood coursed through her veins wanting to erupt. *How dare he? He promised he had changed. I was an idiot. I believed him.*

"Rebecca? Rebecca!"

She flinched and rewound the last bits of conversation. *Escargot, finished with dinner, join us.*

The man, Collin she presumed, was holding out his hand. She extended her arm and he took her injured hand.

"Nice to meet you," he said.

She pulled back and rubbed her neck, trying to keep her head from exploding. Her role was to fill Mitch's ego, and nothing else. It never would be anything more. Collin called over two couples from the bar. Chairs and tables were moved to make room.

Rebecca pushed her food aside. When she looked at Mitch again, he was staring at her. He made a fist with his hand. She looked away, down at the table. Her hands were holding the table's edge as if it was the only thing keeping her upright.

She heard one of the men mention that they'd eaten dinner at a local restaurant and were back for drinks. They made introductions and Mitch fell into easy conversation with the men. None of their names stuck in her mind. It was too filled with rage. Anger bubbled and steamed. Fear of Mitch had been replaced with hatred. She watched as Mitch ignored her. He treated her as if she was insignificant, but now she knew she was not. Her life meant as much as Mitch's.

The room spun. Nauseous, she rushed to the bathroom, just making it. She fell to her knees and retched. She pictured Mitch as she vomited, repulsed by him. She gripped the toilet, disgusted as memories of their love-making spun through her mind. Her hair fell forward. Vomit caught at it. His touch on her skin—revolting. She was sick until there was nothing left inside. Nothing left inside her heart. No feelings for Mitch other than hatred. Vile hatred. Pure loathing.

Her heart was empty, void of love.

When she could stand without falling, she moved to the sink and cleaned her face and hair. Looking in the mirror, she caught her reflection. Ashen.

She'd adapted and changed to protect herself. She'd survived by taking on the characteristics of a hunted chameleon, adapting to the environment in order to live. Her relationship with Mitch, a dominating, abusive monster, transformed her into the weak woman she was today. How stupid she was. How stupid to be manipulated and controlled by Mitch.

No. She wasn't being stupid. She'd been protecting herself from a horrible, repugnant man. She straightened her shoulders and marched out to their table. Mitch sneered at her and squeezed his hands together in a strangling motion.

Rebecca stood tall. "Apparently the escargot didn't agree with me. I'd better get back to the cottage before I lose my steak, too. Nice to meet all of you." She spun on her heel and escaped the room.

She started back toward the cottage, looking over her shoulder to make sure he didn't follow. She should have stood up to Mitch long ago, when he started putting her down and controlling her. But she'd loved him. She thought he'd get better. She thought he was better. She thought everything was better. He'd told her that she was always messing up. He made her feel isolated and confused. And she'd believed all of his putdowns. He'd preyed on her vulnerabilities and drove the old Rebecca away.

He'd taken advantage of her naivety.

He'd taken her innocence.

He'd taken her dreams and turned them into nightmares.

He was a venomous snake and he'd bit her time and time again. And she'd let him.

"How could this happen to me!"

The thoughts were too much to bear. She changed direction, turning away from the cottage and walking toward the beach. She tripped on a stone on the trail, stubbing her toe. She howled and grabbed her foot, ripping off her sandals. The moon barely visible in the dusk sky mocked her. She whipped one shoe in its direction, then threw the other.

When her feet touched the sand, she ran until she couldn't anymore. She collapsed on the beach, clutching her chest. Sobs came. So many. Tears poured down her cheeks, and tiny droplets speckled the sand. She fell into a fetal position, the waves just reaching her feet.

Her mind played tricks on her. Her father. Death. She'd run to the beach and collapsed after his death. All alone. The guilt. It had consumed her. Swallowed her whole. She was alone again, alone with the grief of a broken marriage and a broken life.

She rolled over onto her knees and pounded the sand. It would not loosen. She pounded again wanting it to hurt, to bleed. She pounded and pounded, and pounded some more, crushing her stupid choices.

Why? Why had she hoped? Why had she dared to dream?

Time. She hadn't been living the last few years. She'd been existing, surviving, with all of her dreams on hold, keeping her past life at bay.

All those precious days I gave to Mitch.

The wet sand wouldn't budge. It was as stubborn as she had been. Too stubborn to see. No, she had been terrified. She had been manipulated. She clawed with both hands, wild and fast, as fast as a dog digs a hole for its bone. The sand loosened and she scooped up a handful and threw it into the sky. "Why!" It poured down on top of her. She let it hit her body, as Mitch had done so many times. She dug again, and a sand pile grew.

"I'll destroy you!" She clenched her fists and beat the earth, tears spilling into the mound. "I hate you!"

She wanted to be buried in the sand. Buried with all the past. Go to a life with no more pain. Feel no more fear. She stood, kicking at the sand, sending it flying just as fireworks explode in the night sky. She howled a brutal sound and ran straight into the chilly water. She jumped through the water like a tired hurdler, the current holding her back. But she wouldn't be denied and swam through the breakers. Her arms pulled her through the waves. The muscles in her legs felt the resistance of the water. Every ounce of strength was needed, and she kept going toward the deep ocean. Away from the pain. Away from Mitch. Away.

She cried into the wind, tightened her palms, and punched at the water, until her muscles couldn't move anymore. They were like rocks, impossible to lift. Oars in muddy water.

She'd been robbed of her innocence, her sense of fairness and order, and her life.

What was left?

Suddenly her feet left the sand. It was deep. She swam further into the vast ocean, staring out at the horizon, moving toward her goal.

"Why?" she shouted. "Why did he deceive me?" She gulped in water. The salt burned her throat and she spat it out. Her sore arms thrashed, forcing her body deeper into the ocean. The cold water tightened her muscles.

"I can't live like this anymore." A wave washed over her head, pulling her under. She came back up, sputtering. She yelled until another wave knocked into her again. Loneliness and regret covered her like a bandage. The beatings, the bruises, the birth control pills. The lies, the choking, the threats. What to wear, how to act, who to be. Living without choices, secretive behavior, no trust.

It was too much.

"I can't do this for one more second." Her words floated away in the wind. It was time to say goodbye.

A huge wave pulled her body below the surface and she went slack. Her broken heart and damaged soul weighted her down. Her body drifted under the water, arms and legs splayed out, with the tide pulling her further away from the beach.

She said goodbye to her loved ones, to her dreams, and let her heavy heart help sink her.

Mother, brother, nieces, David, Joan, Kelly, Barb ... Ben ... Scout...

Her lungs screamed in pain, but the will to fight was gone. It was over. Mitch had won.

Daddy! Nan!

She waited.

A sharp pain tore through her head, worse than ever before. She closed her eyes and Anna's face appeared. Anna motioned her to come close, extending her arms.

"Rebecca! Stop this! You have to fight. Fight for yourself. Fight for your dreams."

The vision disappeared, but she still felt Anna's presence. Her body fought her mind, refusing to head back to the surface. She was tired. She needed to sleep. She needed to be nothing.

"Bec, look around you. Now."

Rebecca opened her eyes as a flash of lightning in the dark sky illuminated the water. Life was everywhere. Starfish beckoned. A dolphin. Its majestic body and tail. Beautiful creatures inhabiting this world, surrounding her. Things worth fighting for.

"You need to survive. You can do this."

"I can't take it anymore."

"Think, Rebecca. Think about who you were. You can become that person again. You need to bring the old Rebecca back into your life. It's time."

No! It was too painful to think about how far she'd fallen, how much control Mitch had gained.

Her father holding her in his lap. Her mother cooling her forehead when feverish. Being taught to ride her bike. She'd been a pitcher and a cheerleader. Straight A's. A best friend. A scholarship. The purple scarf from her cheerleading days. The trip to Disney World. She remembered everything. The person she used to be, the old Rebecca, resurfaced. Things that she valued became clear. The dream she'd had was about her, not Anna.

Happiness. She'd been happy.

Confidence. She'd been confident.

Courage. She'd been brave.

Love. Respect. Friendship.

She thought she had to be swallowed up by the ocean to stop the pain, but stopping the pain was her responsibility. *She* had to fight. It wasn't too late. She was worth fighting for. The old Rebecca had to save the new one.

Another wave hit her and the current pulled her further under. She gulped in another mouthful of salt water and her right leg cramped.

Her arms flailed as she broke the surface. She'd released so much energy; she didn't think she had enough to get herself back to shore.

"Rebecca," Anna said. "Don't give up."

"Anna!"

"I'm still here," Anna said.

She searched around for Anna, but she was not visible.

Rebecca's body went slack. "I'm sorry."

"Fight, Bec. You can do it."

Exhaustion seized her muscles. "I can't anymore."

"You'll get through this and you'll leave him. Just do what I say," Anna said.

"I'm so confused. I'm dead inside."

"No. I'm inside you. We're not dead and we'll get through this."

Her arms were on the verge of quitting. "I can't. I don't have the strength."

"You're strong and have the will to survive. Dig deep into yourself."

"But I don't know which way to go."

"I'll help you."

"Then, I'll try. I promise."

"Find the beach and slowly move parallel. You can do it."

She looked around and found it behind her. "The current is too strong."

"No, you're fighting the water. You can survive. Use me for your strength. I've been here with you for years. Now you need to let me help you."

For years? Anna? Anna was her, part of her past.

"When your body is out of the current, let the waves bring you in."

Another wave went over her head and the current pulled at her.

"Just stay parallel."

"Stay with me, please. I can't live without you."

"I'm here for you. I always have been."

Her arms struggled to push the water. She willed her weak legs to kick. Like weights, they started to sink into the water. She had hardly moved. "Please forgive me."

"Don't say that! Just follow my instructions."

Rebecca floated, trying to catch her breath.

"Swim!"

She tried.

"You're doing it."

"I'm not."

"Yes. Look. The beach is closer now. Look."

Darkness had set in. Lights from the resort were visible.

"Keep letting the waves guide you in."

She floated again and then kicked with every ounce of might she had left. The lights came closer. "It's working."

"You'll survive this and you'll leave Mitch. Be done with him for good. No more abuse."

Rebecca allowed the quiet waves to carry her toward the beach. She was almost there. In and out, forward and back with the waves and the tide. Suddenly her hand ran along the ocean floor and she clawed at it before the tide could take her back again. Was she free? Alive? She'd made it and thanked God.

Crawling onto the beach, she gasped for breath, gagged on the salt water in her lungs, and vomited. Her dress clung to her, weighing her down. Salt water mixed with tears ran down her face. She pushed her wet hair back and wiped her eyes.

Everything was clear now, where before it had been cloudy, like sand in salt water.

She had to leave Mitch. Immediately. She'd given him five years of her life, and she wasn't giving him *one more minute*.

Anna said, "It's time, Rebecca. It's time."

"Yes. Let's go."

Chapter 50

Anna gave directions. Left. Right. Left again. Chilled to the bone, but with a fire burning inside, Rebecca found her way through the darkness to the cottage. The stairs squeaked under her feet. Rebecca's soaked dress left puddles in its path. No light emanated from the windows.

"Looks safe, Bec," Anna said, helping her in. "Go in and grab a few things. We'll call David as soon as we're off the resort."

Rebecca burst through the door. She snapped on the foyer light and the room illuminated.

Mitch.

On the edge of the sofa, he sat like a statue. Quiet. Still. Seething. Then those hands she had felt around her neck oh so often, closed into fists, then seemed to grow like the talons of a hunter. Rebecca's sandy feet slipped on the tile floor. Anna caught her.

Anna said, "Ignore him. Keep moving."

Rebecca stood still.

Anna tried to push her. "Go!"

She couldn't.

"Run!"

She didn't.

His crazed expression immobilized her, rooted her to the ground. The aspirin bottle sat on the coffee table in front of him.

Oh, my God.

Rebecca tried to move, but her legs wouldn't cooperate. Her wet dress clung and wrapped and chained her to his presence.

"Bec, stay with me. We're in this together," Anna said.

Flaring tempers, vicious kicks, hits. They flashed. Rebecca drifted deeper inside herself.

"Don't leave me again," Anna begged.

Broken dishes, angry words, threats, insults. The past consumed her, glued her, caged her.

"How dare you?!" He picked up the bottle. "I knew you were hiding something. Did you really think you could outsmart me?" He dumped the pills into his hand and turned his palm downward. The pills scattered to the floor.

"Remember the ocean? You overcame it. You can do this, too," said Anna.

The waves crashing over her. The salt water in her lungs. Despair. But then the sea creatures. The living organisms. The lightning. Fighting the waves. Making it to the beach. Victory.

"You betrayed me," said Mitch. "And now you're going to pay."

His fists, kicks, insults, verbal assaults. A weak and insecure man bullying to get his way.

"Turn around and run back out the door. Now! We can do this."

"I told you never to deceive me." He threw the bottle in her direction.

She didn't flinch. She saw Mitch clearly for the first time in years. She lifted her chin.

"Give him hell," said Anna.

Rebecca inhaled. The air felt fresh and easy. "No, Mitch. You betrayed me the first time you abused me and every time since!"

His mouth opened. He said words, none that Rebecca heard, for she, too, spoke.

"You took away my innocence. You took advantage of my commitment to our marriage, making me believe the abuse was my fault. I wasn't to blame." She jabbed her finger in his direction. "You had no right to hurt me!"

"Keep going, Bec," Anna said. "Tell Mitch how you feel."

Mitch's face turned scarlet. His body unfolded like a ladder, growing with each step.

She stood straight. For the first time, she would not be intimidated. "You deceived me, Mitch."

"Liar!"

"I was protecting a child from you. From you ... you ... you monster."

"Me?" He screamed. "You're just a little nobody, Re-bec-ca. I made you special by marrying you, you ungrateful bitch. You deserved every punishment I handed out."

Rebecca stepped forward. "I am somebody. And that somebody is better than you. You're evil."

"Keep going, Bec. This is your chance. Tell him what he took from you," said Anna.

Rebecca said, "Yes. I'm telling him everything."

"Who are you talking to, you crazy bitch?"

Anna said, "Go ahead. Tell him what he's done to you."

"You took my confidence and happiness and beat it out of me until I became a shell of the woman I was before. You threatened me and took away *my* choices." She pointed to her chest, and then to his. "You're the coward."

Mitch snorted, shortening the distance between them. "You're—"

She put up her hand. "You controlled everything I said and did. You controlled where I went and with whom I talked. You're a manipulative bastard. I'm done with you, for good."

"No you're not. You wouldn't dare leave me."

Anna said, "Tell him you are."

"I wouldn't stay with a man like you. You've never loved me. You just used me." Word by word, Rebecca's voice became one with Anna's. They spoke in unison. One voice. One strong, confident voice. "You're incapable of real love. You only know how to dominate. To be above someone else. I've found my voice. I'm using it. We're through with you."

She turned to escape and slipped on the tile.

Mitch lunged forward and caught her arm. He squeezed tight.

She wiggled from his grasp and took three giant steps toward the door, reaching the handle.

"Hurry!" Anna screamed.

When she pulled on the knob, Mitch's hand pushed against the door, slamming it shut.

"Open the door! I'm leaving!" She struggled to get his arm off the door. She kicked backwards, connecting with his shin.

He let go to grab his leg. "You bitch!"

She opened the door, but he gripped her around the waist. She squirmed, couldn't break free. He tossed her into the small living room. She stumbled, knocking into the glass table. She shook off the pain. Adrenaline pumped through her.

Eyes darting around the cottage, she searched for an escape.

He came toward her, his hands open and ready. When she scooted behind the sofa, he rounded the table. She circled the sofa. The door was the only way out. It was in reach. She flung the door wide open and hurried across the porch.

"Run! He's right behind you."

Footsteps grew louder.

She looked over her shoulder. Mitch was there.

"Scream for help, Bec. Maybe someone will hear us."

"Help! Someone!" they screamed.

The palm of Mitch's hand closed around her mouth.

"Bite it!"

Instead she kicked her foot back again, but he was ready. He swung her around, gripping her arms. She wobbled on the top step.

"Let me go!"

He pulled her face next to his, eyes boring into hers. "I told you that you'd never leave me!"

He pulled her toward him.

"You're evil, Mitch. I'll never stay."

With his muscular arms, he threw her down the stairs, like she was a bucket of water being tossed on a fire.

Her arms spread wide open, hands reaching, trying to grab hold of something, anything. The back of her head hit the corner of a wooden stair and her body tumbled over itself. She hit another stair, her skull gashing open. With each tumble her head bounced again. The tumbles ceased. Her crumpled body landed on the beach. Blood flowed from the gash in her head, mixing with the sand.

Her eyes met Mitch's as he stood on the porch with arms crossed. No remorse. No compassion. There never had been. He never knew how to love, only to control. She had finally seen the truth.

Rebecca struggled to breathe. She whispered, "I found my strength. I stood up to the monster."

Anna said, "You are brave. You've always had it inside of you. Mitch wore you down through his control, put downs, isolation. He made you feel guilty. You wanted to take away his pain. He knew your vulnerabilities. Then came the threats."

"I tried. I tried so hard."

"He's a manipulator, but *you* overcame unbelievable obstacles and left him."

"I did. I finally found my voice."

Anna held her hand as they took their last breath.

Rebecca looked up at the sky. The clouds parted and the bright sun strained her eyes. She shielded them with her left hand. Her diamond sparkled in the sun. A spectrum of colors streaked through the sky. A faint glow appeared through the cloudless opening.

The wet sand beneath her chilled her skin. It contrasted the sun's rays soaking into her body. The breeze blew wisps of hair into her face. She wiped the strands away, leaving gritty sand behind.

Conflicting emotions warred inside her as the glow slowly approached, until a sense of calm swept over her. She felt him before she saw his figure evolve from the light.

"Daddy."

"Reba, I'm here to take your pain away." He held out his hand and she took it. "It's time. Come with me."

"I've needed you."

"I'm here now." Her father looked at her with teary eyes. "I love you more than life."

Epilogue

Ben

Ben cried out, punching a pillow, after he clicked off the phone. Jonathon Fields' somber voice echoed in his mind. He'd listened to the devastating story of Rebecca falling down the stairs and hitting her head. The funeral would be on Saturday and Jonathon expected everyone there. Of course, he would attend. He'd be there for Rebecca.

Why didn't Rebecca listen to his advice? Why did she have to go on vacation?

No.

He was asking the wrong questions. She wasn't to blame.

Why did Mitch have to be abusive and controlling?

He rubbed the back of his neck, replaying each encounter he'd had with Rebecca. He should have insisted on helping her out of the relationship, but instead his own damaged soul prevented him from doing so. He'd been jaded by his own experiences.

"He killed her. I know it." The words spat out of his mouth. "Bastard! He won't get away with this."

Ben looked up at the heavens and said to Rebecca, "I'll get justice for you."

David

"I know he killed her. Please investigate further," David said. The vein in his temple bulged.

"David, you're a good friend. I'll continue to check it out, ask around at the resort, but I don't see anything coming of this. His story is believable. He found her like that after returning from the restaurant," Detective Paul Melrose said.

"I know. But the history of abuse—"

"I get it, believe me. I know how these things work, unfortunately. It doesn't help that she never reported it."

"That's normal. She was afraid."

"Such a common problem."

"She was also giving him some unwanted news."

"What's that?"

"She was taking a promotion. He didn't want her working. Her new independence would have worried him."

"A shift in power in the relationship. I know. I'll see what I can do."

"Thanks, Paul. Let me know what you find out."

"Will do."

David clicked his cell off and poured himself a whiskey. He held the glass toward the heavens and said to Rebecca, "I'll get justice for you."

Evelyn

"Oh God! No!" Evelyn collapsed to the floor, holding her midsection. "Not my baby!"

"Ma'am? Ma'am!" Detective Melrose said. "Your son is on his way. Please call a friend to stay with you in the meantime."

The phone fell out of her hand. She lay on the floor, moaning. In between broken sobs, she cried out, "That horrible man. He killed her. I know he did."

Scout

Angela and Nicole approached Scout's cage.

"I don't know, Angela. They're late picking Scout up. It's three days past when she was scheduled to go home."

"Maybe they stayed longer on vacation and forgot to call."

"The strange thing is, I ran Rebecca's credit card through the machine and it came back as having been canceled."

"That is weird. Well, we'll give it another couple of days and then take her to the animal shelter."

Angela whispered to Scout. "You've been whining for a few days now. So sad. You must miss your mama. She'll be back soon."

Scout cried a long and desperate meow.

The End

Dear Reader,

Thank you for taking the time to read *Drowning*. I really appreciate it. *Drowning* comes from my heart and writing it has been a long journey. I was inspired to write this story because I've seen abuse and I wanted to give victims a voice. No more silence.

Sometimes we must take a stand for what we believe in. I believe that Rebecca's story is all too common. I want to change that. I need your help. Did you know that 'on average three women are murdered by their intimate partners in the United States every day'?[1] We need to stop the violence.

How can we do this? We can talk about the problem. Educate ourselves. Volunteer at the local domestic violence organization. Just be aware. Sometimes the smallest action can ripple and make an even larger impact. Sometimes it can save a life.

If you are in a domestic violence situation, please seek help. Most importantly, have a safety plan. Rebecca didn't need to tell Mitch she was leaving. You don't need to tell your abuser that you're leaving. In fact, he should have no hint that you are. You can go to the grocery store and never return. But a safety plan is crucial.

I've blogged extensively on domestic violence issues. You can read the blogs at www.katelinmaloney.com. Please sign up to receive future blogs and book updates. Also, you can email me at katelinmaloney@yahoo.com.

Please consider leaving a review on Amazon or Barnes & Noble if you feel *Drowning* will help another woman.

If you're being abused or know someone who is, please call the National Domestic Violence Hotline for help. 1-800-799-7233.

Remember, if we can help just one woman, we've done our job.

Katelin Maloney

1)Bureau of Justice Statistics Crime Data Brief, Intimate Partner Violence, 1993-2001, February 2003. Bureau of Justice Statistics, Intimate Partner Violence in the U.S. 1993-2004, 2006.

For more information about the author, please visit
www.katelinmaloney.com.

Acknowledgments

Drowning has been a several year project that I would not have completed without the help of many people. My husband, Rodney, and two sons, Branden and Justin, have supported me from the beginning and have pushed me to keep going.

My mother has read and edited **many** versions and has patiently worked hard on each one. She has been invaluable. My father's confidence in my abilities inspired my growth in learning the craft and motivated me to continue writing.

Family members and friends have endured reading *Drowning* several times as well. Family members Anne and Don, Linda, Jen, Karen, and Heather H.; old friends Sarah and Nancy; and new friends Cindy, Alisa, Heather R., Lillian, Sandra, Susan, and Jean all played a role in helping *Drowning* come to fruition.

A special thank you to PT Editing.

I couldn't have done it without **all** of your help.

Thank you!

Printed in Great Britain
by Amazon

57806997R00187